J. E. MCDONALD

Caged Fury

GOLDENLACH RIDGE SHIFTERS BOOK 2

MYSTIC OWL

AN IMPRINT OF CITY OWL PRESS

CAGED FURY

J. E. MCDONALD

MYSTIC OWL

CAGED FURY
Goldenlach Ridge Shifters, Book 2

MYSTIC OWL
A City Owl Press Imprint
www.cityowlpress.com

Cover Design by MiblArt. All stock photos licensed appropriately.

Edited by Heather McCorkle.

For information on subsidiary rights, please contact the publisher at info@cityowlpress.com.

Print Edition ISBN: 978-1-64898-266-8

Digital Edition ISBN: 978-1-64898-267-5

Printed in the United States of America

To Coline and Simone.
Because sisters are everything.

PRAISE FOR J. E. MCDONALD

"*Ghost of a Gamble* is a contemporary, gothic tale filled with sparkling wittiness, budding romance, thrilling suspense, and scary ghosts!"
— *InD'tale*

"Bree was funny, and quirky, but also independent, which I loved. I enjoyed the quirky atmosphere, the hauntings, and the hot romance between these ghost hunters. A great read for fans of paranormal romance!"
— *J. E. Hunter, author of The Torc*

"I adored *Ghost of an Enchantment*! Fun, magical, and romantic. Stella is everything I look for in a witchy romance heroine, and Wickwood is a delightful setting for these books. The pacing was perfect, and the magical mystery was right up my alley. Well done!"
— *Lisa Edmonds, bestselling author of the Alice Worth series*

"J.E. McDonald comes out swinging with *Captive Wilderness*, the first in a new paranormal romance series featuring shifters, plenty of spice, and forced proximity done right."
— *Gabrielle Ash, author of The Family Cross*

"McDonald's cast of supernatural characters are always impeccably crafted and leave you eager for the next installment of this delightful series."
— *Ashley R. King, author of Painting the Lines and Forever After*

"Bree is utterly charming right from the beginning, and her

dynamic with Zack makes for a wonderfully compelling story. *Ghost of a Gamble* is easy to sink into, with a supernatural plot that escalates all the way to the end."
— *K. Caine, author of A Study in Velvet and Leather*

"McDonald busts this worldwide open and brings it to new heights and dimensions. She easily navigates blending in all of the different plot points and relationships (romantic, family, and friendship) together into a fun and 'enchanting' story."
— *E.E. Hornburg, author of The Night's Chosen*

"A heartfelt paranormal romance about a skeptic teaming up with a paranormal investigator, *Ghost of a Gamble* is sure to make you smile. Bree and Zack have perfect chemistry and their banter is irresistible."
— *Kat Turner, author of Hex, Love, and Rock & Roll*

"Stella is a witch who doesn't trust cops. Unfortunately, Lucas is a cop--and the sexual tension between them is scorching hot, making *Ghost of an Enchantment* a fast-paced, compelling read."
— *K. Caine, author of A Study in Velvet and Leather*

"Transporting readers to a thrilling romance filled dimension, *Ghost of an Enchantment* is a breath-stealing page turner set in the magical town of Wickwood! With characters that provide touches of humor and a plot filled with mystical intrigue, readers will be enticed to move in and peek from their windows in anticipation of what will happen next!"
— *InD'tale Magazine*

"A fast-paced read with a tension-filled romance and high-stakes plot, *Ghost of a Summoning* is a paranormal love story you don't want to miss."
— *Gabrielle Ash, author of The Family Cross*

"A devilishly fun romance. Highly recommend."
— *Luna Joya, author of the Legacy series*

"Wickwood, a quaint town with a paranormal twist that I'd love to visit."
— *J.E. Hunter, author of The Circlet*

WORKS BY J. E. MCDONALD

PROLOGUE
WALKER

Darkness shrouded the trees surrounding the warehouse, keeping me cloaked in shadows. The quiet sounds of the woods tickled my senses as my heart beat an accelerated rhythm. I used to live for this shit.

What the fuck was going on in this place? Guards circled the structure, flood lights illuminating the space between the barb-wire fence and the building—a mini prison. My instincts told me it wasn't good. What had Landon gotten me into?

The human woman I was tracking, Jolyn Mahn, was a ghost. When we were kids, she'd been quiet, but it was kind of hard not to notice her with her bright red hair that spiraled out in every direction. But now, she was either very good at existing in the shadows or someone had killed her and gotten rid of the body. If that was the case, Landon was going to be pissed.

I'd done some research, found her service record. She'd joined the Canadian army four years after me even though she was only a year younger, but she hadn't seen as much action. As soon as her four-year contract had ended, she'd moved to Detroit, then disappeared. That was this past year. No record of employment, no activity at the apartment leased in her name, no travel trail, just *poof*. Gone.

Because she'd turned into a ghost, I'd focused on her brother. All of us had grown up together in Goldenlach Ridge, a town nestled in the Canadian Rockies. Emerson Mahn was the same age as me, and I remembered him as a nerdy, little kid. If he had some contact with his sister, then I could pinpoint her location, let Landon know, and go nurse a beer at my favorite bar in Vancouver until the next time he had a menial chore for me to do. I knew he gave me these odd jobs to keep me busy, but, it had seemed personal for him.

I didn't know what thing he had for the woman, and frankly, I didn't give a flying fuck. He could moon over and screw whoever he wanted. When I found her, he'd send money direct to my account—money I barely touched. More importantly, once I found her, I'd return to that barstool with my name on it, maybe convince Landon to go to the shooting range again, or allow him to finally take me golfing like he's been pestering me.

But right now, Jolyn Mahn remained a ghost.

Which was what led me here. In tracking her brother, I'd found the listing for this property in a roundabout way. It was strange. For one, no one was supposed to be here. According to city records, it was abandoned, slated for demolition. But someone went to the effort of the guards, security gate, floodlights, and barbed wire fence. It definitely wasn't condemned.

Snap. I tensed, listening. Someone walked through the woods a couple meters away. Annoyance rippled through me. I should've heard them sooner.

I stilled. A feminine, feline scent slammed into me like a physical thing. *Shifter.* It made every hair on my body stand on end. My heart galloped in my chest, and I developed the sudden need to go to her, wrap my arms around her body, and *claim*. A growl began low in my chest and worked its way through my throat. I bit it off before the sound could escape.

I stepped toward her without thinking, about to reveal my position, when I shook my head and forced myself back into my hiding spot within the bushes. *What the hell is happening?* Every instinct I owned wanted me to touch her, to take her. I was getting a damn hard-on, and I couldn't even see her properly. Nothing like this had ever happened to me before, and I didn't understand it.

Gritting my teeth, I clenched my hands into fists, willing myself to stay put. It didn't stop me from inhaling deeply as she passed three steps away from me, so close if I reached out, I'd have her. My hot blood pumped through my veins. I couldn't even recall why I was here in the first place. All I wanted was the woman in front of me.

I slowly exhaled, trying to keep my shit together in the face of this unexpected need, her intoxicating scent. *Peaches and cream.* She didn't notice me, her gaze on the warehouse. I shifted my eyes to see her better. Her long brown hair was swept up into a ponytail, curling slightly as it cascaded down her back. Dark wash jeans and a blue plaid shirt clad her petite form.

She kept going down the hill toward the warehouse, only stopping by the outer chain link fence. Even though we were shadowed by trees and bushes, she was way too close. My instincts to protect her came from the same place as the need to claim. I wanted to rip her away from that fence and take her from whatever danger lurked behind the walls of that warehouse.

She stared at the building for a long minute, then lifted binoculars. When she lowered them, she ran a hand over her head, agitated, like she was deciding what to do. If she made a step toward the warehouse, I'd have to stop her. There was no way she could get inside without being seen.

Another twig snapped, this one from her other side. She'd distracted me so much, someone had snuck up on us. *Fuck.* What the hell was happening to me? Why was I acting like such a rookie?

She spun around at the sound. A man gripped her by the throat a second later, pressing her against a tree. Fury snapped through me so fast it blinded me for a moment. I stood, my instincts telling me to attack, to protect what was mine, when I realized there was more than one person out there.

The scent of shifters swamped the area, and I recognized them as my own kind. Three cougar shifters surrounded her in a loose circle. Every muscle in my body bunched, ready to fight. My instincts warred with my training. I wanted to charge forward and rip out the man's throat for touching her, but I also needed to stay concealed, to find out more about what the hell was going on.

"Look what I've caught," said the one with his hand around her throat. He wore a cowboy hat and spoke like a Texan. "Another kitty for the hunters to skin. You've been poking where you shouldn't. Have you told anyone where you are? Your sister or mom perhaps?"

Hunters? Primal rage ripped through me. When the one in the trucker hat adjusted his crotch like he was getting turned on by what his friend said to her, I couldn't contain myself any longer.

I ran and shifted, my cells morphing in a flash of heat, one molecule at a time. With every sense enhanced, the world brightened around me. Canines lengthened and muscles realigned, ripping my clothing from my body. My fighting screech tore through my throat. I attacked the one touching her first, my teeth tearing into his shoulder. In the next instant, he shifted, the flesh knitting back together in a horror show suture. Before I could launch again, another shifted, only the third remaining human.

The woman's footsteps retreated into the distance. She ran away through the forest, not even bothering to be quiet about it. A shot of betrayal made me stumble. I didn't know why I would've thought a woman I'd never met before would stand beside me while I took on these fuckers. It was safer for her to run. But it stung anyway.

Story of my life... Everyone always left me in the dirt while they moved on.

The pair of cougars weren't letting up, charging over and over again. I got in a few good bites, but so did they. I shifted partway, healing the gashes. Snarls cut through the night. Claws came at me from every direction. I tried to stay in front of them. This wasn't the first time I'd been outnumbered, and I usually came out on top.

I knocked out one with a kick of my hind legs and was turning to take down the other cougar when something jabbed me in my ass cheek. I whipped my head around. A hypodermic needle stuck out at an odd angle from my rump. To have that syringe at ready and in hand... They'd planned on using it on the woman.

A new wave of fury crashed over me as my movements slowed, my muscles lethargic. My paws wouldn't hold me up. My knees were made of rubber. It was all slipping away.

But at least the woman was free.

"Find her," was the last thing I heard before my vision blackened.

1

SABRINA

I shifted one claw, the pain spearing through me to settle in my stomach. *Please don't throw up again.*

The loud drone of the airplane's engine filled my head. I checked my sister again, her cage next to mine, to make sure she still breathed. Brooke lay so still, but her chest moved in a shallow rhythm. I swallowed against the panic burning my throat and focused on my task.

I could hold the shift, but just barely. My vision blurred. My stomach rolled. But I had no other options. We needed to get free.

Concentrating on my claw as it manipulated the mechanism inside the padlock, I tried to block everything else out: the chattering of the monkey two cages down, the agitation of a wolf and fox across from me—all ordinary animals, not shifters. Every cage was used, and crates lined the back wall. It smelled like shit, a zoo left unattended.

My gaze skimmed to the door to the cockpit of the large cargo plane, expecting one of those shifters who'd abducted us to come through at any second. They'd given me and Brooke something to make us sleep, and it had made me sick. As soon as I'd woken up,

I'd puked through the bars of the cage. The scent of bile wafted up to me every so often. I tried to ignore that too.

The internal mechanism inside the lock clicked. I froze, holding my breath. It didn't release. Fighting the despair threatening to swamp me, I tried again. I kept my gaze on the lock and away from Brooke whose miniskirt rode up high on her thighs, her ass hanging out. I wished I'd found my sister at home in sensible clothes instead of grinding with a guy at a dance club. But of course, I hadn't.

The truth grabbed tight to my throat. This was my fault. If I hadn't gone to my sister, then Brooke might have remained free. She didn't know anything. Hell, I barely knew what was going on. I just knew my investigation of a missing shifter couple had turned into something dangerous. Something that threatened my family.

God, I hoped Mom was okay.

I'd found the warehouse outside of Detroit and knew something bad was happening there, I just didn't know what. Then there had been those men, those shifters, they'd tried to take me. Three of them? Four? It had gotten so confusing at the end, I'd just run. But running hadn't mattered. They'd caught up with me just as Brooke and I left the dance club.

The spike of pain jabbing through my skull and into my stomach from holding the small shift became too much. I dropped my hand, sat back on my heels, and dragged deep breaths into my lungs. My eyes stayed glued to the cockpit door as I waited for my insides to settle, then I glanced at the row of black parachutes behind the cages across from me.

As soon as I'd seen those chutes hanging there, the plan to escape had formed in my mind. We needed to get free. The shifters might have kept us alive so far, but they'd abducted us for some reason, and it couldn't be good. They'd spoken of hunters when they found me at the warehouse.

The thought made me breathe in and out slowly, attempting

to settle my stomach. We didn't have time for me to feel sick. I needed to get us out of here.

When it seemed like I wouldn't hurl again, I attempted another claw shift. A cold sweat broke over my body. It hurt so much. These collars delivered the worst kind of pain I'd ever felt, but I couldn't give up now. I had to break free.

In the cage next to me, Brooke stirred. *Good.* She'd been lifeless for so long. Slowly, she reached for the collar around her neck. Then, suddenly frantic, she yanked at it.

"Don't touch it," I said, keeping my gaze on the lock but watching Brooke out of the corner of my eye. I was making progress with the internal mechanism and didn't want to start over again, not with so much pain shooting to my stomach. And I didn't know everything these collars could do, but I'd seen the frequency gauge. They were likely armed.

Brooke froze, her eyes wide, breathing panicked. In a flash, she heaved, puking through the bars of the cage and onto the metal floor of the cargo plane. She looked so lost and scared in that cage. I wanted to go to her, to comfort, but right now it was impossible. I needed to remain strong and steady and get us out of here in one piece.

"The drugs they gave us did that," I said as a way of explanation when Brooke turned horrified eyes to me.

She held tight to the bars separating us. "What's going on?" Her voice came out hoarse and scratched.

There wasn't time to go into everything. A couple had gone missing, but not just people getting lost when they'd hiked off-trail. They were shifters, bobcats like us. Bobcats didn't get lost; we followed our scents back home. The couple hadn't.

But I couldn't tell the local authorities they were shifters. We instinctively kept our abilities secret from humans. It was in our nature. That was why I'd started investigating their disappearance on my own.

And I didn't want to admit to Brooke our current situation

was my fault. That would make the hopeless feeling inside me swell again. I needed to focus on the possibility of escape.

The second Brooke tried to shift, she gasped and curled into herself.

I winced at the pain on her face. I knew how bad it felt, like someone had speared a javelin through her brain and into her stomach. I fought against the bile rising in my throat with my one claw out, sparks going off in my head. "We can't shift with the collars on."

Brooke panted through the pain. "Could have told me sooner." Her jaw was locked, her words forced.

The apology was on the tip of my tongue. But if I apologized for that, I should be apologizing for a whole hell of a lot more. "We need to get out of here." I tried to keep my voice calm over the roar of the engine. "If we don't escape, they'll kill us."

Kill us or something even worse. With all the animals here, and from what they'd said to me when they caught me at the warehouse, I knew they weren't planning a surprise birthday party with cake and presents.

The locking mechanism clicked. *Yes!* A shot of adrenaline made my limbs jerky. I scrambled to remove the lock and open the door.

The rush was something else, almost a hindrance. Stars danced in front of my eyes as I crawled out of the cage then stood on weak and shaky legs. How long had they kept us drugged?

"Get me out of here." Brooke rattled the bars.

I swallowed the bile rising in my throat and crouched in front of my sister's cage. As soon as I shifted my claw again, the pain spiked through me. I breathed through the sensation, trying to ignore it. Escape was more important.

Through the bars, Brooke's eyes pleaded with me, but thankfully, she remained quiet instead of bombarding me with questions. Her usually perfect blonde hair was a haloed mess around her face, matted and tangled. The sequined halter top she wore picked up the overhead fluorescents and glinted shards of light at me. Her usually perfect makeup was smeared across her face, her desperate expression pleading. It made my heart clench and my claw falter.

No. I couldn't get distracted. I cast another quick glance toward the cockpit, then concentrated on the lock.

Click. Easier to pick the second time. My adrenaline-infused fingers yanked at the lock until it tumbled to the ground. I stood and backed up so Brooke could crawl out.

As soon as my sister stood, she swayed. I reached out with a steadying hand. "Are you going to be okay?"

After a moment, Brooke nodded.

"Good. Because we're not free yet." I crossed the metal floor of the cargo hold to the parachutes. The sight of the black cable running above the door eased some of my tension. If I clipped us onto the line before we jumped, I wouldn't need to worry about Brooke getting so freaked out she'd forget to pull the cord.

I grabbed two of the packs and threw them at her feet. I didn't have time to inspect the chutes to make sure they were packed properly. This would be a leap of faith.

"You've got to be kidding me." Brooke's voice cut through the drone of the engine.

"This is the only way out." I picked up one pack and forced the harness between my sister's legs and over her shoulders. Brooke stood limp, allowing the act, her eyes dazed.

"I've never done this before." Her voice was small, terrified.

Fear ripped through me, threatening to consume. I needed Brooke to remain calm. "It's easy. I've done this before. I'm going to clip you onto this line." I gestured to the cable above the door. "It's going to pull your chute open for you at the right time, all you need to do is jump."

Brooke blinked, then a giggle bubbled from her lips.

This was not the time for hysterics. I placed both my hands on her shoulders. "You need to pull yourself together. We only have one shot at this. They'll make it impossible to escape if they catch us."

After her expression sobered, she gave me one nod. However flighty Brooke appeared most of the time, she had a will of steel. I was counting on it to see us through this disaster.

Giving her a nod of my own, I buckled the straps across her chest, clipped her onto the cable, then stepped into the harness of the other parachute to pull it over my shoulders. I was about to give my sister a quick tutorial of how to direct the chute when the door to the cockpit opened.

Fear made my breath catch. We'd run out of time.

Two men came through the door, one decked out like a cowboy, the other wearing a trucker hat. I recognized them from when they'd attacked me at the warehouse. My heart pounded. There wasn't time to think.

I turned away and yanked on the handle of the emergency exit. A thundering noise enveloped the cargo hold, along with terrifying pressure. Loose supplies suctioned toward the door. Brooke reached for me, her eyes wide.

A great force smacked me in the middle of my spine at the same time as Brooke was snatched away from me, out the door, into the night sky.

My heart stopped.

I didn't have time to even process the sight when my own pack was ripped off my shoulders with a growl. I lost my balance, falling toward the door, now without a parachute.

I couldn't stop my momentum. *I'm going to die.*

Wind swirled around the cargo hold. I inched toward the door, closer and closer. Maybe it would be better to die than whatever they had planned for me.

Sharp pain along my scalp made me see stars. I screamed. My whole body was yanked from the edge by my hair, into a pocket of space where the wind wasn't as strong.

A growl made me turn my head. A cougar loomed above me, his face in a snarl. He spat out my hair and bared his teeth.

I wasn't going to thank him for saving my life.

Movement caught my attention. The cowboy was putting on a parachute. *No!* I wouldn't let him go after Brooke. My sister needed to remain free of this.

One move in his direction, and the cougar yanked me back with his teeth in my shirt. I kicked and screamed, trying to break free. The need to protect Brooke outweighed everything else. I wasn't defenseless. I was a trained forest ranger and had taken karate half my life.

He released me for a second, only to grip my calf in a bite. I gasped in pain.

The cowboy yelled something over the noise in the plane, then grabbed a smaller bag from beside the parachutes. I strained to stop him, crawling, trying to grip the slick floor, but the teeth on my leg tightened, the cougar dragging me. I got a kick to his jaw, making him loosen his grip, then scrambled away.

I'd almost reached the parachutes when my hair was wrenched again, my scalp screaming. He spun me away until I hit the wall. My breath left me, and I crumpled to the ground. Everything hurt.

The cougar had shifted back to human and stood above me, naked. I glared at him, ready to attack. I would fight dirty if I had to, and his shriveled, little balls were right in my line of sight.

Before I could do anything, he crouched in front of me. I flinched. A grin spread across his face as he picked something off the floor. A remote. He aimed it at me.

"Bad kitty."

Pain seared my brain before I sank into blissful oblivion.

2

SABRINA

COLD METAL PRESSED AGAINST MY FACE, THE SENSATION EERILY familiar. Even before I regained my senses, my instincts told me I was in a bad place. My stomach clenched in fear.

Before opening my eyes, I took stock of my surroundings. Gone was the heavy drone of the airplane. We'd landed. I extended my legs, and my bare feet hit something cold. Bars. I was in another cage, and they'd taken my hiking boots and socks. My heart picking up tempo. I swallowed, reaffirming I still wore a collar.

My head ached where my hair had been torn out. My calf throbbed too, and I realized my pant leg had been rolled up to expose the bite the cougar had given me. Slowly, I reached down to touch it. My fingers met the soft material of a bandage. If they meant to kill me, why would they bother treating the wound?

I tried to take a steady breath. The scents here were different too. A strong cleaner and something medicinal, not the zoo smell of the cargo plane. The place sounded hollow and metallic.

Finally, sensing no one close by, I opened my eyes. Metal bars of a different cage, bigger than the last, filled my vision, a cinder block wall beyond them. These bars were thicker than the ones on the plane but closer together so I wouldn't be able to reach through. On the other side of the room sat a heavy metal door, a desk beside it. Clutter littered the top, and I tingled in awareness at the sight of the remote the cougar had used on me.

I sat up. My head swam, and acid churned in my stomach. Even though the cage was bigger than the one on the plane, there was no way I could stand in it. Extending my arms, I could touch both sides at the same time. I wouldn't be able to stretch fully in any one direction.

Two more doors flanked either end of the long room, each with a narrow window above the doorknob. Which way was the exit? The door on the right had two keypad security locks, one on either side. The other two doors had none. This place felt like a holding room, something impermanent about it.

I need to get out of here. At least Brooke had escaped. Maybe.

The memory of Brooke falling into the sky made me close my eyes and press my forehead to the bars. Had she survived? If they'd caught her again, then they'd bring her here, right? But the other cages beside me were empty.

I swiveled to examine the wall of metal behind me, a small, rectangular door inset inside of it. Desperate, heart pounding, I grabbed at the edges, trying to find purchase and force it open. When a fingernail tore at the effort, I gave up, trying to swallow my panic.

The door to my right opened. I stiffened, the urge to extend my claws and protect myself making my head feel split open. A man strode in, his skin pasty white. He wore a lab coat and held a clipboard, looking like some kind of doctor. Square-rimmed glasses were topped with a receding hairline, and the cut of his pants did nothing to hide his potbelly. The scent of human came at me.

A *human* had me in a cage.

He paused, his posture straightening when he saw me sitting there.

"You're awake." He sounded mildly surprised. "You burn through our serum quite quickly. Interesting. Must have a high metabolism." He smiled like he'd made some sort of joke.

I gripped the bars, wishing it was his neck. "Let me out of here."

He stepped to the desk, then continued like I hadn't spoken. "We'll need to adjust the dose if we want to keep you under longer." His conversational tone made me hunch my spine. "It could take some study. The question would be, is your whole species this way or just you?" He shot me another smile over his shoulder.

My skin crawled with the need to get out of here, to hide myself from human eyes. What else did he have planned for me besides a drug study?

"Let me out of here," I repeated, my fingers tightening on the bars until they hurt.

Two more white men came in through the door on the right, and he turned to them. "She's awake."

I recognized the one, the cougar. He was working with humans. I snarled at him. He grinned, tipping his trucker hat in my direction. The man beside him, another human, wore an air of power along with his expensive suit. The other two seemed to defer to him.

"I can see that," said the one in the suit as he walked toward my cage. He kept his tone mild and his expression placid, but his eyes held a coldness that rose my hackles.

Dangerous. My instincts told me to stay away from him, but I had nowhere to hide.

"I'm hungry," I said, needing to know how he'd take the request. My stomach protested the thought, but I knew I hadn't eaten in many hours because of the way it clenched. I had no clue how long it had been since I'd last had a meal.

"Sharpe," he said as he glanced to the man in the trucker hat. "Go find her something."

Cocking his head, the cougar shifter walked to the door on the left. I noticed a clip at the base of his skull, the same place my collar attached to me. Did it do the same kind of thing? He disappeared through the door. While we waited, the doctor passed the man in the suit a clipboard. Their blasé attitudes made me want to scratch their faces off.

I shook the bars. "Let me out."

He didn't even lift his head or act like I'd spoken. I was nothing to him.

Sharpe returned, a bowl in his hands. My stomach panged. Then he grinned at me as he slid a saucer of milk in the gap under the bars.

All three of them stared at me, waiting to see what I would do. I wanted to pick it up and throw it, but it was almost like they expected that. And if I did what they expected, it meant they won.

Whatever they planned, I couldn't let them win.

Instead of giving in to my anger, I scooted back until my spine pressed against the flat metal of the back wall and hugged my knees to my chest.

They looked disappointed. *Good.* That's all they would get from me—disappointment.

After a moment, the guy in the suit turned away, and Sharpe shrugged before following. The doctor stared at me, his eyes assessing, as they left. He made me feel like an amoeba under a microscope. I hated it. I hated them. I wanted to tear them to pieces.

Swallowing, I tore my gaze away from the leering doctor and watched the two men at the door. That was my exit. They swiped their keycards at the same time, then punched in a four-digit number to get out.

The keypads were so far apart, not even a neanderthal with an eight-foot arm span could reach both at the same time. Two people were required. I was so screwed.

The humans stared at me as if I were an insect.

And I'd seen their faces.

There was no doubt in my mind they meant to kill me.

The milk wasn't sitting well due to my lactose intolerance, but I'd needed some sort of nutrients. Now my bladder swelled to the point of bursting. There was nothing in the cage with me. Nothing. I had no way to relieve myself and refused to pee my pants.

As soon as the doctor returned, I grabbed the bars. "I need to use the bathroom." He paused for a second but didn't look at me as he sat as his desk. I hated thinking of him as a doctor because I was positive he didn't give a shit about my health.

I slapped the bars, palms stinging. "I said I need to use the bathroom, dammit."

The shushing sound of the metal door at the back of my cage startled me as it slid open. I spun around and saw dirt and grass beyond. My entire being screamed at me to escape.

Scrambling through the small opening on my hands and knees as fast as I could, I stood, intent on making a run for it.

My reflection greeted me, the sight shocking in its rawness. I was a mess, my chestnut colored hair everywhere, my face drawn and haggard. I fisted my hands. It wasn't a mirror, but a one-way window. Someone was on the other side. I could feel them watching me but couldn't see them.

Frantic, I glanced around. It was a habitat like a person would see at a zoo. Grass and dirt lay beneath my bare feet, one fake tree with branches took up the center. The wall in front of me was made up of reflective glass, and the other two at my sides were metal. A small door was inset to the wall to my right, no doorknob. I was trapped.

And that wasn't the worst of it. A litter box was tucked in one corner, two bowls beside it full of water and kibble. My face heated. They were determined to treat me like an animal.

There was no privacy, everything open. The trunk of the fake tree was only six inches wide, not big enough to hide behind. But the bottom part of the window was made of metal, almost two feet's worth. Dear God, I had no other options.

Lifting my chin, I picked up the litter box and moved it to the bottom portion of the window. It was the only place where I could keep it concealed. Leaning against the window, I slid down until my bottom half was out of sight.

I wouldn't let them break me.

3

WALKER

A FEMININE, FELINE SCENT WOUND ITS WAY TOWARD ME. *FAMILIAR.* Peaches and cream.

I lifted my head and it hit me low in the gut.

No. Not her. Not here.

I strained, and the shackles and chains around my wrists rattled. I needed to break free, to fight, to protect. Rage coursed through my veins, hot and explosive. If I were free, no one would be safe from my wrath. A growl started low in my chest and rumbled past my lips.

Her scent had come in with Croskey, the man in the lab coat who'd introduced himself when I arrived. I couldn't see him because my eyes were swollen from the beating two cougars had given me, but I heard him putter around the desk across from my cell.

My hands fisted as much as they could in the tight shackles. If they planned to do to her what they'd done to me...

Another growl ripped from my chest. I yanked against my restraints, testing their strength for the thousandth time. They didn't give an inch.

Croskey paused in what he was doing. If I got too rowdy, I'd pay for it, but with her scent wrapping around me like a blanket, it didn't matter anymore. I needed to get her out of here. My heart sped up, and I loosed an involuntary shudder.

The collar around my neck wasn't just a shock collar. I didn't understand it. It injected me with drugs, sometimes to knock me out, other times to do...something else—the sensation of creepy crawly things under my skin, the hot flashes and burning eyes...

Was that how they got those cougar shifters to work with humans? I'd seen the chips in the back of their necks when they'd beaten me.

I'd smelled other shifters in this jail cell who were now long gone, probably dead. The scents were like that of the woman, feline. I was starting to think the only way out of this place was death. But I couldn't surrender to that thought now. Not when she was trapped here with me. I needed to keep my wits and find a way to break free.

The squeak of the chair told me Croskey sat at the desk. Before my eyes had swelled, I'd noticed a machine with clamps, jumper cables, and a lot of buttons and dials stood against the wall. I'd seen something like it once before, when I'd been captured in the terrorist camp with Jordan. The thought of my dead friend made my heart squeeze tight. I might have failed him, but I could *not* fail the woman stuck here with me.

What I wouldn't give to be able to shift and heal my bruises, cuts, and cracked ribs. But the collar around my neck prevented it. The chains connecting me to the wall from my ankles and wrists were secured tight when they'd beaten me, stopping me from fighting back or using my legs. When they were done with me, they'd allowed them to go slack, and I crumpled to the floor, unable to move.

I vowed they'd never break me. I wouldn't scream. I wouldn't plead. Whatever their end goal, they wouldn't win. I'd break free, get the woman out of here, and take them all down.

The door opened, and I lifted my head. A new scent

proceeded this person, human mixed with an expensive after-shave. I tried to open my eyes, but everything remained a blurry, red color. I thought maybe my eyes were bleeding. During my last beating, the cougar coward in the trucker hat had worn brass knuckles, and I'd made sure to tell him how much of a pussy I thought he was for it.

The man stopped in front of the cell, and through the blur, I noted his suit and the mild disgust on his face. He looked famil-iar, but I couldn't place him.

"Do you remember me?" he asked in a pleasant voice, like he was inquiring over the health of my mother.

I tried to shake my head, but it wouldn't cooperate. "Must have a forgettable face." At least that's what I'd tried to say. It'd come out garbled. My mouth was too swollen, and I realized my jaw might be broken. Through the pain, I tried to keep my eyes on him.

"We used to go to school together," he said, flicking a piece of lint off his shoulder.

This new information conjured images from elementary and high school in Goldenlach Ridge. I remembered him now—Emerson Mahn, a human. *Fuck.* The job Landon had sent me on. Was that what this was about? Mahn's sister? Bloody hell, if I told him I hadn't touched her, hadn't even laid eyes on her, would he let me go? All they had to do was ask.

No. This was something else. This facility, the torture, the other shifters. Something bigger was going on here. I just happened to find my way into this bullshit at Landon's direction. *What the hell?* Was Mahn in charge of everything? A human torturing and killing shifters? My skin crawled with the need to conceal myself, to keep our lives a secret.

Back in elementary school, I'd tried to be friends with Mahn, but like so many others who lived on the other side of tracks, I hadn't been good enough.

"I see you do remember," Emerson said after a time, a small

smile ghosting over his face. "It's interesting my men found you nosing around one of my properties along with the woman. Do you know each other?"

I didn't react, didn't blink, didn't move a muscle. Because honestly, I didn't know who she was, only that she'd stumbled into this shit heap at the same time I had.

"Why were you there? At my warehouse?" When I didn't attempt to answer, he asked, "Who else knew you were there? Your friends from our hometown, perhaps?"

Still, I didn't answer, wouldn't give him the satisfaction. I vowed to give him nothing, even if he demanded the best brand of protein powder, my favorite football team, or challenged me to a round of *Halo*.

He turned his head, addressing Croskey over his shoulder. "I think it's time to move on to phase two, don't you agree?"

I thought I saw Croskey smile but couldn't be certain with my vision still so hazy. Mahn focused on me again, then nodded once, his face impassive, before turning and heading to the door. I spit a glob of blood in his direction. It didn't make it all the way to him, but he paused mid-step, and I knew he'd received the message loud and clear.

I'd never felt such pain. Nothing prepared me for this. Whatever information they wanted, I was sure they'd gotten it by now. I didn't know what they were looking for. I didn't know what they wanted. I just knew I needed the pain to stop.

I'd thought I was so badass. I thought I could handle anything. *I survived terrorists, and look at me now, blubbering and crying.*

I was back in the dirt hole in the ground watching Jordan get his head cut off. They were doing it to send a message, televised on local television and on the Internet. The screams—they wouldn't stop. I just wanted it all to stop.

Were they even asking me questions? Did they want to know where my unit was? I didn't know. Hadn't seen them in weeks, but I told them everything. Every bit of intel I had inside me. I even made shit up.

I just wanted it to stop.

It's just the three of us, me, Landon, and Kane. Even though they don't know it, I've never felt more whole than when I'm with them. I never thought I'd have a best friend—no one ever cared enough—and now I have two. I'd do anything for these guys.

"You're making a mistake."

Landon said the words to Kane and I agreed. My hands clenched and unclenched at my sides. Kane was leaving, just like everyone else, and he made no indication he'd heard Landon's words as he threw all his clothing into a suitcase and a duffel bag.

When he didn't respond, I couldn't hold my tongue and longer. "So you're just going to give up?" I asked, my tone bitter, but I couldn't help it. "Cut everyone off? Make it so no one can find you? It's selfish, Kane."

With a half snarl, he signed, "What do you care? You're leaving next week."

That was completely different. I might be on leave, my first, but I had no other options to get out of Goldenlach Ridge. These two did. They were smart and could earn scholarships and shit. If I wanted anything better for myself, the military was the only place for me.

My whole body tensed, my hands remaining in fists. "That doesn't mean I'm giving up on life." I turned away and slammed the door to the apartment on my way out.

"Suck it! Suck it!" Jordan jumped up, waving a finger in my face as he yet again beat the crap out of me at a video game.

Across the room, Verdugo and Chi laughed at his antics. No one got as competitive as Jordan. At least he wasn't a sore loser on top of it, though.

I smiled and tossed my controller onto the coffee table, spreading my arms wide in defeat.

"Which one of you fuckers is going to take me on?" Jordan challenged the pair across the room.

But Lavigne stepped into our living space with his serious expression. We all quieted. "We're on," he said with a nod.

Time for another mission.

The scent of dirt and blood surrounded me. I heard Jordan's screams. Our captors shouted in our faces, nothing we ever understood. I don't know why they preferred to torture him over me, but I needed it to stop. I swore at them, screamed every insult I knew so they'd focus their attention on me instead. Jordan was already missing half his leg because of the land mine. Starved and injured, neither of us had enough energy to shift.

They'd eventually kill us. I knew it. We could only hope to stay alive long enough for the rest of the team to find us. Except, I knew there was little chance of that. We'd failed. And now we were paying the price.

Our country would deny our existence. We knew the risks going in.

Dirt filled my mouth, my body hung heavy, chained to the wall, my jaw broken. They beheaded Jordan. I was next.

I couldn't see her, but I knew she was close. I could tell from her scent. I followed her shadow, trying to touch it, hold it, but she was always just beyond my reach.

Pain, unimaginable pain, kept me from her. But it didn't stop me from reaching out, trying to catch a glimpse. I knew if I finally caught her, the pain would stop. I'd feel whole for once in my life. I *needed* her.

And she needed me.

4

SABRINA

THE SCREAMS WOKE ME.

They were tortured and primal, coming through the door across the room—a man's screams. The noise made my teeth clench and my heart pound. Whoever made such a sound had to be near death.

I was back in my cage. My time in the habitat had allowed me to stretch, but when they'd wanted me to return to the other side, I'd refused. They'd shocked me unconscious, and I'd woken up in here.

The lights above me flickered. I never knew what time it was because they always stayed on. Right now, it was like a great force drained them of electricity.

The screaming stopped and the lights above me stabilized.

I'm next. Whatever they were doing to the guy on the other side of the door, they would do to me too.

Not happening. I'd wait. I'd watch. And I'd find my moment to escape.

A sense of agitation went through the compound, putting everyone on edge. Something must have happened, but I didn't know what. I caught snippets of conversation when the door opened.

"How does a whole helicopter go missing?"

Anger and disbelief tinged the words. Somebody said something I couldn't hear, then the same voice spoke again, "I don't care. She's worth ten million. If you don't—"

The door closing cut off the words. Dread pounded in my chest. Were they talking about Brooke? *Please be alive. And safe.*

Every few hours, the screaming would wake me. It physically hurt to hear it. I wanted them to stop. I covered my ears. At some point, I starting hoping they'd kill him and put him out of his misery.

But these humans were not humane.

"You're not going to break him."

A new voice, a feminine one. I lay on my side in my cage but pretended to be asleep. Holding still, I cracked open one eye. A short redhead wearing a black T-shirt and jeans faced off with the man in the suit. I'd heard people call him Mr. Mahn. She wore a fierce frown and her curly hair went in all directions. Freckles the same color as her hair stood out against pale skin, so many they covered most of her face. Maybe Irish ancestry or something.

"We'll see," Mahn said, his voice idle, like he didn't care about what she had to say.

The woman appeared worried, maybe the first person to wear that expression in this place since I arrived. *A weak link.* I could exploit weak links. If the redhead had sympathy for the person being tortured on the other side of the door, then maybe she'd help me.

"You never heard the stories. He's survived this and worse."

"He's like the others. He'll crack," Mahn said, moving away from her.

The redhead's gaze slid to me, and I quickly shut my eyes. I learned more when they thought I was asleep. Their footsteps moved to the door, and I opened one eye in time to watch them swipe their keycards at the same time then punch in the code. This time I caught a four and a six. The door unlocked.

"It would be nice if you listened to my opinion once in a while," the redhead said, stepping through.

"It's simple. He turns or he dies. Those are our only options. He's too dangerous for the arena. We can't have—" Their voices cut off when the door shut behind them.

The door to the habitat slid open. I didn't hesitate. Being cramped in the other cage made me appreciate the short spans of time they allowed me this scrap of freedom.

I stood and stretched, easing the ache of my sore muscles, then froze. The sensation of being watched screamed at me even more than normal. I walked up to the window, and my glaring face reflected back at me. I refused to be their entertainment.

"I don't want to hunt a woman," a man's voice said, muffled, but I'd heard him.

"Is this better?" This was Mahn. I would recognize his voice anywhere now.

My skin rippled, a familiar feeling that made me take a step back. Dread and nausea filled my stomach. *I'm changing.* My molecules tingled, each like a grain of sand moving quickly through a small space. No matter how much I fought, it was out of my control.

I usually loved to shift, but not now. This was a violation.

Every piece of me transformed until I was covered in fur. My bobcat form was smaller than my human one, and my clothing trapped me. My feline instincts made me back up to escape, shaking my head back and forth until I hit the wall. My claws tore into the material near my face. *Rip.*

Finally, I was free, my paws digging into the dirt, my spine arched in a defensive stance. Horror made my stomach clench.

A chuckle tittered on the other side of the glass. Humans had watched me shift, and now they laughed.

Anger swept through me, intoxicating in its intensity. They could make me shift on demand? Shame followed the anger, my instincts screaming at me to hide. Or kill them. I snarled and dove at the window.

"Much better."

I charged the window again, wanting to tear them apart.

"Then don't try to lowball me. It's ten million. She's worth the money."

"I'll consider it."

I climbed the tree and launched myself at the window again. I wanted to rip them to shreds, every one of them. I'd never even thought of harming a human in my bobcat form before, but in this moment, all I could think about was tearing out their throats.

The metal door at the side opened. A box slid inside before it shut with a slam.

I watched that box, foreboding making me tense. When I heard the rustles inside, a soft squeak, I knew what they'd given me—mice. The box was full of mice.

Despite the loathing I had for everyone on the other side of the window, my feline instincts perked up. When the first mouse popped its white head out of the box, I pounced on it.

Days passed, I didn't know how many. A knot of nausea settled in my stomach when I realized the longer I was here, the more chance there was I'd go into heat. What would they do to me then?

I hadn't heard the screaming from the other room in a while. I hoped they put the man out of his misery. No one should have to suffer like that. These people were monsters in every sense of the word. I started praying for my own death. Whatever they wanted to do with me, it would be as bad or worse as what they'd done to that man.

Angry voices woke me. The door to my right was open, and the man in the lab coat, the one they called Croskey, eavesdropped on whatever occurred in the hallway beyond.

"I don't care what happened," Mahn said. "You don't lose a ten-million-dollar piece of my property."

I lay still and silent like I'd learned to do, to find out as much as possible about my captors.

"No one said she was mated." A new male voice said.

"That shouldn't matter."

"You didn't see this guy. He flipped over a car by himself."

Silence reigned.

Croskey stepped away, the door closing.

"Get out of my—"

After that, tensions ran high through the compound. I didn't know what had happened, but it wasn't making anyone here happy. Something that was bad for them was probably a good thing for me.

It wasn't long before the attitude in the compound changed again. It became buoyant. *Not good.*

I understood why when the door to the hallway opened and I heard the next piece of conversation.

"We ship her out tomorrow. If you can—" The door closed.

My heart pounded. I needed to escape or I'd end up dead.

Time's up.

5

SABRINA

My heart had raced with panic every second since I'd heard of being shipped somewhere. I didn't have a plan—or, at least, a good one—and the terror of what was to come made my skin feel tight on my body.

I lay in my cage in human form, my habitat closed. The only way to get out of this place was through the door that took two people to open, two keycards. No matter how much I listened, no matter how much I saw, no other way presented itself.

I needed help and my options were limited.

When the door opened, I expected Croskey, but two men came inside. One I recognized from before, Sharpe, the other I hadn't seen before now. He was a smaller guy with a wiry frame. Both seemed pissed.

I still hadn't learned anything about why these shifters worked for humans.

They strode toward my cage and I stiffened. At least these two didn't look at me like I was lower than low. They both smelled the same, both cougars. Sharpe's expression was filled with derision. But the other guy's eyes held interest. My senses went alert. Keeping his gaze, I slowly sat up.

"Let's go," said Sharpe, tugging at the other's arm. "We've got work to do."

"Sure." He stepped away from the cage. His eyes lingered on me until he turned toward the door and punched in the code.

I kept my eyes on them, my mind racing. They both had those clips in the back of their necks, ones that looked similar to my collar. They were controlled somehow, same as me. When the one glanced back at me, I gave him a little wave and a smile. His eyebrows rose before he stepped through the door.

It closed with a clang. *Shit.* I gripped the bars, pressed my forehead against the cool metal. I'd thought I'd had a chance and I'd lost it. Defeat made my limbs heavy. I leaned against the back wall and hugged my shins to my chest. Tomorrow, I'd be shipped like a piece of merchandise to God knew where. My head fell forward on my knees. I bit my lip, trying not to cry.

When the door opened again a while later, I glanced up. A bolt of hope speared my chest. It was the same wiry guy as before, and this time he was alone.

"Hi," I said, perking up, but then toned it back. I didn't want to appear too eager. I also didn't want to appear disinterested.

He nodded, his gaze scanning the lab then landing back on my cage. We stared at each other for several long moments. I licked my dry lips. I couldn't screw this up. This was my only chance to get out of here. And it didn't matter what the hell I needed to do—I needed to get out.

After a while, he gave himself a shake and turned away, heading toward the door.

"Please stay," I said, trying to adopt a sultry tone. He turned a bit. "I don't want to be alone right now."

His eyes scanned me up and down. I knew I probably looked a mess. My plaid shirt was torn, my hair going every direction. Dirt smudged my jeans. I'd felt like I'd been here for weeks and hadn't been offered a bath, shower, or even a clean wash cloth in all that time.

"Where is everyone?" I asked, keeping my voice soft. "It's quiet."

He shrugged. "Home mostly. It's late." Which meant civilization wasn't far. That was good.

Hesitating for a moment, he pulled the chair away from the desk and straddled it to face me, his elbows propped up on the back.

"How are you going to get out when you're here by yourself?" I asked jerking my chin toward the door.

He shrugged. "The guard is right outside. He'll give me a few minutes." He steepled his fingers. "I met your sister."

My whole body tensed. *Brooke is alive.* It was so hard to keep my expression neutral, to not scream at him to tell me more.

"Oh?" I asked, adjusting to a kneeling position, my hands so tight on the bars they ached. "What happened?"

"That bitch bit me." He rubbed his hand distractedly even though there wasn't a bite there now. He'd probably shifted since then, healing it.

"She was always the disobedient one," I replied, keeping my voice soothing even as my stomach bubbled with mixed emotions. Not that it was true at all, but the guy looked like he needed an ego stroke.

"You don't look much alike."

Actually, we resembled each other a lot. My sister's friend, Corey, called it the Elsa/Anna Effect. If we shaved our heads, we were the same doll. My sister's hair was almost platinum blonde, mine a rich brown like our mom's, but our features were extremely similar. "Everyone says she's the pretty one."

The guy cocked his head to the side. "I don't think so."

I took a deep breath. "Where is she now?"

"Hell if I know."

Even though the answer brought me so much relief my vision swam, I knew I needed to change the subject. He was becoming testy. I needed him relaxed. At least I knew my sister wasn't coming to this place. Now I must focus on escaping.

"Why did you come back in here?" I kept my voice soothing, trying to channel my sister's way of luring guys in, even as my stomach rolled with nausea.

He shrugged and didn't answer.

"You seem like a nice guy," I said, leaning back.

His eyes turned hard, skeptical. "Do I now?"

I nodded, not wanting to lose him. "It's my last night here. I don't want to spend it alone."

"Yeah, they're shipping you out to the arena in the morning."

I tried to keep my face neutral, to not reveal what the word "arena" did to me, that I wanted to know what the hell that meant, like I was fine with what was about to happen to me.

"I don't want to go without at least one good memory, considering what might happen to me there." I kept my voice soft even though I wanted to scream.

He didn't answer, just kept staring at me. I couldn't tell what he was thinking, but words weren't working. I needed to try a different tactic.

I leaned away from the bars and unhooked the top button of my shirt. The guy's eyes narrowed. I undid the next one, then the next, all the way down to my navel, until the torn shirt hung in two panels, exposing a hint of the beige bra beneath.

I waited for him to say something, but he kept staring at me.

"Let me out of here and I'll show you more," I whispered, fighting the nerves that made me shake.

"I'm not stupid."

"Didn't say you were." I parted the material and let it slide over my shoulders to the floor of the cage. I shivered in the cold air of the room.

And still, he didn't say or do anything, just watched me with those hard eyes.

I need to get out. Steeling me spine, I reached for the top button of my jeans. Whoever had been on the other side of the window of my habitat all this time had seen more than I was revealing now. I shimmied out of my jeans until I wore only granny panties and bra.

The guy's eyelids lowered.

"Do you like what you see?" I asked, forcing my voice to become husky.

He nodded once.

"Let me out and you can see more." I emphasized the point by squeezing my breast through the material of my bra. "You can touch more."

He stood so fast the chair almost toppled over. It settled back with a *bang*, making me twitch. He stalked toward me. Instead of opening the cage, he grabbed my jeans and shirt through the gap at the bottom of the bars and ripped them free, tossing them across the room.

I had nothing to hide behind.

But still, he didn't open the cage, the indecision plain on his face.

Frustration making me desperate, I cocked my head to the desk behind him. "You've got the remote. You hold the power." I glanced at the door, then back at him. "You said there was a guard right outside. What am I going to do?"

He straightened and walked to the desk. "I've got the remote." He picked it up. "I hold the power." Tucking it into the back pocket of his jeans, he strode toward me.

My eyes went to the camera in the corner. The usual red light on it was out. Had he done that? Had he come in here with some sort of plan for me? I held those questions inside as he punched a code into the panel at the front of my cage, the first time anyone ever had. The lock released and my heart raced.

One hurdle down. When the door swung open, I shimmied to the edge. His hands on my waist, he helped me down, keeping my body pressed against his. My skin crawled.

I would have stepped away, but he yanked me back against him. My breath left me in a huff. His hand gripped my ass, and he pressed my pelvis against his erection.

Bile gathered in my throat. "I like it from behind," I said to his chest, swallowing. If I looked at him directly, my revulsion would show.

"Me too."

He spun me around and pushed me roughly toward the desk and over it. His hand on the middle of my back forced my face down. The bile climbed higher as I reached blindly in front of me. The sound of a belt buckle unfastening made my chest tighten. When he pulled down my underwear, I swept my hand across the top of the desk's surface, searching for something, anything, I could use as a weapon. Limbs shaking, I made contact with a pen.

My grip tight, I spun. All the rage I'd held inside since I'd arrived in this godforsaken place gave me the strength of a rabid bear. My martial arts, then forest ranger training, told me where a human's weak points were.

The pen sank into the flesh of his neck. With a garbled shout, he straightened. But the stab wound didn't incapacitate him. In the next instant, I pulled it out. Blood gushed. I drew back my fist, punching him in the throat before he could shout for help.

He bent forward, his hands moving up to his face. I jerked my knee upward, connecting with his nose. A loud crunch echoed, followed by a muffled howl. I ran at him with all my strength, pushed him over, then followed through until I straddled his torso. I ignored the fingers grabbing at me, trying to shove me off. My knees squeezed tight to keep my place. With the force of both hands, I drove the pen into his eye socket.

Silence followed the sickening sludge sound. Everything went still in the room, even the air around me. Then I reached for gulping breaths, gasping as stars sparked in my eyes.

Reality slowly settled. My hands still clutched the pen. Blood and clear jelly oozed from his eye. I let go, scrambling back and off of him. My spine hit the wall. My heart pounded in my chest. My breaths came out fast. Every surface that touched me was freezing. I stared at the door, expecting the guard to come charging through.

It remained closed. I inhaled deep into my lungs, the shock of having my plan work making me weak. *Thank God for karate lessons.* I stared at the dead man's feet. Anyone who passed by and looked through the small window would see the body.

The thought made me move. Heart pounding, I went back to the guy, strained to roll him over enough to pull the remote out of his pocket, and tried not to look at the pen in his eye or blood gathering on the floor. As soon as I had the remote in my hand, I stared at it. The thing could shock me, drug me, and force me to shift. I hated it as much as the people who kept me captive.

I pressed the disarm button. My collar beeped. Then I pressed release. A gasp escaped me as the two prongs in my spine retracted. The remote fell from my shaking fingers as I frantically pulled the collar away from my neck.

As soon as I was free of it, it felt like I could breathe easier. I tossed it away from me, then stood. Adrenaline made me light-headed. I wasn't out of the woods yet. And I couldn't escape without help. At any second, someone would come in here or see the body.

I scurried to the door across from my cage and yanked it open. Stale air pressed against my face.

I stepped into a hallway with two doors. Up on my toes, I peeked in the narrow window of the first one. Jail cells, empty ones, but I pressed my face against the glass to see farther along and noticed a prone form.

I pushed the door open and poked my head inside. The scent of blood, piss, and shit slammed into my senses, making my throat close up. Breathing through my teeth, I stepped inside.

A naked body lay on the floor of the last cell. The desk across from it was similar to the one in my room. I crept closer, urgency and caution warring with each other. Some sort of electrical device was in the corner, complete with cables and prongs, wires and clamps. My stomach rolled when I thought of how the lights had flickered.

I stared at the person inside the cell. Was he dead? It looked like it. But if he was, then I was so screwed. I needed help or I'd never get out. But this guy might be more of a hindrance than assistance.

Even if that was true, I couldn't leave him here. Not after hearing what they'd done to him.

His arms and legs were shackled to the wall with chains. There were other hooks, some on the ceiling, others high up on the wall, some on the floor—a torture chamber. I rattled the bars, trying to open the door, but it was locked.

My gaze moved to the desk. There were lots of things on it. Keys, papers, books, pens, a remote. I grabbed the keys, trying the first one in the lock. It took three tries, but finally, the locking mechanism clicked. The hinges squeaked in the quiet of the room when I pulled the door open. I took a step inside, then paused. He had a collar on too, one like mine.

Before I did anything else, I needed to get his collar off. I returned to the desk, grabbed the remote, and hit the disarm button, followed by the release button.

The man didn't move as the collar clicked open.

Swallowing, I dropped the remote and went back into the cell. The man's face was turned away from me, his skin scraped and bruised everywhere. Long, thin marks ran across his back, some older than others, like he'd been whipped or caned. It didn't look like his chest rose and fell with breaths, but I needed to know for sure.

Cautiously, I crept forward until I crouched beside him. I removed the collar, throwing it away from his body, then pressed two fingers to his throat to check for a pulse.

It happened so fast, I had no time to react. I was squatting one instant, and in the next, I lay flat on my back, an enraged man above me with days' worth of stubble competing with the swelling on his face. His hate-filled glare was the only thing I could see as he gripped my wrists over my head with one hand, his other tight on my throat.

6

WALKER

My tormentor would finally die.

Soft, supple flesh. Cool hands struggling against mine. Small hips between my thighs. The scent of shifter filled my head. *Familiar.*

Reality was slow to sink in. My gaze finally focused through the swelling in my eyes. It was a woman beneath me, not Croskey or one of the others who'd participated in my torture. Her brown hair spilled over the floor of my cell, eyes widened in panic.

Our gazes collided and my breath caught in my throat. An electric zing went through my body from touching her. And her scent—*peaches and cream.* It was a triple punch straight to the depths of my soul. *Mate.*

I'd been about to choke her. *Fuck.*

Horror splashing through me, I let go and rolled onto my back. The concrete pressed against my wounds and made me hiss. My whole body shook with adrenaline, barely feeling the cold air on my naked flesh. Beside me, the woman sucked in deep breaths.

My fault.

When I rolled onto my side to see her face, she shrank away

from me, still gasping. I didn't ask if she was okay. I could very well see she wasn't. Wearing only underwear, a beige bra and white panties that covered everything as much as underwear could, her golden eyes glared at me.

She pressed a palm to her chest, and I noticed the red chafe marks around her throat. Not from my hands. No, those were from the collars they'd made us wear. I touched my own throat as my eyes spied the piece of metal a few feet away.

Rage spread through me like lava. They'd hurt her. They'd tortured me. I wanted everyone responsible to burn, starting with Croskey and Emerson Mahn. All of them would scream just as much as I had. I wouldn't stop until they were all dead.

But first, we had to get out of here.

My training kicked in. Everything clicked into place inside my head. She was breaking me out. She'd removed our collars. No alarm had been set off yet. We still had time to get free if I didn't fuck it up worse than I already had.

Adrenaline spiked, and I rolled to my feet, assessing. I was a mess, could barely see out the slits of my eyes. They'd kept me weak so a full shift would be tricky. Someone had been feeding me, but barely. A piece of bread here and there, shoved into the corner of my cell when I hadn't been hanging from my wrists, like they were trying to keep it a secret. Whoever it was, it was the same person each time, the same human scent.

Gritting my teeth, I shifted enough to start the regeneration process on my body. Pain shot through my limbs and back, but it was nothing compared to what they'd already done. As soon as the swelling of my face went down and I could see properly, I shifted back. The energy expended made me stagger, and I braced a hand against the wall, taking a deep breath. Shit, they'd messed me up.

My eyes went to the woman who'd freed me. "Are you okay?" My voice came out like gravel.

The only indication she gave me that she'd heard the question was a small nod. I could finally see her properly. My heart raced in my chest. Even in her ragged state, she was beautiful with flowing, dark brown hair, delicate limbs, and a fit and trim form. High cheekbones were struck with a flush, her wide lips pressed together. She was more gorgeous than any of my imaginings could've made her.

But she looked anything but impressed at seeing me for the first time. She sat with her spine pressed against the bars of the cell, her hand at her throat, glaring at me with fire in her eyes.

Yeah, I'd fucked up the introduction.

I extended a hand to her and she shrank away. What had they done to her? Now wasn't the time for questions or answers, but I couldn't have her afraid of me. "I'm assuming we need to hurry if we're going to get out of here alive."

Her jaw tightened, but she nodded again and pressed against the cell bars to stand without my assistance. I dropped my hand, turning away to stride out of this hell hole. "What about other shifters? Are any others being held here?"

"I haven't heard or scented any except you." Her voice came out raspy and I shivered.

If there weren't any in the immediate vicinity, we didn't have the resources right now to do a big search. What we needed were weapons and clothes. I slunk to the door and listened. No sound. I poked my head out and saw two doors on either side of the hallway.

The soft sounds of bare feet on concrete came up behind me. "Do you know where the exit is?" I asked quietly without looking at her.

"To the left," she said. When I glanced back, her skin rippled slightly, muscles undulating to heal the marks on her throat in a partial shift.

Quickly, I headed to the door on the left. A glance through the narrow window revealed a man down, blood on the floor around his head.

I glanced behind me. She'd done that? Grim, golden eyes stared back at me.

With a nod of acknowledgment, I opened the door, listening for a moment, then pushed it the rest of the way. It was a lab of sorts, empty cages lining the one side and a desk on the other. There were three doors, the one we'd stepped out of and two more opposite each other on either end. Everything was cold and clinical, the scent of cleaning fluid almost overwhelming all else. One of the cage's doors stood open, milk and kibble visible in the corner. *That's where they kept her.* I fisted my hands, ready to punch something.

When I got a good look at the dead guy, I snarled. He was one of the shifters who'd beat the shit out of me. And with his belt and top buttons of pants undone, I could only assume what he'd wanted to do. I growled. Even with the wound in his neck and the pen in his eyeball, his death had been too easy.

Quickly, I crouched beside him, searching for weapons. No gun, but there were odds and ends in the pockets of his cargo pants: a Swiss Army knife, a wallet, and a set of keys. I untied his boots, yanked them off, then loosened his belt and did the same thing with the pants. He was smaller than me, but tight pants were better than none.

"We need to swipe two keycards at the same time," she said, pointing to the belt I'd yanked from its loops. "There's another one on the desk."

Palming the keycard, I nodded then watched her button up a plaid shirt, the same blue one I'd seen her wearing that night those cougars had taken me down. That meant we'd been here the same amount of time, however long it had been. I ran my hand over my jaw. It was covered in thick stubble. Multiple days. Weeks maybe.

Quickly, I buttoned up the pants and was reaching for a boot when the one door started to open. As fast as I could, I moved, pressing against the wall. The second the guard in all black tactical gear got a view of the room, he paused. It would be a lot to process in a split second. My half-naked mate appeared vulnerable and alone even with the dead body between her and him.

Jeans in her hands, she froze, eyes glued to the guard. Either she was too shocked or too smart to look at me.

"Hey!" The guard took another step inside and raised his M16.

I grabbed the barrel, pointed it upward, and slammed the door against him at the same time. Shots went off, flaring into the ceiling, glass raining down from the fluorescent lights above. I ignored the way my hand burned from the heat of the barrel. It was nothing compared to what I'd been through. I widened the door, then slammed it again and again until his grip loosened. As soon as it did, I ripped the gun away from him, turned it around, and fired.

His face received the brunt of the shots, shattering in a burst of flesh and bone. He fell backward.

An alarm sounded. *Fuck.*

I glanced at the woman. "No time," I said when she reached to pull the jeans on. She hesitated, then dropped them, moving toward me to pick her way between shards of glass.

Slinging the gun over my arm, I searched the guard for more weapons, keeping my eyes and ears open to anyone else coming down the hallway from the crack left open by his leg. *Guess we didn't need the keycards after all.* I would hang on to them anyway, just in case we found any locked doors. The guard wore a holstered handgun at the small of his back, and I checked to see if it was loaded, then grabbed a magazine from his belt before pocketing it.

"Do you know how to use this?" I asked, waggling the gun without looking at her.

"Yes." She held out her hand when I stood, and I set the butt of the weapon in it.

Like an expert, she too checked it was loaded before pointing it at the ground and giving me a nod. She had to know some shit if she took out a guy with a pen. A thrum of pride made my blood hot. "Which way now?"

"No clue," she replied in a soft rasp.

That wasn't good. But if she'd been locked up in one of those cages this whole time, what did I expect? The fact that she'd gotten us to this point was pretty amazing.

I glanced to the left, a fifty-fifty chance we'd find the exit. Needing to move, I headed in that direction. "Stay close," I said over my shoulder. There might not be any guards ahead at the moment, but that would change with the alarm blaring like an air raid siren.

We neared the corner and I snugged up against the wall. When I shot a quick glance at my mate, I noticed the trail of blood behind her. She must have stepped in some of the glass. I closed my eyes. So much for stealth. Anyone who came looking for us would know which direction we'd gone.

"Heal your feet," I barked at her before checking to make sure the coast was clear.

"Sorry," she murmured.

I didn't look back at her again as we headed down the next hallway. Movement ahead caught my attention, and I fired two rounds at the fucker coming our way. He went down. I glanced behind us. Another advanced on our six. The woman lifted her gun and fired before I had a chance to warn her, making the guard duck for cover. We both slid around the corner. Another thrum of pride raced through me. Nothing like a badass woman with a gun.

"Run to the next hallway, then stop," I said when she turned to me. This place was a maze. Who knew what we'd find ahead?

When the guard behind us fired again, I waited a heartbeat, turned the corner, and fired twice, getting him in center mass. He went down. Lucky for us, these guys weren't wearing Kevlar. Guess their boss was cheap.

I caught up to my mate pressed tight against the wall. I

checked that the coast was clear, then grabbed her hand, hurrying her along. A redhead appeared around the corner ahead of us. Her eyes jumped from us to further beyond. She lifted her gun, fired, then tucked herself behind the corner. I fired, hitting the wall in a spray of concrete, but missed her head.

Her shots hadn't come anywhere close to us, and I surveyed down the hall. A guard was down. Neither I nor my mate had fired at him.

"Stand down!" the redhead shouted in the ringing silence.

Like hell. But she hadn't fired at us when she had the chance. A fist appeared around the corner. I held my fire. The redhead poked her head around the corner.

The scent of a familiar human came at me. I'd smelled her before. Even more than that, I recognized her from the picture Landon had given me: Jolyn, Emerson Mahn's sister. For that alone, I should shoot her for whatever her part in this operation. She was the one I was supposed to find. Well, my job for Landon was over. I'd found her and looked forward to my paycheck.

Beside me, my partner in crime lifted her gun to fire. I stayed her with a hand on her arm. "She was the only one who gave me food."

The three of us stared at each other, assessing, the alarm still blaring around us. After a moment, Jolyn cocked her head to the side. "This way."

"We can't trust her," my mate said beside me.

"No," I agreed but lowered my gun. "But we're going to follow her anyway." Neither of us had a clue as to where the exit was. This might be our only chance to get out of here without recapture or death. "Are there any more like us here?"

Jolyn shook her head. "You two are it right now."

With a jerk of her head, she led us through two more corridors before stopping to address us. "Turn right. Go to the end of the hallway. The last door on the left leads to the garage. You can find a vehicle there." She pulled a set of keys out of her pocket and tossed them at me. "These will work on something. Head southwest to Fairbanks."

Fairbanks. What the fuck were we doing in Alaska? When those cougars had captured me, we were in Detroit. And Jolyn was making it clear she couldn't come with us. My gut told me that wasn't a good idea, but short of another shoot out with her, there wasn't much I could do. I had my mate to protect, and being a shifter here was more dangerous than Jolyn being a human surrounded by human trash.

I had questions, a lot of questions only Jolyn could answer, and no time. But she'd helped us, and I felt like I should return the favor. Once Landon learned about this place, about what she was involved in, I doubt he'd be happy.

"Someone's looking for you, Jolyn." Her eyes widened, the only reaction to my declaration. "I'd run if I were you."

I didn't say anything else as I ushered my mate down the hallway where Jolyn had told us to go.

"What's going to happen to her?" my mate asked quietly, glancing once over her shoulder. Jolyn was already gone.

7

SABRINA

THE GUN FELT HEAVY IN MY HAND, THE WALL COLD AGAINST MY back. Adrenaline and anxiety coursed through me in equal measures.

The man I'd freed, the shifter, blocked me with his body as we stood near the door the redhead had told us led to the garage. It made me feel both protected and gave me the urge to punch him on the shoulder and tell him I could protect myself.

How had he known that woman's name? She'd looked surprised when he'd said it. Did he know anyone else here? Had the man I killed been an old friend?

My body shook, the images of the pen sticking through his eyeball imprinted in my mind. I'd never forget it, the sludgy sound it made when I'd stabbed him. My stomach rolled.

But I didn't have time to lose it right now, not when we still needed to get out of this place. The man in front of me took a quick glance through the window of the garage, then leaned against the wall, assessing.

"This is going to be tricky," he said quietly without looking at me. I wondered if he was talking more to himself than me. I didn't know if his voice was always this husky, but it made me shiver in a way I didn't have time for right now—a strange reaction with danger surrounding us.

When I'd first seen him, when he'd pinned me down, he'd been a mess of bruises and swelling and I hadn't been able to determine what he looked like. Now that his face was healed, I saw he was handsome in a stark and brutal sort of way. Long nose, sharp jaw that ended in a pointed chin, green eyes rimmed with yellow—he might have been called beautiful if it wasn't for the savage calculation in his gaze.

Before my mind could wander too far, he opened the door. *Ratatat.* I flinched at each shot fired, then glanced down the hallway from where we'd come. No movement. I waited, watching, not knowing if I should follow him or remain in place to make sure no one came from behind. This guy obviously knew what he was doing, but he'd given me no instruction. My hand tightened around the gun.

After a heartbeat, the noise in the garage stopped. With one last glance down the hallway, I poked my head around the doorframe to see if he'd survived.

The first thing I saw was the dead man near the door. He wore an all-black outfit like the others we'd encountered in the building, and his eyes stared right at me, vacant. I swallowed. My gaze moved past him to my shirtless companion who skulked through the space, his athletic body low to the ground, always assessing, grabbing more guns off the fallen.

The place was filled with all sorts of vehicles: SUVs, Jeeps, a couple Hummers. I stepped fully inside, allowing the door to close behind me. When I noticed the deadbolt, I locked it.

"Come here," he said without looking at me, climbing into a black Jeep without its soft top, the roll bars exposed.

I hopped over the dead man, then another one, skirting around a dead woman before I arrived at the Jeep. He'd killed six people in the space it had taken me to think him beautiful.

The indifferent assessment he wore on his face chilled me.

Taking these lives meant nothing to him. I was grateful he was on my side, that I'd made the right decision in freeing him, but the fear of this place was quickly becoming superseded by alarm toward the man helping me. But I knew now I wouldn't have been able to get this far without him.

As soon as I climbed into the passenger seat beside him, he shoved a machine gun at me. "Shoot anyone who comes through that door," he said, trying each of the keys in the ignition. He paused and tipped his head. "Except the redhead."

Maybe not so indifferent, but the severity of his focus was unnerving. I pointed the gun at the door, but my hands shook, making the weapon bob. Seconds ticked by, each feeling longer as I sat there and tried to make my arms hold still.

"Just keep it together a little longer," he murmured under his breath, and I again didn't know if he was talking to himself or me.

It seemed like such a long time before the engine roared to life. He shifted into gear at the same time movement caught my attention on the other side of the window. Someone was trying to get inside the garage.

Clack, clack, clack came the sound of someone shooting the deadbolt just as the Jeep launched toward the garage door. We screeched to a halt a second later. Even with my hand on the dashboard, I almost went through the windshield.

"Hit that button," he said, turning with his gun in hand. *Ratatat.* He aimed at the two guys who had broken through the door. I ducked when they returned fire.

"The white button!"

Head down, I peered to my right, trying to figure out what he was talking about. Then I saw it, a red and white button beside the garage door. I hopped out, my legs almost collapsing beneath me, then stumbled toward the door. Using the wall for balance, I slapped the white button. The massive door groaned, then began lifting an inch at a time.

Rat a tat tat tat. Bullets sprayed toward me, and I screamed, crouching low. My companion returned fire, then shouted for me to hurry.

The door was up two feet now. *Too slow.* More people could come through before we could get the Jeep out. I stumbled toward him, my legs unsteady, my head light. *Just keep it together a little longer.* I didn't know if I could. Everything seemed to be happening to someone else, nothing felt real.

I managed to pull myself into the passenger seat, then he was pushing my head down as he returned fire again. The Jeep rocketed forward, my body plastered to the seat from the force. The roll bars thwacked against the bottom of the garage door, but he didn't slow, just stepped on the gas. We burst through with a clang and groan of metal that made my teeth ache and my head throb.

Freezing air slapped at my face and bare legs. I curled into myself. It might have been mid-May when my sister and I were abducted, but it felt like winter here. I glanced behind me, to where we'd been. The compound was lit up like a Las Vegas strip show, its buildings sprawling on and on. To the right of it was an airstrip where a cargo plane sat. Was that the plane I'd arrived on? Was it the one they'd planned to use to take me to the arena? My stomach twisted and rolled.

I didn't have any more time to examine my surroundings because we were turning at such a high speed, if I hadn't braced my hand against the dash, I would have fallen right out. Then he stepped on the gas so hard my body jerked backward.

We headed toward a gate made of chain link fence and barbed wire. It looked like the whole place was surrounded in the same type of barrier. Two guys with guns stood next to a guard house.

"Head down," he shouted, pushing me toward the floorboards when they fired at us.

The windshield clanked, then shattered. He stepped on the

gas, heading straight for the guys with guns. Someone shouted. I could still hear the damn alarm.

We hit the gate in a screech of metal. Something tore at my leg, and I screamed. As we bounced and rumbled down a dirt road, I touched my burning thigh, and my hand came away covered in blood.

The shots receded behind us, and I braved looking over the back of the seat. The glaring lights of the compound shrank as we traveled away from it. Straightening, I faced forward. Cold wind whipped through my hair and burned my cheeks, making tears gather in my eyes.

He drove without the headlights. Clouds covered any light from the moon that would have aided us, and the sensation of heading directly into blackness made my heart climb into my throat. We could hit an animal or roll into the ditch at a curve. I glanced at my driver. His irises reflected what little light there was in the darkness, and I realized he'd shifted his eyes to see better.

I did the same, and some of the tension eased from me when I could make out the outline of the road ahead of us, the wide ditches running alongside it, and the forested areas beyond.

Tick. Tick. Twang. I flinched and ducked. A taillight shattered. Keeping my head down, I glanced behind us. Two vehicles followed with headlights blazing, making me squint. They seemed bigger than what we drove, maybe those Hummers I'd seen in the garage.

My driver ducked and swerved. "We need to get off the road."

More shots pelted the Jeep, and I covered my head.

"Return fire." The words made me sit up. "But keep your head down."

In the high stress of escape, I'd forgotten the machine gun in my lap. My hands still shook, but I pointed it behind us and fired, not even looking if I hit anything. When I cast a quick glance in my driver's direction, he tilted his head at me. "You can do better than that." Above the roaring wind and whining motor, his tone chastised.

Narrowing my eyes at him, I gritted my teeth and glared where I fired. The vehicles were way closer now than I thought they'd be. Some of my shots pinged off their front fenders.

"Nice."

The praise was short lived, because in the next instant, one of our tires was shot out.

The Jeep skidded, fishtailing. He tried to keep it on the road, but the tires on one side lifted. A lightness overcame me, like for a second, I'd been transported to outer space with no gravity, my hair and skin lifting away from my body. Dread made me close my eyes. I wasn't wearing a seatbelt.

I barely had the time to process the thought when he shouted, "Shift!" in my ear. I didn't think I had the energy to make a full shift. Strong arms came around me as we flew through the air, propelled by the speed of the Jeep as it rolled over onto itself. The world around me spun. This was it. I knew I was going to die.

"Shift!" he roared again, his arms a relentless band around my chest as we sailed through the air, his spicy scent filling my head.

Adrenaline spiked. I connected with my instincts and let the shift happen. It took every ounce of energy I had inside me. My claws tore through my clothes, even as hopelessness over-whelmed me. Whether I hit the ground at eighty miles per hour as a human or a bobcat, I wouldn't survive.

The Jeep landed first, the crunch of metal and glass deafening enough to send a spear of pain through the front of my forehead. The air in my lungs left in a whoosh, like someone squeezed me from the inside. I couldn't breathe. Then I was being propelled forward by strong arms. Somehow my paws landed under me so fast my ass was trying to get ahead of my shoulders. The momentum made me keep running several yards before I could slow enough to turn around.

The Jeep continued to roll down the embankment, the two

other vehicles slowing on the road. Their lights cut through the dark beyond the ditch.

The man who'd helped me escape hadn't shifted but took the brunt of the crash through his body. With my heightened eyesight, I could see his whole back was shredded from where he'd skidded across the hard-packed dirt.

I had no clue how he'd managed to make sure I wasn't harmed at all. Even the wound on my leg was gone because I'd shifted. But I wouldn't have enough energy to return to human for a long while, not until I ate and slept.

My companion was so still I thought he might be dead. Then he moved, staggered to his feet, and was shifting fully in the next moment. His cargo pants tore away from him as he ran straight toward me.

A *cougar*. He was a cougar. Like the ones who'd abducted me. Like the man I'd killed. Like the one who'd used me years before.

Pure, unadulterated fear made me turn and run.

Away from him.

The ground slapped beneath my paws as I made my way across the ditch toward the trees. Dirt and grass sprayed behind me. I ran as fast as I could, but no matter how hard I pushed myself, I could hear him hot on my tail. The people from the compound fired into the dark.

I chanced a glance behind me. They pursued us, flashlights cutting through the darkness in wide slices. But they weren't fast, and the noise of their voices became more and more distant. I knew that might not last. If they sent shifters after us, they could close the gap.

Focusing forward, I put one paw in front of the other, dodging bushes, puddles, and dips in the uneven earth. Mountains rose up in the distance, dark shapes against the midnight sky. The brush changed into a more wooded area, stunted trees twisting like gnarled fingers as they reached upward.

The different terrain made me slow my pace, but I didn't

reduce my effort. Not only did I need to flee from those who'd captured me, but my gut told me to get away from the cougar I'd come to rely on for my escape. We were free of the compound. There was no need to stick together. In fact, it would probably be best to split anyway, divide our trail and double our odds for success.

Abruptly, I veered to the left, aiming for another part of the forest even though I had no clue where we were or where we should be headed. I didn't get far before the cougar sidled up beside me and pushed my body back in the direction we'd been running.

Fine. I veered right, intent on going the other direction. I wasn't surprised when he cut me off that way too. Huffing out a breath of frustration, I focused in front of me. Every footstep I was aware of him, of his body twice the size of mine and his heavy breaths misting in the cool air.

There'd be another time to get away. I just needed to wait for it.

8

WALKER

IT DIDN'T TAKE LONG TO REALIZE THE GORGEOUS BOBCAT WAS trying to get away from me. A flash of uncertainty made me hot and cold at the same time. My mate was rejecting me?

Just like everyone else in my life, she was going to leave me. She'd run when I was first attacked in Detroit. She was trying to run now.

Why would she do that? I could *feel* the bond. Instead of acknowledging it, she veered away from me, trying to escape.

My instincts told me not to let her. A growl rumbled through my throat, a warning. Her head whipped toward me, golden eyes wide, then I nudged her again, urging her in the right direction.

After a hesitation, her head bent as she picked up her pace, but she didn't try to flee. A wave of relief made my legs move faster. She wouldn't fight me. For now.

Why would she reject me in the first place? I almost tripped in the dirt. Maybe she didn't recognize the bond, feel it like I did. These circumstances we were in didn't lend well to getting to know each other. Hell, I didn't even know her name. And if she did get to know me, she'd probably reject me anyway. I was a washed-up ex-soldier with no future plans.

But couldn't she sense our connection deep in her belly? If I told her what I felt, what would happen?

The urge to shift, to stand in front of her and declare she was my mate, almost stopped me in my tracks. But that could scare her even more. She would have the chance to officially reject me. *No.* As much as I wanted to shout it to the whole world, now we were free, I needed to let her figure it out on her own. I didn't have enough energy to return to my human form anyway.

We still had a long way to go before we were safe enough for me to ask her questions, including ones about her involvement in all of this shit. The farther we traveled from the compound, the better. Emerson Mahn knew about shifters and employed them. All shifters were natural trackers. Why the hell they would work for the sadistic douche, I had no idea. But I was going to find out. This had become personal.

That familiar rage I'd felt when she'd first freed me came rolling back. I soothed myself with what I'd do to Croskey and Mahn when I got my hands on them. Every deranged thing they'd done to me would be gifted back to them tenfold. Getting even would be the only way to fill the aching emptiness they'd left inside of me. And at least the thoughts of revenge kept me from dwelling on the potential rejection of the bobcat running beside me.

She had impressive stamina and kept my pace for a good two hours. Even when she needed to slow, she pressed on. I didn't want to stop any more than she did. It still felt like we were way too close to the compound.

There was no sign of civilization. No lights or roads or towns. Just trees and a distant mountain range, its peaks highlighted by the blue-black of the night sky and bracketed in gray clouds. I spotted a large outcropping of rocks to our right, and I nudged her in that direction. It would be harder to track us across the rough terrain. The moment she realized where I wanted her to go, she picked up her pace again. Eyes flashing, she jumped up onto the first rock.

We kept climbing. She slipped, and I nudged her back up with the top of my head. Turning, she snarled. I grinned, perversely delighted by her aggressive reaction. She hissed at me before trotting higher. Okay, so I'd gotten a bit close to her rump there, but it wasn't like I was copping a feel.

The rock formation turned out to be a boon, large enough we'd be able to jump off a fair distance from where we'd climbed up. Finding a lake or a river would be an even better way to mask our scents, but this was a close second.

Our luck held when it began to drizzle. It might've felt like shit to be wet in the middle of the night, but if it rained hard enough, it would erase all our tracks from earlier.

When it started to pour, she slowed to a walk, her body shaking with cold. I didn't really care about the water or the cold. I'd lived in worse conditions in the army. But this little bobcat in front of me looked about to collapsing. We needed to find shelter for a while, hunt some food, get some sleep.

The rocks angled toward the ground again, and I loped beside her to give her a nudge. Stopping, her lashes flinched with each splash of rain against her face, golden eyes glinting at me. I tossed my head toward the left. She glanced in that direction, noting the slope, then trudged toward the edge of the rocks. It was about a ten-foot drop, nothing on a usual day, but with her so exhausted and wet, I wasn't sure she'd be able to make it without face-planting.

I was about to nudge her onward to find a lower spot when she launched herself off the slick rocks. A yelp echoed up to me the second before I followed. Snout to snout, she snarled at me, favoring her front leg.

Okay, this had been a shit day for her. She could be pissy at me if she wanted. I scanned the area around us, looking for shelter. Further along, the rocks made a sort of canopy, the area far underneath it relatively dry. I nudged her toward it, and she snarled again.

Huffing out a frustrated breath, I trotted over to the space and tossed my head toward the dry spot. After a moment, she hobbled her way toward me. Why didn't she shift and fix her foot? Maybe too low on energy. If that was the case, even more reason for me to find something to eat. It would be hard in the rain, but I might be able to hunt smaller nocturnal animals.

I scanned our surroundings, looking for any sort of movement in the bushes and trees. *There!* A hare burrowed under a pine. I took off, reaching low with my jaws once in range. With a snap, it dangled from my mouth by its hind leg. I flicked it up into the air, breaking its neck when I caught it again. I jogged back to the bobcat, who hadn't moved, and dropped it at her feet.

She glanced at the hare, then at me, then back at the hare before settling down on her tummy, paws placed primly in front of her. When she dug into the meal, I turned back to the terrain, looking for another kill.

I skulked around, searching for more movement in the pouring rain. In the end, I only found another hare. *Enough for now.* I ate the meal in record time, then jogged back to the outcropping.

For a moment, I thought she'd run off. Panic grabbed my throat. But then I saw her silver-gray fur and black spots blending in with the rocks. The hare devoured, she'd tucked herself as far under the outcropping as she could go.

Relieved, I approached at a cautious lope, not wanting to scare her off. She was already jumpy enough, and I hadn't even begun to ask my questions. Her head lifted at my approach, but otherwise, she didn't move. The closer I came, the more I noticed the trembling of her body. She was freezing.

When she rested her head on her paws, I drew near, out of

the slanting rain. I shook my body, trying to get the majority of the water off my fur. She startled again as a few stray drops splashed her. No help for it. I didn't want to freeze.

And more importantly, I needed to make sure my little bobcat didn't either.

9

SABRINA

THE COUGAR STEPPED TOWARD ME. I WOULD HAVE SHUFFLED BACK more, but there was nowhere else to go with the rocks pressed against my side. I don't think I'd ever been so cold. With my fur damp, every shiver that went through me felt bone deep. When he took another step, I bared my teeth.

I knew I was being unreasonable. The space under the rocks wasn't big, and he deserved to be dry just as much as I did. But I was wet, and tired, and sore, and I didn't trust him no matter what we'd already been through together.

He slunk closer until I could smell the damp of his fur, then his rich and spicy scent. His molten green eyes studied me before he took the last step separating us and hunkered down beside me —around me.

I yelped and tried to get away, but his body blocked me, curling like we were two croissants in a too-small container. My limbs stiffened at the contact, halfway between getting up and lying down. No sooner did I have the thought about attacking him to get him to back off, my body realized how warm he was. For a moment, the shaking in my limbs intensified at the added heat.

With his tail tucked in around him, he laid his chin on his paws and closed his eyes.

My heart galloped in my chest. It took me several minutes to decide what to do. In the end, the needs of my body won. Slowly, I settled into the position I'd been in when he found me, curled in on myself to keep as warm as possible. As soon as I stilled, he shuffled even closer, every inch of his body coiling around mine. The added heat made me melt.

A rattling noise startled me. When I realized it was my purr, I stiffened. If I'd been in my human form, I would have blushed. The purr was involuntary and unstoppable, a physical reaction to being content. Not that being on the run was a great situation, but my body didn't know that. It was just happy to have a heat source.

I turned my head and lifted my gaze to his. Reflective green eyes stared back at me, steady, solid. Pushing my embarrassment aside, I settled back down, exhausted. There would be time enough to get away from him in the morning. I just needed a few minutes to rest.

The next time I opened my eyes, the rain had stopped, and the sky lightened with hues of pink and gold. It had been so long since I'd seen a sunrise, my heart ached for a moment.

Locked in a cage, I'd missed this so much: the sights and sounds of nature, the smells of it. My job as a forest ranger at Sleeping Bear Dunes kept me outdoors all the time. And before this, I'd had no problem spending weeks alone in the forest— with the proper supplies, of course. I'd give almost anything for my pack and hiking boots.

Birds tweeted a soft morning song. The ground emanated a fresh, damp scent, full of life. A bird flitted from one pine to another, and I poised to jump. The movement woke the cougar beside me. His body tensed with predatory alertness, feet braced as he surveyed the dangers around us.

As we'd escaped the compound, I'd realized he must have had some sort of military background. He'd been too adept at killing for that not to be the case. Despite that cougars couldn't be trusted, I thanked fate he'd been the one to help me instead of some Joe Schmoe who would have been more of a hindrance than an asset.

When he realized I was only staring at birds, he turned his head to me, chuffed a breath, then tore off a second later.

The birds scattered, but that wasn't where he headed. Behind the trees, there was a yip and yelp, then he returned with a fox dangling from his jaws. Unceremoniously, he tossed it at my feet, then tore off again.

I stared at the fox, my body needing food. I didn't usually hunt this way, preferring to eat human food when I went on long hikes, like protein bars, dried fruit, and beef jerky. But my bobcat body needed nutrients. Without them, I'd be useless. I wouldn't be able to shift or run, and both of those things were necessary for survival. We weren't free yet. Not until I was out of Alaska and safe at home. Not until I knew Brooke and Mom were safe.

Settling down, I dug into my breakfast. About ten minutes later, the cougar returned, licking his jaws. He'd caught something for himself too, but had already finished it off. I stood when he neared, wondering what he would do next.

When his skin rippled, I realized he was about to shift back to human. I braced myself, watching, expectant. The cougar stretched, moving into a standing position, then his fur receded, turning into taut skin over muscle. Hair covered his thighs and legs, but his chest was smooth and bare.

I tried not to stare lower than his chest, but it was kind of hard not to when what hung between his legs took up so much space on its own and I was looking upward from my place near the ground. Awareness and appreciation curled low in my stomach.

The marks he'd received in that jail cell were now gone, his skin flawless. He must like to keep his hair really short, like a buzz cut, because he didn't have much hair on his head, the same amount as the scruff on his face.

Seemingly undisturbed by his nudity, he casually crossed his arms over his chest and leaned against the rocks beside me. I stared at the ground, heat flooding my face, glad for the fur to hide it. Especially when it wasn't just embarrassment, but admiration of his very muscled body.

"I've got some good news and some bad news," he said, the words making me look up at him again, his husky voice causing a shiver to run through me. "We needed to head southwest to get to Fairbanks. We didn't go southwest."

I'd just run last night, not thinking where I was headed. Glancing to the trees in front of me, I cursed my own stupidity. It would have only taken a moment to check which side the moss grew on. I could have saved us a lot of time.

"The good news," he went on, "is that southwest is probably where they'll expect us to head, so maybe the mistake will give us some extra distance."

I blinked, unsure if he was trying to be nice about my mistake or not. He studied me long and hard, and I was tempted to look away first.

"What's your name?" he finally asked.

In order to answer, I would have to shift. Without clothes or a blanket, I had nothing to shield myself. I knew most shifters probably weren't modest in that regard, but I hadn't grown up around them. It had been just me, my mom, and my sister.

He looked away, toward the trees where the birds had returned to their nests. "I'm Walker, and I'd really like to know why you got me stuck in that place."

The shock of his words made me shift without thinking about it. Like a morning stretch, I was in my human form in the next instant, incensed.

"I didn't get you stuck there," I said, advancing toward him.

He met my glare. "Sure you did." His voice was calm, but there was steel in his eyes. "I could have left you to those three cougars and gone my merry way. Instead, I helped you, and you ran away, leaving me to get drugged and hauled off in a crate."

I froze. He was the one who'd helped me at the warehouse. The fourth cougar who'd attacked. The truth chilled me. I clenched my jaw.

He was right. I'd run, hadn't helped. I'd been too confused as to what was going on and too scared for my family to do anything but make sure they were safe. I'd run right to Brooke, thinking I was protecting her, and instead, I'd led them straight to her. They'd taken us both, put us in collars and cages. I pressed a hand to my forehead. God, I hoped she'd made it somewhere safe.

Swallowing, I dropped my hand and opened my mouth, thinking to apologize, then stopped. He'd been at that warehouse for some reason. I hadn't put him there. He was trying to piss me off, to make me shift to human, and it had worked. I fisted my hands.

"What's your name?" he asked again.

"Sabrina," I said, my voice hoarse.

"Okay, Sabrina." He said it reverently, like he tasted my name on his tongue. "Here's what we're going to do." I shivered at his husky tone and wrapped my arms around my middle. "We're going to do our best to find some sort of civilization before we hit Fairbanks because we need supplies before we get there. Clear?"

I nodded once.

"And we're going to stick together."

My eyes flicked to his.

"I have too many questions," he went on, "but now's not the time. Not out in the open like this when we have no weapons. Understand?"

I nodded again.

Some of the tension seemed to leak out of his shoulders. He'd expected a fight from me. But I'd bide my time, maybe answer those questions, and as soon as I had the opportunity, I'd leave him on his own. I needed to find my sister, to make sure my mom was okay. My family was my number one priority. Nothing he could do or say would change that.

"Okay, all right." He pushed away from the rocks and strode closer.

I lifted my chin, refusing to back away. God, he was tall. It hadn't really hit me before. Everything had happened so fast at the compound, and we'd been in our animal forms after. But right now, his body blocked the sunrise, blocked everything.

"Did any of those fuckers back there touch you?" he asked, his voice low.

The question surprised me, but it probably shouldn't have. I'd rescued him in my underwear. He'd been tortured. But except for the one I'd propositioned, that was a line none of them had crossed. I would have scratched out their eyeballs and taken all their testicles if they had.

I shook my head.

He stared at me a long while before nodding. "We're going to head west, then circle back south, try to get as far away from those motherfuckers as possible. Sound good to you?"

"Yes."

His eyes on my face, he backed away. "Then let's run."

Fur replaced skin, and he shifted smoothly into his cougar form just as the sun broke over the horizon. He galloped a few paces, then turned to me, waiting.

I shivered, telling myself it was from the cool in the air and not the way his eyes assessed me. Focusing inward, I shifted, my paws hitting the dirt a moment later. When he turned away to run west, I followed.

10

WALKER

I CHOSE A PACE I THOUGHT SHE COULD KEEP BASED ON LAST NIGHT'S run. We weaved in and out of trees. All the while, I kept an ear out for her, making sure she followed.

Okay, so I was a bastard for telling her it was her fault I'd ended up in the compound. On the surface, it might have sounded like the truth, but really, when it came down to it, I put the full blame on Landon. If it hadn't been for him sending me to track down Jolyn, then none of this would have happened. I wouldn't have been at the warehouse the same night she'd been. Those cougars would have drugged her instead of me.

I wasn't a saint, and I'd use every weapon in my arsenal to keep her close. I couldn't have her working against me. Even though she may have looked stricken for a moment, her anger quickly replaced it. But I wouldn't backtrack or apologize. Anger would keep her focused.

The sun continued to rise as we headed out of the forest and into a more open area. I didn't like being this exposed, but we didn't seem to have a choice if we wanted to circle back south. At least we were headed away from the compound. I'd go back there soon to burn the motherfucking place to the ground, but right now, my priority was to keep the woman beside me safe.

We ran side by side, avoiding trees and dodging wetlands. Smaller animals raced out of our way. It was tempting to hunt more since our breakfast had been small and we burned off calories with each passing mile, but we needed to push onward.

The white-topped mountain range remained ever-present in the distance on our left. Being this far north, the sun barely made it above us before it began its descent. We stopped once at a creek, drinking its clear water, catching a bite to eat, before continuing on. Not long after that, the mountain range turned into foothills, and I decided to start arcing our path toward the south.

The sun glared at us from the right as it set, almost blinding. I hoped we could find a safe place to stop before nightfall. Beside me, Sabrina's energy began to wane, our pace slowing to a trot. Her stamina surprised me. I didn't believe she was military trained, but she pushed herself more than some of the people I had served with.

As the sky turned a combination of reds and pinks, I saw it: a two-story house nestled amongst trees and rolling hills. We both slowed, then stopped together. On the one hand, we needed supplies, food, and a safe place to sleep. On the other hand, this was the first mark of civilization we'd seen. If we came across it, what were the chances those fuckers at the compound knew it existed? From how organized they were, I wouldn't put it past them to know all the private residences nearby. Hell, one of them could live here. We had to be careful.

The way Sabrina panted beside me made up my mind. We needed to rest. With a toss of my head, I veered toward the house. It was a simple design, elegant, like someone had sunk a lot of money into it even though it was out in the middle of nowhere. A road snaked its way to the front door. Later we could follow it to civilization, hopefully Fairbanks. Gravel lined the whole front of the property. A double-wide garage sat to one side, an RV covered in a tarp beside it, a shed beyond next to a long patch of garden. Power lines ran away from the house to the road. It was on the grid.

No lights declared no one was home. I slowed, then jogged around, looking for signs of life or a trap. I couldn't smell anyone, shifter or human, and didn't see anything move. Heading around to the back, I bounded up the steps of a deck with two Adirondack chairs nestled beside a matching table and a perfect view of the sunset on one side.

I sniffed the ground, waiting for something to clue me in that this was a bad idea, but everything remained calm. With a glance at Sabrina as she came up the stairs, I shifted, my body sighing at the transformation. My next steps took me to the back door. I tried the knob—locked. I knocked and waited, but there was no movement inside.

The soft sound of bare feet on wood told me Sabrina had shifted too. The temptation to turn and soak in her nude form in all its glory made me swallow. I barely resisted the urge.

Bracing, I punched through the windowpane closest to the doorknob. Sabrina gasped behind me. I wasn't sure if it was because we were breaking in, or because of the blood on my knuckles from slicing through glass.

I didn't look at her as I tapped as much of the shards out of the pane as possible before reaching in to unlock the door. It swung open on a squeal. No other sounds greeted us. I stepped over the glass and inhaled a deep breath. Only stale, human scents filled my nostrils, a few days old at the minimum.

"Mind the glass," I said when I heard Sabrina follow. There was a pause behind me, then a dainty hop.

The owners had gone with a high-end rustic look, fitting for its location. We stood in a kitchen that spread out into an open-concept dining and living area. It was clean, not even a stray plate sitting on the counter, but it appeared to be well-used. Small appliances were lined up neatly on the counter, pots and pans hanging on the back wall on a tidy row of hooks. A butcher-block island, an aloe vera plant in a white pot in the middle, housed three bar-height stools.

Someone lived here, daily. It wasn't abandoned.

I didn't know how long we would have before the owners returned. It wouldn't be safe to linger.

"Find as much as you can: food, water, clothing—anything we can use," I said, crossing to the front door.

"That's stealing." Her tone was snide.

When I turned to face her, I knew I couldn't hide my disbelief at her words. "It's called survival. If we don't have supplies, we're dead." When she didn't move, I ran a hand over my face. "We have people who kill without hesitation hunting us, and you're worried about stealing?" I knew my tone was harsh, but I couldn't help it. Her misplaced morality in this situation pissed me off. Looking around this place, these people weren't hurting for money. This could be their second home. Or was Sabrina trying to mess with me on purpose? After what I'd said to her about my capture being her fault, probably.

Her throat bobbed up and down as she swallowed. I turned away. I might be being cruel, but this was no time for softness. Mahn could be minutes or hours behind us. My fists clenched, I nodded to the kitchen cabinets. "Move."

"Asshole," she muttered.

The insult shouldn't have bothered me, but it twinged something in my chest. I ignored it. When I chanced another look at her over my shoulder, I got an excellent view of her perfectly formed ass before the kitchen island blocked my gaze. She could call me all the names she wanted as long as she quit playing the morality card and followed instructions so we could both survive this.

I stopped next to the table by the front door, finding a bunch of mail nestled neatly in a basket. At least two people lived here—

both a man and a woman were listed on the front of an assortment of bills. They shared the last name of Johnson. What really interested me was the stack of brochures and papers beside the basket and a flight itinerary originating in Fairbanks with a connection in Anchorage. This couple was booked for a two-week cruise to the Virgin Islands.

What day is it? I lifted my head, searching through the open space for something to tell me how long we'd been in captivity. My eyes settled on the TV. Crossing to it, I grabbed the remote and turned it on.

A football game blared, a bunch of men lining up on the ten-yard line. I immediately muted the sound. Behind me, I noted the stilling of Sabrina's movements as I hit the button for the guide. The date popped up in the corner of the screen.

Her soft gasp echoed at the same time as I swallowed my bitterness. *Two weeks.* They'd been torturing me for two weeks. They'd trapped Sabrina in that tiny cage for two weeks. A renewed rage simmering below the surface, I turned off the TV and tossed the remote on the coffee table.

"They're on a cruise in the Caribbean," I said over my shoulder without looking at her. "Won't be back a few more days. We can rest here for a bit."

When she didn't answer, I turned toward her.

She'd piled a few things on the kitchen island: a box of granola bars, graham crackers, apples from the fridge, a package of beef jerky. But her eyes were still glued to the blank TV screen, all color leeched from her face.

She was going into shock, either from how long we'd been caged or the glaring discrepancy of what we'd gone through compared to normal life.

There was always a disconnect from trauma. It wasn't that I was used to it, but I'd experienced it enough I'd gotten good at pushing it aside. When I'd returned from overseas and saw friends, old co-workers, and classmates, very few had cared about what I'd gone through, what I'd witnessed. They had their perfect little lives and resented anything or anyone who disrupted it. They didn't care about the land mine, or that Jordan and I had been captured and tortured. Or that those terrorists had forced me to watch while they'd cut off Jordan's head. Or that my whole team had been discharged because they'd disobeyed direct orders and come to rescue me.

No, everyone else had been worried about their fantasy football team, the barbecues, the little league practices.

I saw it in Sabrina's eyes, the need to scream and not stop screaming. But now wasn't the time. She was right, I was a total asshole, because the only way we were going to get out of this mess was if she could keep it together. She could break down all she wanted when we were free of this place. But right now, I needed her angry and focused. As much as it made my stomach churn to act the villain toward her, I'd sacrifice her kind regard in favor of survival.

"Enough dawdling, peaches," I said to her, and her eyes whipped to me. "It's a good start"—I jerked my chin to the pile in front of her— "but we need other things like flashlights, packs, clothes, shoes. You can watch *The Real Housewives of Miami* later."

She clenched her jaw, eyes simmering. *Good.* I hope she tore into me with that fire.

"You might be the biggest dick I've ever met."

Since I was standing there in front of her without a stitch on, I couldn't help but smile. "Thanks for the compliment."

Face flaming, she broke my stare, gaze going to the staircase by the back door. Fists clenched, she marched to the stairs, then stomped her way up like a toddler. If the look on her face hadn't been so tortured moments ago, it might have been funny.

Running my hand over the two weeks of growth along my jaw, I spied a set of keys by the front door. Time to check out what was in the garage and shed. With any luck, it would be a hoard of weapons and a tank.

11

SABRINA

MY SURROUNDINGS BARELY REGISTERED AS I STRODE THROUGH THE top floor of the house. All I wanted to do was punch something, preferably Walker's face, with his too-calm demeanor, his smug expression. Like he was saying, *Oh yeah, I escape from homicidal humans all the time. Oh yeah, I shoot my way out of compounds all the time. Oh yeah, I break into houses all the time. Everything's fine.*

Everything was *not* fine. Not even close. I was walking around naked in someone's house, stealing their shit. I stopped in the middle of an open space and shuddered.

Those people in that place had laughed when they'd turned me into my bobcat on a whim. They'd *laughed*.

Hatred made heat lick through my veins. I clenched and unclenched my fists. Wanting to rip something apart with bare hands, I took a deep breath and closed my eyes. This wasn't productive. I needed to get a grip. Clothes, shoes, packs—that's what I needed to focus on.

Opening my eyes, I scanned my surroundings. Like the first floor, it was mostly open concept, an office and bedroom spread out between two windows on either end, the eaves angling toward a peak on the ceiling. An en suite bathroom was tucked into one side, a walk-in closet on the other.

I stepped toward the closet. The sound of the front door opening and closing made me pause. At first, pure, unadulterated panic took hold of me. *They found us.* When I realized it was Walker leaving, not someone new coming inside, another wave of panic brought stars into my eyes. Was he abandoning me?

It took all my strength to move toward the window and look out. Light reflected off the keys dangling from Walker's fingers as he headed toward the shed. *Supplies.* He was just looking for supplies. Even as I told myself this, a tightness encircled my chest, making it hard to breathe.

This is stupid. I'd wanted to get away from him only hours ago. If he left me here, I should be thankful, not horrified.

Despite that truth, I stood frozen at the window, watching as he opened the shed and disappeared inside. Seconds later, he started setting things outside the door: an orange jerry can, rope, a tarp.

With the adrenaline ebbing out of my system, I took a good look at him. Toned ass, thick thighs, smooth skin—every part of him seemed to be designed as a predator, even in human form. He looked as fit as one of those gym rats who alternated between leg day and arm day. My feline side purred.

Blinking, I shoved down the unwanted reaction and turned my attention to the room around me. My movements almost robotic, I stepped to the dresser and opened the top drawer: women's underwear. I shut the drawer. I couldn't take someone else's undergarments. After everything, that was probably a strange place to draw the line, but I couldn't help it.

I opened the next drawer: T-shirts and tank tops. I grabbed three shirts and threw them on the bed. Next drawer was yoga pants and jeans. I held the yoga pants up in front of me. The woman who lived here was both wider and taller than me, but hopefully, the elastic would keep them up. I tossed two pair on the bed. The drawer below was socks, and I put a few pair of those on the bed too.

There wasn't anything I could use in the way of clothes in the walk-in closet, mostly dresses, but I did find a pair of runners a couple sizes too big. I grabbed the duffel bag wedged between two suitcases and placed it on the bed too, then stared at the bathroom.

Walker said we would have some time here. That meant I could have a shower, right? I didn't know if it was a good idea to spend the night, but at least I could get clean. Stepping inside the rectangular space, I turned the taps until warm water blasted out of the fixture.

God, it felt good. I'd never been so grimy before, not even while camping. It had been over two weeks since I'd showered.

My entire body stilled at the reminder. When Walker had turned the on TV, utter shock went through me to realize I'd been at the compound for that long. Those bastards had toyed with me, debased me, made me pee and shit in a litter box, fed me mice like an experiment, forced me to shift, drugged me, and shocked me unconscious. They'd been in total control.

Despite the warm water, my limbs shook. I adjusted the tap until it turned scalding. The heat didn't chase the memories away.

A sob erupted from my chest before I was even aware it had been building. Where was Brooke? Was she okay? My mom? Tears mixed in with the hot water. Now that they'd started, I couldn't stop them from flowing. If what I'd gone through meant Brooke remained free, then I'd gladly do it again.

Even as I acknowledged the thought, I couldn't stop the wave after wave of despair washing over me. They'd put me in a habitat. They'd meant to kill me. When the man I'd stabbed said I'd be taken to an arena, I could only think he meant I'd be some sort of entertainment—for hunters. They would have controlled me with my collar and killed me like a helpless animal.

I'd stuck a pen in someone's eye. I'd killed a man. Maybe more than one if my random shots in the night had hit anyone.

My fingers scratched against the slick, tiled wall. Every moment since those cougars found me played like a movie in my head, all my bad choices, *everything.* They kept going until I wasn't even sure I'd escaped at all.

I didn't even notice when my legs gave out and I slumped to the shower floor, didn't notice the puddle I sat in or the way the water sprayed out into the rest of the bathroom through the open glass door. I didn't realize I shook from head to toe without a way to stop it.

12

WALKER

A GUN SAFE WITH A COMBINATION LOCK STOOD TALL IN THE A corner of the garage. I tried a few different combos of numbers but knew it would be a major fluke to actually get it open. After a half dozen attempts, I gave up and moved to the worktable that took up the whole back of the garage. A flashlight sat on the one end. I picked it up.

Before I could move on, the row of tools on the wall snagged my attention. Four different kinds of pliers captured my gaze. I flinched as I remembered how it felt when Croskey peeled my skin away from my body, his expression turning to one of fascination as he used the collar to force me to shift enough to heal. The handsaw beside it recreated the images of Jordan's beheading, his gurgled screams, his eyes becoming lifeless even before they finished the job.

Turning away, I swallowed the bile rising in my throat. I'd thought I'd moved beyond what had happened to me and Jordan, but the weeks at the compound had brought it all back. The past became fresh, living memories inside my head. When I saw Croskey again, I'd make sure to use pliers.

A tug in my belly told me to check on Sabrina, redirecting my focus. I embraced the sensation, needing it to erase the ache in my chest the memories had created. Flashlight in hand, I turned away from the row of tools and headed out of the garage. The shed had revealed quite a few things we could use. The Johnsons liked to be prepared. They lived in the middle of nowhere and it showed. They stocked useful, common items, which turned into good luck for us. I wasn't taking everything, just enough to survive the next couple of days until I could get help.

Unfortunately, our choice in vehicles was limited. The only one in the garage was an ATV. We could use it or the behemoth of an RV outside. Neither was inconspicuous. Neither was as fast moving as I would've liked. Each had their own advantages and disadvantages.

I told myself it was the rapidly dropping temperature and my lack of clothes that made me jog back to the house, even though I knew it was something else. The connection with Sabrina she didn't seem to reciprocate told me to find her.

When I closed the door, I made sure it locked behind me. A shower ran upstairs. I didn't begrudge Sabrina the luxury, I needed one too. At least she'd gotten over her initial aversion to taking advantage of everything this house could offer us.

After I made sure the back door was locked, as well, even though it was broken, I paused at the bottom of the stairs, glancing upward, then surveyed the ground floor. We'd lucked out with this place, but if it turned out to be the closest civilian residence to the compound, then those fuckers were bound to check here.

It was beginning to get dark, the dim of twilight seeping through the blinds, but I didn't want to turn on any lights and give the impression someone was here. Beyond the guys chasing us, the owners might've sent someone to check on it once in a while.

The shower kept going.

Clothes. That's what I told myself I needed as I made my way up the steps. The staircase opened into a long space, mostly a bedroom, partly an office. She hadn't turned on any lights, which was good, and shadows bathed the whole area.

The uninterrupted sound of the water led me to the en suite bathroom. She'd left the door wide open. Even as I told myself to give her privacy, I stepped close enough to see through the shadows.

"Shit." My blood freezing in my veins, I dashed inside and turned off the water. "Sabrina?"

She lay on the bottom of the shower, curled in on herself, naked and trembling. The water had been freezing even though it had been turned all the way to hot. Her eyes were glazed and unseeing, fixed on a point that didn't exist.

As quickly and as carefully as possible, I lifted her out. Our naked skin slid from the moisture on hers. I grabbed a towel hanging on the bar on the wall and wrapped it around her as best I could without setting her down. I wasn't sure her legs would hold her.

She was in shock. I'd thought I'd made her snap out of it earlier, but it had obviously been a short-term fix. I should've known better. I should've been here to help her.

An assortment of clothes and a bag lay on top of the bed. I kicked it all to the floor and set her in the middle, wrapping the comforter around her until she resembled a human burrito.

It wasn't enough. She still shook. "Sabrina?" I tried to catch her eye, but she stared vacantly at the wall. Hell, if the freezing water hadn't been enough to snap her out of her shock, then I didn't know what else would.

Running a hand over my face, I climbed in behind her, wrapping my arms around her. Then I squeezed her tight.

She gasped. Finally, some sort of reaction. But her body still shook.

I'd been fantasizing about torturing Croskey for what he'd done to me, but what had he done to her? She'd said they hadn't touched her, but she'd been wearing only underwear when she'd gotten me out. I hadn't seen another electrocution device by her cage, but that didn't mean they hadn't done things as equally messed up. I swallowed.

Rage and anguish battled for dominance inside me. I couldn't fix the past. I couldn't erase it, but everything inside me wanted to.

"You're okay," I said into her sopping wet hair. "You're safe." My thigh went over hers and I squeezed her a little bit more.

It took a long time, but finally, her body made a different kind of shudder. Then she sniffled. Then snuffed. Sobs escaped her lips. I wasn't sure if I was making things worse. I loosened my arms.

"Don't let go." Her words came out ragged and raw. "Don't let me go."

"I won't." I squeezed her again. "I've got you." When her sobs made her body shake even more, I just held on, my throat tight, my eyes hot and stinging.

We lay there until the shadows lengthened, then dark smothered the room. Slowly, her sobs dissipated. Little by little, the shaking of her body eased. Her breaths lengthened as her limbs became heavy. She let go of what caged her emotions, melting into my arms.

I didn't move again until I was certain she was asleep.

13

SABRINA

EVERYTHING INSIDE ME FELT LEADEN. MY EYES WERE GLUED SHUT, and for half a second, I thought I was back on the plane, captured, that my sister was beside me, helpless, and I only had moments to get her free.

But silence surrounded me, not the droning of an engine. Warmth cocooned my body, softness beneath me. I wasn't confined in a metal cage.

Not only warmth, but a weight pinned me. I should have panicked, tried to get away from whatever it was, but my instincts told me I was protected—*safe*. I really wanted to trust those instincts right now.

Opening my eyes, I surveyed my unfamiliar surroundings. Pre-dawn light filtered in through the slats of blinds, highlighting a dresser and a closet in front of me. I exhaled slowly, remembering arriving at this place, this house we were stealing from.

We. I stiffened, realizing who the heaviness behind me, *around* me, was.

A soft snore warmed the back of my head. I turned slightly, trying not to wake him. Walker's arm lay over my ribs. Not that it was untoward. The thick comforter wrapped around my body, trapping my arms against my sides, gave neither of us an opportunity to be inappropriate.

I barely remembered how I had gotten into this position. There was a shower, I'd felt overwhelmed...then everything after was a blur. Did I have a panic attack? I'd never had one before and had nothing to compare, but it had felt as if I'd been drowning. I remembered crying, Walker murmuring things to me.

I closed my eyes briefly. God, I'd really broke down in front of him like that. Heat scalded my cheeks.

Looking downward, I noted his arm was bare. Was he still naked? The fresh scent of soap surrounded us. I lifted my head to see him more clearly.

The movement woke him. His eyes, so close to mine, flew open. I froze, captured by his gaze. I realized he'd shaved, the weeks' worth of growth gone. He was even more handsome now.

Long heartbeats passed between us. His scrutiny created a tingling sensation throughout my body, and it was then I realized I was naked beneath the comforter.

My cheeks burned anew, my throat becoming dry.

Before I could say anything, he gracefully rolled away from me and off the bed to stand. He'd donned a pair of jeans, but they were ill-fitting. Whoever owned them was shorter and wider than him.

I sat up, clutching the comforter to my chest when it started to slip. The need to thank him for helping me burned on my tongue, but I bit it back. He'd seen me at my weakest, and it was hard to be thankful for that.

Even though I didn't say anything, he nodded once and grabbed something off the side table beside the bed—a Swiss Army knife. He clicked it closed and turned away.

While we'd slept, he'd been prepared to defend us at a moment's notice.

Another wave of embarrassment flushed through me. It wasn't like I didn't have skills, even though he wouldn't have known that from the way I'd been acting over the past day. I knew how to survive on the land. I knew how to take care of myself.

"We need to get moving," he said over his shoulder as he grabbed a shirt out of the duffel bag and slid it over his head. "We're still too close to the compound to relax."

Silently, I agreed. The farther we could travel, the better. But I wasn't getting out of the bed until I was alone. It didn't matter that he'd seen me naked more than once. I had some semblance of pride left, and I needed to hold on to the last shred of it if I was to ever look him in the eye again.

He headed down the stairs with the duffel bag in hand before I could think of a response. Letting out a slow breath, I untangled myself from the comforter. The clothes I'd chosen from the day before lay in a neat pile on top of the dresser.

Quickly, I used the bathroom, then dressed. I found a hair elastic and brush in a drawer and neatened my hair, securing it at the back of my head. When I examined my face in the mirror, I tried not to wince.

I looked so tired. Wide, purple circles lived beneath my eyes, the rest of my face wan. After everything that had happened, I should have been more forgiving of my appearance. At the end of the day, it didn't really matter, but it still made me cringe.

Turning away, I stepped into the bedroom, made the bed out of reflex, then headed downstairs. I found Walker chewing on one of the granola bars I'd procured yesterday. Another one sat on the counter in front of him. The rest of the food was packed in the open duffel bag beside the aloe vera on the kitchen island. He only glanced at me, his attention focused on the map of Alaska spread out beside the bag. I tentatively walked over to scan its creased surface.

"As far as I can tell," he said between bites, "we're only a few hours away from Fairbanks." He'd found a bomber jacket and some runners to round out his already ill-fitting clothes.

"That's good news." I cleared my throat, scratchy from my cry the night before. "I'd like to get as far away from here as possible." I didn't say *from them*, but it hung in the air between us.

He tossed the second granola bar at me. I caught it against my chest. "I'm going to need to ask you a few questions," he said, the husky quality back in his voice.

I paused in the act of opening the bar, then nodded. I'd been expecting that and had a few questions of my own.

"What were you doing at the warehouse in Detroit the night those cougars attacked?"

His eyes didn't leave mine as I swallowed my first bite. It tasted like sawdust. "I was investigating the disappearance of a couple."

His eyebrows popped toward his hairline. "You're a cop?"

I shook my head. "No. A forest ranger."

His head tilted like he wasn't expecting that.

"This couple, they were shifters, bobcats like me," I went on in explanation. "And they went missing on my turf at Sleeping Bear Dunes National Park. They'd been missing for over two weeks. Everyone was giving up, saying it was an accident, that they'd gotten lost and died on the trail somewhere, that if we did find something eventually, it wouldn't be much."

"But shifters don't get lost," he cut in.

"Exactly!" Finally, someone could see what I could see. It felt nice. "I knew they weren't in the park anymore, and all those searches were for nothing. Their trail ended at the highway, but they'd left all their stuff at their campsite."

He watched me, assessing, as I took the last bite of my granola bar and set the wrapper on the counter.

"That doesn't explain how you ended up at the warehouse."

I ran a frustrated hand over my head. "I knew if their trail ended at the highway, then they'd been snatched for a reason. I started digging into their lives, their work history, something the local police refused to do because they were just hikers lost in the woods." I paced to the wall, then back again. "The man, he worked at an accounting firm. Nothing came of that. But the woman, she worked for a pharmaceutical company."

I felt more than saw the tension racket through Walker's body out of the corner of my eye.

"Was it Mahn BioIndustries by any chance?"

I spun to him. "Yes! It was. She worked at their lab in Detroit. I went there, started asking questions. They'd heard of her disappearance, were saddened by it, but ultimately, my questions didn't result in answers." A slow breath passed through my lips. "I don't know what made me keep digging, but I did. I kind of..." I avoided his scrutiny by looking at my hands. "I kind of got obsessed with the company, started researching everything about them and found a list of secondary properties. That warehouse was supposed to be abandoned, but it obviously wasn't."

"No," he agreed.

My eyes met his, and I wasn't sure what I saw there. Respect maybe? Wariness? It was a mixture impossible to decipher. "What were you doing there?"

He started to say something, paused, then continued on with, "I was also looking into Mahn BioIndustries, sort of...for a friend."

"And what did you find?"

"Not a hell of a lot." He ran a hand over his now-smooth jaw and seemed to be considering how much to tell me.

A shot of anger made me inhale quickly. "After everything, I deserve as many answers as you do."

A quick, assessing gaze was followed by a nod. "That woman we ran into in the hall? Her name is Jolyn Mahn. Her brother, Emerson, owns MBI, inherited it when his father died a few years ago."

"It looked like you knew her." Kind of. The redhead had been startled he used her name.

He nodded and rubbed the back of his neck. "The Mahns grew up in the same town as me, Goldenlach Ridge."

My eyes narrowed. I knew I wasn't responsible for what happened to him.

"I'd also been hired to find her," he added.

"Like as a private investigator?"

"Sort of." When I glared at him for being vague, he added, "I freelance."

"Freelance what?"

"My skill set."

It didn't look like he wanted to elaborate, so I let it drop. "Did you see either of those bobcats, the missing hikers, while you were at the compound?"

He shook his head. "You?"

"No sign of them."

He tensed, hesitating.

"What?" I asked.

"When I first arrived, there were other scents in my cell. Someone had been there recently. They smelled a lot like you, but I'd never been around bobcats before to know. I'd thought lynx maybe."

A cold sensation spread through my chest. "If they were there before you but gone by the time you got there..." I couldn't finish the sentence. They'd been about to send me to an arena. Was that what had happened to the couple? Had they been killed for sport like I thought was going to happen to me?

Even though the missing couple had led me on this path, they weren't my only concern now. I met Walker's gaze square on. "When I was taken, my sister was too. I made her jump off the plane, but those cougars, they stopped me from doing the same. And one went after her. I know they never brought her to the compound. The one I—" I paused as the image of the man with a pen in his eye flashed in front of me. My stomach rolled, the few bites of granola bar feeling like cannon balls inside me. "The one guy told me he didn't know where she was."

"Let's hope that's true."

"I need to find her."

He stared at me for long moments. "How about we worry how to get out of this state alive first?" Crossing his arms, he continued, "We have two options, we can fly out of here, or we can drive. I have contacts in Canada who can help us."

It didn't escape me that he'd skirted the issue of my sister. Finding Brooke might not be his top priority, but it was certainly mine. I'd do anything to find her, including ditching this guy. When he seemed to want a response from me, I nodded that I understood, not that I agreed.

"Secondly, we have two options for vehicles to get us off this property: the RV on steroids and an ATV. My vote is the RV. Even though it's huge, it offers us protection if we need to stop somewhere."

He'd already said we were only a few hours away from a city, so I didn't see the reason we'd need to stop before then. I nodded my agreement anyway.

My eyes drifted to the phone behind him mounted to the back wall of the kitchen, and my heart picked up tempo. It hadn't even registered when we'd arrived. I don't think I knew anyone with a land line anymore except for the one at the office at work.

"On the downside," he continued, "it's huge and noticeable. When the people who live here return, they'll report it missing. That means we only have a day or two with it tops. Not that I'd want to hang on to it long, but it's like a whole other house inside, and we could utilize that. And we'll leave it in Fairbanks, all safe and sound, when we're done, which will make you happy, I'm sure. Hell, we can even leave gas and grocery money inside."

Heart racing, I swallowed. What were the chances my sister would answer if I called her? My shoulders slumped. None.

Those cougars had taken our phones. But my mom? I could try her cell.

As helpful as Walker had been these past two nights, I needed to get away from him if he wouldn't help me find my sister. She could be in this state. We could be moving away from her.

"The ATV might be more maneuverable," he added, "easier to hide, and it can offroad, but it doesn't give us any protection."

He said he had contacts, but so did I. Our neighbor growing up, Frank, had become a mentor of sorts, had started me down the path of becoming a forest ranger. Former military, then a contract worker, he was always one of those guys who knew someone in every state, who would get the job done no matter what. In a way, Walker reminded me of him.

I also knew a lot of people through the forest rangers. The people I worked with would help me if they knew I was in trouble. They'd spent those weeks tirelessly searching for the missing couple without a thought to themselves.

Instead of saying any of this, I chewed on my granola bar, watching Walker. He'd stopped speaking, giving me an expectant look. Shoving the last of my granola bar in my mouth, I realized he was asking my opinion.

I nodded. "The RV is fine." Especially after he said he'd leave gas money. My eyes returned to the phone. I had people I needed to call. People who would drop everything to help me.

When Walker turned his head to see what I was staring at, I snapped my eyes back to him. "We should call the police and tell them about the compound."

He shook his head. "No police. Not with this. I have friends who can help with this sort of problem. We just need to get to Fairbanks first." He assessed my face for a moment, then said, "I'm going to start loading up the RV. We'll take more food with us since we have room. Box up what you can, but don't take more than half."

My hands braced against the counter, and I nodded once. For

a moment, it seemed like he would say more, then he strode off, out the back door. I didn't move until I heard the gravel crunch under his feet as he headed toward the garage.

Skirting the kitchen island, I picked up the phone and dialed my mom's number. It rang and rang, then her voicemail picked up. Not knowing what to say, I hung up.

I didn't realize my hands were shaking until I held the receiver again. I punched in Brooke's number. It wasn't a surprise to hear the automated message saying her phone wasn't in service, but it made my heart lurch in my throat anyway.

I hung up. *This is dumb.* I was sicker to my stomach for my family's wellbeing than ever. Swallowing my frustration, I dialed my own voicemail number. My mailbox was almost full. Not surprising after being in captivity for two weeks.

There were a couple mundane messages from people at work and one from a store where I'd ordered some books. No one was really worried about me right now. I'd taken leave from my job to investigate the bobcats' disappearance, and it wasn't unusual for me to go off grid for a week or two at a time. I wasn't expected back at work for a few more days. Only Brooke knew what had happened to us.

I froze when I listened to the next message. It was like my thoughts conjured Brooke's voice. She'd recorded the message only a day ago. I shook as her words sank in. She was telling me to call her at a new number. That was it, the message ended.

My heart pounded hard in my chest. Had I imagined it? Hands shaking, I pressed the button so the message would repeat.

The same message slapped against my pounding head. "Sabrina. Call me." Then she recited a phone number with a 604 area code.

It took me listening to the message a third time to regain my senses enough to grab the pen and paper beside the phone and write down the number.

My fingers almost shook too much for me to punch it into the phone. It rang once, twice. I kept shaking.

"Hello?"

My sister's tentative voice hit me in the gut. "Brooke. Thank God you're okay." My knees were so weak I used the counter to remain standing.

"Sabrina." My name came out of Brooke's mouth on a whoosh of breath. "Where are you? Are you okay?"

I closed my eyes and pressed my forehead to the cabinets. "Yes. I'm okay for now." I swallowed. "When I heard your message... God, Brooke, I was so worried about you. Are you somewhere safe?"

"Yes. I'm protected."

"Thank God." Relief made colors shoot behind my eyelids. They popped open a second later. "What about Mom? Have you heard from her?"

"Yes, she's okay. She's safe. Where are you?"

The back door slammed. I straightened and spun around. Walker stood there, an empty box in his hand and violence in his posture as he stared at me holding the phone.

"What the hell are you doing?" he asked, his voiced edged with fury.

My grip flexed on the phone. "I don't have a lot of time to explain," I said to my sister. "I got free, but I have some things to take care of."

"What things?" Brooke's voice turned high-pitched. "We can help. Just tell me where you are."

"No!" The thought of Brooke coming to Alaska, closer to that compound, made panicked fire race through my body. "I don't want you anywhere near here. If you're safe, you stay safe. I'll contact you again when I'm done with this."

Walker strode toward me, his body rigid and his jaw clenched.

"What is 'this'? Sabrina, you're scaring me."

I took a breath. If I didn't end this call now, Walker was bound to murder me. From the look on his face, he was already thinking about it. "Just know I'm okay," I said into the phone. "I've got to go. I love you, Little Sis." I hung up just as Walker reached to do it for me.

I lifted my chin and met his stare.

14

WALKER

"I didn't think you were stupid."

It was a mean thing to say, but I was so angry I wanted to break something.

Her eyes flared at me. I should've been happy to see some other emotion there instead of the vacant one she'd had last night, but her using the phone was one of the most foolish things she could have done right now.

Her words erupted from her lips like a volcano. "I was checking my voicemail and my sister left me a message. I had to call her!"

"You did not have to call her." My fingers flexed. "You put both her and us in danger." Frustration and worry for her safety made every word I spoke harsh.

"She said she's safe! If she's safe, then she's not in danger. I could have found out where she is." Her jaw clenched, her body vibrating with bottled aggression.

"Thank fuck you didn't, or you could put her in even more danger. If you've been researching MBI for a while, they could've been watching you. People you care about could be monitored too. And I definitely don't want them to know where we are right now. I would expect more sense from you." From someone who freed us from that hellhole on her own.

Her expression faltered for a second, but then she exploded again. "You don't know anything about me!"

I wanted to. I wanted to know everything about her, but my anger was making it impossible to think straight. I wanted to tear into something with my bare hands because I needed to keep her safe and she was making it extremely difficult. "You're right, I don't. And your selfishness doesn't make me want to know you."

She gasped. "My selfishness?" Her eyes narrowed into slits. "I only want to make sure my sister is safe, and you're calling me selfish?"

I took a step toward her. "If you want your sister safe, then don't fucking call her!" I roared the last bit, my gut tangled up in worry and frustration. How could I protect her if she actively worked against me?

Sabrina pushed against my chest, but I didn't budge, didn't give her an inch.

"Back off," she growled.

I growled back. "No."

The sound of a car engine made us both freeze.

"Shit," I breathed. My anger melted away as I moved to the front door. A quick peek out the drapes revealed two Hummers coming down the drive. "Fuck." Was it too much to hope it had been the couple returning and not the assholes from the compound? Of course it was. There were at least of eight of them.

When I heard Sabrina coming up behind me, I turned and herded her to the back door. "We have no time."

"It's them?"

"Yeah." I'd packed up the RV with our stuff, but it wasn't an option anymore. There was no way we could outrun them in the beast. "Change of plans." When we neared the kitchen, I stepped to the side and grabbed two knives out of the knife block. I passed her the chef's knife without a word.

The only advantage we had right now was they didn't know we were here—yet. I hoped they were just doing a sweep of the area surrounding the compound. It was what I would've done in their place.

A shout sounded, someone barking orders, a sense of urgency, then feet scrambling. My hopes fled. They knew we were here. Which meant they probably had at least one shifter with them, and they'd scented us.

Palming the fillet knife, I steered Sabrina away from the back door and up the steps to the second level. "Another change of plans."

"We're just going to hide?"

"*You* are going to stay out of the way so I don't need to worry about you getting shot." At the top of the stairs, I turned her until her body was tucked to the wall, out of sight. "If someone comes up here, you do what you do best."

She scowled at me. "What's that?"

I grinned at her fierce expression. "Stab them in the eye."

Her jaw dropped, but I was already halfway down the steps before I heard her squeak of outrage.

A shadow cut across the back door. Silently, I floated the rest of the way down the stairs, my spine pressed against the wall. I pulled the Swiss Army knife out of my pocket. With two knives in hand, I kept my limbs loose. Long seconds passed, the knob jiggled, then someone reached through the broken pane to unlock it.

Just as the door swung wide, another shadow crossed the window of the front door. I'd barely completed the thought when two guys skulked their way through the back door, fanning out in a familiar military formation. I only had seconds before they'd see me.

Training and instinct governed my actions. I stepped up behind the first guy, grabbed his left wrist, the one holding the barrel of a M16, and found the space between his helmet and jacket with the Swiss Army knife in my right hand.

Shots sprayed from his weapon. I angled my body so they'd hit the guys near the front door. The second guy was there, aiming at me, but my body was mostly blocked with the guy bleeding out in front of me. I ducked behind his helmet before the second asshole could go for a head shot, then put all my force behind making the bleeding guy move.

We headed straight for the second dude, right toward the bullets he sprayed into his companion. I didn't stop until we trapped him against the kitchen island. A startled *"oof"* left the guy as he scrambled to free himself from the now dead weight.

I heard glass shatter and knew the guys were breaking through the front door. Dropping the knife, it took me a second to reach for the handgun at his waist. Too long. By the time I unclipped it, the others were coming in the front door. I ducked and dodged, slinking behind the kitchen island as bullets flew right at me. One nicked my biceps. I hissed with pain.

Gritting my teeth, I took care of the guy near the island first, shooting him in the throat. While he tried to stop the blood from seeping out of his neck, I fired blindly over the counter just to get them on the defensive. My spot behind the island did nothing to shield me from the back door, and I knew there would be more coming that way.

Heart pounding, I peeked around the counter, then ducked down in a hail of gunfire. They blocked my way to the stairs and the front. I couldn't stay in one place for long. Opening the cupboard behind me, I grabbed the first thing I touched—a mixing bowl—then threw it against the far wall.

Shots rang. I moved, firing at the guy near the stairs, then the one by the door; two shots each, aiming for their heads in case they had body armor. From the heft of the guy I stabbed, I was pretty sure he was wearing.

I waited, heard a thump, then poked my head out to assess

the results of my four shots. Both guys were down, but that didn't mean they were dead. I waited another heartbeat, then carefully slunk out from my place behind the counter.

Nothing moved. With my gun aimed at each of their bodies in turn, I advanced toward them. My shots had reached their targets. I squatted down, taking what I needed from them—two M16s, two handguns, and tactical knives. As quickly as I could, I relieved the one of his utility belt and secured it to my hips.

I'd been wanting weapons.

No one else rushed the house. I knew there were more out there, they'd just changed their strategy. The radio on the one guy's belt made a series of clicks, some sort of code they didn't want me to know. It didn't take a genius to understand they waited for me to make a move or leave. Either way, it would expose me. Expose us.

Loaded up with weapons, I kept away from any line of sight through the windows and made my way back upstairs. My foot hit the top stair, and Sabrina jumped out at me, ready to stab my head. I dropped the guns and caught her wrist just in time, sweeping her hand behind her back until she dropped the knife, her body pressed against mine.

After a tense moment of silence, she swallowed. "Sorry about that. Guess we should have had a secret signal, like a bird call or something."

Despite the fact I'd almost gotten impaled by a nine-inch chef's knife, her words made me grin. "A bird call in a house?" I couldn't resist pulling her closer and inhaling her scent into my lungs.

She shrugged like she didn't care I had her arm pinned behind her. "Whatever works."

I let her go, glad to see she wasn't cowering in the corner. Not that I'd expected her to. I'd seen the way she'd handled herself in the compound. She'd kept her cool. "Would you like to level up?" I passed her an M16 and a Glock.

"Are they all dead?" she asked, dropping the knife and taking the weapons to check them over for ammo.

She wasn't a noob when it came to guns. I liked that about her.

"No." I turned away. "But we can't sit here waiting for them to kill us. We need to go. Grab a jacket."

"The RV?" She crossed to the closet and disappeared inside.

"No. The RV's too bulky." And I didn't want to take one of their Hummers in case they had GPS tracking systems on them. From the way these guys were outfitted and from what we'd seen at the compound, it was a pretty safe bet they were.

Which only left us with one option. The problem was getting from the house to the garage without getting shot.

While she shrugged on a gray puffer jacket, I led the way down the stairs. "Stay away from the windows."

She kept close behind me. My senses attuned to the world outside the house, I carefully peered through the curtains, not wanting a bullet in the head. Movement on the one side of the garage clued me into the two guys there. Two more hid behind the bulk of the Hummers, given away by their feet beneath the body of the vehicle. I waited, listening, to see if anymore were coming to the back door. I didn't hear anything.

"What now?" Sabrina asked from behind me.

A glance over my shoulder showed me her concentration was on me and not on the four bodies around us. She held the handgun in one hand, pointed to the ground, with the M16 over her shoulder like mine.

"We need to get to the garage."

Whatever fear she felt, she smothered. A ripple of pride went through me. It didn't matter she'd broken down yesterday. She was tough, and if she listened to my orders, we might stay alive.

I broke eye contact and swept my gaze back toward the garage. There was about a twenty-foot gap between us and the garage door, giving the guys near the Hummers a clear shot, not to mention the dudes blocking the entrance. I wracked my brain, trying to figure out the best way to approach this. Each pair of dudes would have a fantastic angle at shooting us as soon as we made a dash for the garage. But we needed to get out of the house before their reinforcements arrived.

And I wasn't stupid enough to assume there wouldn't be reinforcements.

I stared at the two dead guys by the kitchen island. Was it too much to ask for a hand grenade or two?

Like someone had been reading my mind, a military-grade canister flew in through the broken window of the front door. Thick, white smoke poured into the room a second later.

"Shit." I stepped and kicked it back. It hit the corner of the foyer with a *thwack*, its contents continuing to pour out in a constant stream.

Actually, I could work with this.

Sabrina stared at me with wide eyes, and I ushered her to the far side of the kitchen where the smoke was the thinnest.

"Stay down," I said, pushing her to the floor. "Don't shoot me."

Scowling, she did as I asked, the handgun pointed at the ceiling.

The whole front half of the house was filled with smoke now. *Perfect.* The fuckers had solved my problem for me.

From the kitchen, Sabrina started to cough. Quickly, I moved to the opposite side of the front door. She must be sensitive to smoke because I could've used the canister for breath freshener and it wouldn't have made me react.

Thunk. My heart dropped. They'd thrown something else and with the smoke so thick, I couldn't see where it landed.

"Take cover!" I shouted to Sabrina before dropping to the ground and protecting my head with my hands.

The blast ripped through the house a second later.

15

SABRINA

Boom.

My head banged against the cupboard door. The aloe vera plant launched toward me, the white pot shattering inches from my head. My ears rang. I couldn't hear or see anything. The kitchen island had protected me from the blast, but I had no clue if Walker was hurt, or if he was even still alive.

Stomach clenching with anxiety, I held the gun in front of me, unsure if I should stay put or find out if he was okay. I'd heard him shout to take cover before the blast, but beyond the ringing in my ears, everything was silent—which either meant he was dead or completely unhurt. He'd be groaning or screaming if he'd lost a vital body part, right?

Long seconds ticked by. The smoke was slow to clear. I felt another cough emerging from my throat and tried to swallow it. This smoke reminded me of getting a mouthful of campfire, creating that same tickling sensation at the back of my throat.

Heart pounding, I listened, but couldn't hear anything. Unable to take the silence anymore, I rolled to my knees, then inched closer to the kitchen island to peek around the edge. I made sure to stay low to the ground but couldn't see anything except the floor tile and a heavy layer of smoke.

Crunch. I froze. That had come from the front door, like someone had stepped on glass. Aiming my gun toward the sound, I was happy to see my hand was steady. Even though I'd never been in a situation like this before coming to Alaska, my forest ranger training had paid off.

Thud. A groan came from the same direction. Then a curse. Walker had to be alive. These dudes wouldn't be fighting amongst themselves, would they?

A shot fired. I flinched. Backing away seemed the most sensible thing to do when I couldn't see shit. Something cold and hard pressed against my temple, and my limbs turned to ice. I couldn't even think what to do next when a powerful arm clamped around my chest and yanked me to my feet.

"Drop the weapons," a hard voice said in my ear. I loosened my grip and the guns clattered to the floor. "We're going to do this nice and quiet like, or I'm going to blow your head off. Understand?"

I nodded. Even though I couldn't see him, I knew his voice—Sharpe. The asshole who'd given me a saucer of milk. My fear swept out of me in a wave, replaced with rage.

It was still too smoky to see the front half of the house clearly. I dug my fingers into his forearm as he dragged me through the back door. I thought about resisting, about kicking and screaming, but the gun pressed to my head made me think twice. And I didn't want to shout out to Walker in case I distracted him at the wrong time.

As soon as we cleared the door, the fresh air swept the smoke away, making it easier to breathe. My feet barely touched the stairs as Sharpe hauled me off the deck and toward a Hummer.

His lips against my head, he growled, "Were you the one to stick a pen in my brother's eye or was it the other guy?"

"The other guy," I said, then immediately felt bad for it, cringing for throwing Walker under the bus.

His brother? No wonder he was so enraged. There was no way he'd be forgiving about it if he found out it was me. I stopped caring about the gun to my head and tried to break free with earnest.

The sounds of fighting came from the house, shots fired. But it was only him and me outside. My too-big runners skidded over the gravel as he dragged me closer and closer to the Hummer. Bracing my feet against the ground, I whipped my head back with a snap, hoping to connect with his nose.

Crunch.

"Motherfucker."

Pain spread through the back of my skull. I may have hit my target, but he didn't let me go. Instead, he manacled my wrists at my back painfully, and pushed me up against the door of the Hummer. My forehead smacked against the window. Stars shot off behind my eyelids.

"You and your bitch of a sister deserve slow deaths, you know that, right?" He wrenched open the door and grabbed something out of a black duffel bag—a collar.

Over my dead body. There was no way I was going to let him put another collar on me.

As soon as he reached for my neck, I shoved back with all my strength, knocking him off balance. My knees followed, thrusting into his side. I wrenched my arms away, then took off. I wasn't even sure where I was running to, but I knew I had to get away from that collar.

I ended up heading for the house, smoke still coming out of the front door and disappearing into the fresh air. When a form came through the smoke, I thought it was Walker. *No.* It was one of the other guys all dressed in tactical black. I veered left, toward the garage.

Shots clacked through the crisp air. Dirt sprayed near my feet.

I kept running. Another shot made me turn and look over my shoulder. The guy at the front door crumpled.

A great force caught me in the middle of my spine as someone tackled me from behind. I went down, propelled forward so much my whole front scraped against the gravel of the driveway leading up to the garage. My skin tore as the loose rocks bit into me.

A feline screech rent the air. Dazed, I tried to escape Sharpe as he pressed me into the stones and dirt. Then his weight abruptly lifted. I could breathe. I could move. I scrambled onto my knees, turning. My chest seized at the sight in front of me.

Walker had partially shifted, his muscles bulking up, his jaw larger than usual, his canine teeth extended above and below his lips, his eyes glowing yellow. He attacked Sharpe with the force of ten men, throwing him across the yard. In the next instant, the other cougar shifted fully, his clothes tearing away from his body.

They both charged at the same time.

Even in Walker's partial shift, he was stronger than the other cougar, faster. They clawed and scraped at each other in a deadly wrestling match. My eyes went to the house. No one came out of it. Had Walker killed them all? Was it just this one shifter left?

I couldn't be sure, so I searched around for a weapon. Sharpe's handgun lay several feet away. I scrambled over, picked it up, and aimed toward where they fought. The cougar leaped, tackling Walker on a screech. They rolled, a ball of enraged fur. I couldn't get a clear shot.

Movement caught my eye. Another Hummer tore toward us. My heart sped up, trapped in my throat.

"Walker!" I shouted. We were about to be outnumbered again.

My shout distracted him enough that Sharpe got in a swipe. The streak of claws across Walker's chest cut deep enough to bleed. I winced. But it didn't seem to faze him as he punched the cougar in the face.

They separated. Just as Sharpe leaped to tackle him again, I fired. The bullet hit Sharpe's flank. He turned to me and screeched, but I kept firing, over and over again. Even as he began to run away, I didn't stop. The bullets that missed made gravel and dust spray up. Satisfaction spread through me at the ones that hit.

Then he was moving too fast for me to hit, but I didn't lower the gun until I'd emptied it. Walker jogged toward me, his wounds healing as he changed back to human.

"Let's go," he said, jerking his head toward the garage and swiping a machine gun off the ground.

We ran inside as the Hummer's engine roared closer.

"You're going to have to shoot a little while longer." He passed me the gun, then straddled the seat. I slid on behind him, my chest glued to his back from the slant of the seat. A moment later, the ATV rumbled between my thighs.

"Don't stop shooting until we're free," he shouted over the growl of the engine. "And hang on tight."

We lurched forward, my one arm tight around his ribs, the other gripping the gun. As soon as we cleared the door, I fired toward the Hummer. It was just coming to a stop behind the other two vehicles. The gunfire I laid down kept them from getting out as we made a sharp turn to the left, then Walker circled us behind the garage, taking us out of sight.

Wind slapped against us. With my hand tight against his ribs, I twisted to aim over my shoulder.

The Hummer burst from around the side of the garage.

"They're coming!" I yelled. My finger pressed against the trigger. Two more shots rang before it clicked empty. "Shit."

We were out in the open. As quickly as I had the thought, Walker veered to the left, toward a more forested area. I let the gun hang useless off my shoulder, then wrapped both my arms around him, fingers aching from the chill. The trees were close together, and it wouldn't be possible for the Hummer to follow.

We just needed to get there first.

Cold air pressed against my clothes and made my teeth clench. Shots erupted behind us, and I flinched, trying to duck lower. If I thought Walker would slow as we neared the tree line, I was completely mistaken. Branches reached for us, tearing against jackets and skin. Uneven ground made us lurch left and right. My teeth rattled in my head, and my fingers clenched around him in an aching grip. And still, Walker didn't slow. He didn't reduce speed for about thirty minutes, then only because we'd come to a creek.

On the edge of the bank, he turned the ATV, then stopped. Both of us were breathing hard as we surveyed the woods we'd just careened through. No sign of the Hummer or any shifters on our tail.

Walker turned enough for me to see his grim face. "We need to keep going."

I nodded and held on tight as he found a shallow spot to cross the creek.

Then we drove south.

16

WALKER

THE SIGHT OF FAIRBANKS IN THE DISTANCE SHOULD'VE GIVEN ME some relief, but after everything, I knew Mahn wouldn't just let us go. His people would be waiting, watching the airports and the bus station, anywhere a person could find a ride out of town.

Mahn might have the manpower, but we were going to be smarter about it.

For one, getting out of town wasn't my number one priority. Mahn would think we wanted to leave Alaska as fast as possible. And for Sabrina, that was true. The farther away she was from this place, the better.

But I had a lot of shit I wanted to burn down on my way out before I could join her. Just thinking about Croskey made my hands clench on the handlebars of the ATV and my gut boil with acid.

And Mahn wouldn't have enough manpower to watch everything. We could find a place to lay low for a couple days. I would call for reinforcements as soon as possible. If they didn't agree to help, I'd go back to the compound on my own, make sure there weren't any other shifters being held captive, then burn the motherfucking place to the ground.

Behind me, Sabrina shivered, the puffer jacket she'd found doing little against the wind. With her body so close, all I'd wanted to do was wrap my arms around her and smother myself in her intoxicating scent.

I really wished we would've been able to take the RV, then she could've been toasty warm inside, resting and eating. Instead, she sat hunched behind me, shivering. When I could, I covered her hands with one of mine to try to warm her, but on such bumpy terrain, it wasn't often.

We didn't head straight into town. Two people riding in on an ATV on the highway would be too memorable. We needed to switch vehicles. The closer we got, the more homes we saw, spread out, each heavily treed on its own acreage. I took a side road and headed down a tree-lined road, the tall birches swaying in the spring breeze. The houses were set back from the road, and lights bloomed from front windows, the people inside preparing their dinners, ready to hunker down for a night of television or reading.

I kept my eyes peeled for the ideal property, one isolated with the lights off. The narrow road wound its way through the trees. It took about thirty minutes of driving around the area before I saw one with potential.

Keeping my eye out for movement, I turned off the road and drove the ATV up the steep slope to the front yard. An old Honda Civic sat to the side of the house beside a garage. Enough trees and bushes hid us from the curious eyes of neighbors on either side. I drove around the garage and parked the ATV out of sight of the road.

Turning off the engine, I stilled as Sabrina shuddered behind me. I wasn't sure if it was out of relief or something else. When she got off, she swayed. I braced a hand against her hip to keep her steady. She shook me off. Trying to shrug off the rejection, I swung my leg over the back, my inner thighs protesting at being stuck in the same position for so long. "Can we try not to destroy the house this time?" she asked, her teeth chattering between each word.

I turned away, scanning the property. "We won't be here that long." I took a moment to watch the house. When there wasn't any movement inside, I strode around to the back and up the steps to knock on the door.

Waiting a full minute, I did it again. No response came, no movement. Sabrina followed, her shuffling pace slow as she trudged up the steps. I took a quick look in the planters and under the welcome mat for a spare key but found nothing. Having no other options, I removed my ripped jacket, wrapped my knuckles, and broke the windowpane.

A dull shattering noise echoed in the quiet around us. Out of the corner of my eye, I noticed Sabrina scan the woods. No alarms went off as I opened the door. We entered a kitchen with rustic decor. The backwoods feel didn't stop there. One more step inside, and we both stiffened.

The owners of this place liked to hunt. The wall above the fireplace held three animal heads—an elk, a doe, and a buck with massive antlers. A bearskin rug spread out in front of the fireplace, its jaws open in a fake snarl. The antlers didn't stop with the shoulder mounts. The chandelier above the dining room table was made of them.

It wasn't like neither of us hunted small game for survival, but displaying it like trophies...

We both looked away at the same time.

"Search for keys, money, and food," I said over my shoulder, already opening drawers.

Sabrina was slow to comply, but eventually, she made her way to the front door.

"No lights," I said when she reached for the switch beside the door.

She hesitated, then nodded right before her eyes glowed with a partial shift. She searched the surface of an entryway table. "Keys," she said after a moment.

"Good. Hang on to them. Hopefully one is for the Civic."

She tucked them into her pocket, then kept looking around, slowly making her way back to me in the kitchen.

The last drawer I searched had a bunch of random things inside, including a white envelope with the name Harriet written on it. I opened it up. *Jackpot.* A wad of cash sat inside. I took it all out.

Beside me, Sabrina made a strangled noise.

I lifted my eyebrows at her, waiting. When she didn't say anything, just stared at me with those golden eyes of hers, I asked, "Aren't you going to say something about how it's immoral to steal, peaches?"

Glaring at me, she crossed her arms over her chest. "No."

Well, that was progress. At least I thought it was until she added, "Because we're going to *borrow* the money, not steal it. We're going to make sure to pay it back."

I scoffed. "If you want to come back and talk to the people who live here about why you took their money, go for it." I jerked my chin at the hunting trophies. "But you definitely won't see me coming back."

Her mouth tightened, but she didn't reply. A small improvement.

I opened the cupboard in front of me and found cookies and cereal. "Grab something quick, and let's see if those keys work," I said as I stuffed the wad of cash in my back pocket, then held out my hand for the keys.

Shooting me a resentful glance, she slapped them into my palm, then grabbed a package of Oreos. I heard her soft steps behind me, then the door close, as I hurried down the steps toward the Civic.

Thankfully, one of the keys had a Honda logo embossed on it. Unlocking the driver's door, I slid into the bucket seat, inserting the key in the ignition. Just as Sabrina opened the passenger side door, the motor purred to life. I fiddled with the knobs. The heat worked. The lights worked.

With a sigh, Sabrina sank into her seat, hugged the cookie package to her chest, then shoved an Oreo in her mouth.

17

SABRINA

WE PARKED TWO BLOCKS AWAY FROM THE MOTEL AND WALKED THE
rest of the way. I understood the necessity of keeping our distance
from a stolen vehicle even though my legs were sluggish, my skin
itchy from the cold, and all I wanted to do was curl up in a ball
and sleep for a while. The last few days, weeks, were taking its
toll. I didn't know how much more I could handle.

The lower the sun set, the colder I became. As we walked into
the wind, I wrapped my arms around my middle, hugging my ill-
fitting jacket closer to my body. Plain, square houses and apart-
ments lined the streets with few pedestrians. Bare birch trees
took up the space between the buildings. Spring had not fully
arrived yet, barely a bud to be seen. In Detroit, people had
already planted their gardens. Here, it seemed as if everything
was put on hold.

I'd never been to Alaska before. Mom had gone on a cruise
once and said she loved it. Even saw a humpback whale breach
and hunks fall off icebergs. I wasn't a cruise type of gal. Now that I
was here, I should want to explore. The great outdoors was my
thing, and this city had a rugged feel to it, at least in this neigh-
borhood. But I wasn't in a sightseeing mood. Not with anxiety

swirling around in my stomach at what we'd escaped from and what we still might need to do.

The motel was a squat shape ahead of us, blue light seeping out the windows of most of the rooms. I could tell this was a dive from half a block off. A horrible, moth-eaten dive that declared its cheap price on a portable billboard with tall yellow letters. I knew there had to be better hotels in this city, but Walker wanted to keep a low profile. Also, the money we stole would last longer here.

We got the last room in the place, and surprisingly, it smelled clean and didn't turn out as run-down as I thought it would be. There was only one bed, but at this point, I really didn't care.

Should I pass out on the bed first or have an incredibly hot shower?

Walker checked all the windows, locks, and crevices, presumably assessing the security of the place. In any other circumstances, I would have said he was being paranoid.

After making sure the curtains covered the entire window, he turned to me. "Are you okay if I leave you for a bit?"

A spike of panic shot through my chest, my skin itching even more—which was ridiculous, because I'd never been dependent on another person in my entire adult life. I pushed the foolish feeling aside and nodded. "Of course."

He stared at me for a long moment, looking torn, then reached for the doorknob. "Stay put." At the last second, he paused with his hand on the knob. "Don't make any calls for right now. We can do more in the morning. Okay?"

He didn't move until I nodded my agreement, then tilted his head toward the doorframe. "Lock the bolt behind me."

When I closed the door behind him and flipped the deadbolt, I realized this was the opportunity I'd been waiting for. There was nothing stopping me from leaving. I could go to the police, tell them what happened, get Detroit PD involved, try to track down my sister, and make sure my mom was okay.

But I hesitated. Something swirling in my gut told me it was the wrong move, that Walker knew what he was doing. Since the compound, he'd only helped me. And yeah, he might have been a dick yesterday at the house, but he'd also snapped me out of my panic attack when he could have left me to it.

Warmth spread through me at the memory of how he held me through the night, heat moving through my limbs to settle in my belly. I rubbed at the tight spot in my chest as I stared at the phone sitting on the bedside table.

Morning. I just had to wait until morning to call my sister again. Heaving a huge sigh, I shuffled toward the bathroom. The tub and shower combo were an older style, but clean. Turning the hot water on to full blast, I stripped and pulled the lever for the shower head, happy to see good water pressure.

I relished the hot water for long minutes, finally feeling my bones warm, then cleaned myself with the tiny bottles of complimentary soaps. It felt so good to have my hands running all over my naked skin. I took longer than I should have, but after a day on an ATV, and the last two weeks, I thought I deserved it.

When I was done, I didn't really want to put my dusty, borrowed clothes back on but didn't have much of a choice. I wrapped one towel around my wet hair.

As soon as I stepped out of the bathroom, the scent of hot, steaming food slammed into my face. My eyes flew to where Walker sat at the little table beside the window. A pizza box took up most of its surface, next to a six pack of Coke and some other stuff in a paper bag.

I walked toward that pizza like a zombie to brains. A hot, gooey slice was in my mouth before I knew I'd picked it up. I groaned, not even caring I'd burned the roof of my mouth on scalding cheese. It tasted so good. I didn't remember ever tasting anything better. Never ever. Closing my eyes, I devoured the piece in under a minute, moaning at how good it tasted with every swallow. When the last bit of crust passed my lips, I sighed, then opened my eyes.

Walker watched me, frozen, his own slice hovering in front of his face. When his hooded gaze met mine, my stomach did a little flip.

The look in his eyes... It was intense enough to make my core clench. We'd been practically joined at the hip for the past two days, everything around us high-octane and life-threatening. I hadn't had a moment to think about how I reacted to Walker. But right now, the primal part of me was perking up her ears and wagging her little, bobbed tail.

"Hit the spot," I murmured, trying to push the feeling aside as I picked up another slice.

"I can see that, peaches."

My stomach flipped again. I'd thought I hated the endearment, but when he said it like that, my whole body warmed.

He swallowed, breaking our staring contest to grab the paper bag. "These are for you."

Taking it from him, I opened it up to find two toothbrushes, toothpaste, and deodorant. "Thank you," I said, setting it on the bed, awareness still swirling in my stomach. "Appreciate it."

I shoved another bite of pizza in my mouth, this one not so hot. Before I'd finished chewing, he popped the tab off a Coke and passed it to me. "Thank you," I said again and sat on the edge of the bed to watch him.

We concentrated on eating and drinking for a while, then he said, "We need to talk about a few things."

I stilled at his serious expression, his grave tone. "All right." I set my Coke on the bedside table and folded my hands in my lap.

"How did you end up at the compound? What did Croskey do to you?" His jaw clenched tight as he growled the name.

I swallowed, looked down at my hands, then back at him. I didn't really want to tell him, but after hearing him scream days and days on end... "It wasn't like what happened to you."

When he didn't move, didn't say anything, I let out a breath and started at the beginning—finding my sister at the club, then everything that had happened since. I told him about the kibble, the saucer of milk, the habitat, the mice, and the litter box. About being forced to shift, losing control of my body. The more I talked, the more the tension eased from my chest. The murderous look in his eyes made me wonder if I should stop, but it felt so good to confide in someone who understood, to talk to another shifter, that I kept going.

I told him everything I knew about the arena and how they'd planned to ship me off the next day, how I'd known I had to escape that night.

"And how did you get out of your cage?" He hadn't relaxed throughout my whole story, the Coke can tight in his hand.

I shrugged. "I was willing to do anything to get out of there."

He still seemed ready to kill someone, but there was respect there too. He knew what it meant to use all weapons at your disposal to survive.

That stare of his warmed me, made the primal part of me purr once more.

I swallowed and looked away from his intensity, needing to change the subject. "Do you know where the 604 area code is?"

"Vancouver."

I swallowed, processing. "That's where my sister was calling from, her new number."

His eyebrows shot up. "I have friends in Vancouver."

"Maybe they can help my sister."

"Probably. Landon is loaded and resourceful. But I don't want to call anyone until we can get a burner phone tomorrow. Nothing's open right now or I would have one already. I was lucky to find a gas station with toiletries and take away pizza." He set his Coke aside.

I nodded, acknowledging he had more experience with this sort of situation. I hadn't even thought of a burner phone. That was what he'd meant about waiting until morning.

Swallowing, I dared to ask, "You said you'd been looking for that woman, Jolyn. Why?" His jaw hardened like he wasn't going to answer, so I added. "I already told you how I ended up there."

He leaned back in his chair, crossing his arms over his chest. "My friend Landon wanted me to track down Jolyn for some reason, he never told me why and I didn't ask. I've done odd investigative jobs for him before, so it wasn't out of the ordinary. What was strange was that I couldn't find her. And when I started digging around in her brother's affairs, I found the warehouse." He ran a hand over his head. "I think I was on that plane with you, in one of the crates."

"What?" My body went still at his statement.

"I remember being in a crate, but as soon as I tried to break free, I was zapped unconscious." His hand touched his neck, but I didn't think he was aware of doing it.

I remembered the crates at the back of the plane, the faint smell of shifter, but I'd thought it was our captors, not someone in the same situation as me and Brooke.

My throat tightened. If I'd known he was there, maybe I could have broken him out. Maybe with his help, we all could have escaped, not just my sister.

"Did you see any ordinary animals at the compound with you?" he asked, snaring my attention.

I shook my head.

A frown wrinkled his brow. "I wonder what they were doing on the plane then."

I shook my head again, unsure, then cleared my throat. "Tell me more about the town you grew up in with Mahn."

He grimaced, then rubbed the back of his neck. "It's a lakeside town in the mountains of British Columbia, but I haven't been back since I graduated high school. I have a place in Vancouver."

"So you're Canadian?"

"Yeah."

I wondered how that might hinder our way out of this state,

crossing customs. I snorted at myself. It wasn't like I had any ID on me either.

"Why did you become a forest ranger?"

His question came out of nowhere but made me smile. "We had this neighbor growing up, Frank, a human. Former military." Elbows on his knees, Walker watched me, his eyes alert, listening to every word. I liked that we were talking about something else besides the hell we'd just walked through together. "He didn't have anyone in his life to dote on, so he took me under his wing when he noticed how much I liked tromping through the woods behind our houses. His nephew did these kid bootcamp things every summer, and he paid my fee. It was like military training for little kids. I loved it."

Walker's face softened into a smile.

I took the towel off of my wet hair and settled it in my lap. "The military aspect didn't appeal to me, but the exercises were fun: the zip lining and crawling through the mud, and wilderness treks with only five things in your pack. And, I don't know, with me being a bobcat, my love for the outdoors, and being good at tracking..." I shrugged. "Frank knew I didn't have much direction as a teenager and gave me a brochure for the forest rangers when I started my senior year. It clicked with me."

"It paid off." His eyes didn't leave mine. "You've handled yourself well over the past two days."

My chest warmed at the praise, even though I wasn't sure I deserved it after my breakdown.

Walker stared at me for a moment more, then rose to his feet. "I'm going to shower. Get some sleep." Picking up the bag I'd set on the bed, he jerked his chin at it. "You need it."

I might have found the statement insulting if it hadn't been the truth. With the carbs from the pizza settling into my system, I didn't remember ever being so sleepy. We were safe and warm, and the faded floral pattern on the bedspread looked inviting as hell, which spoke to my desperate need for a good night's sleep.

The door to the bathroom shut, and after staring at it a moment, I closed the pizza box, tidied the Coke cans, and hung my wet towel on the back of the chair. Then I took everything off but my shirt and slid between the covers.

God, it felt good, but I didn't go to sleep right away. Instead, I listened to the sounds Walker made as he showered. Heat crept through my cheeks as I imagined how he'd look with water sluicing over his naked body.

I gave myself a mental slap. This really wasn't what I needed to think about right now. The sound of a shower running shouldn't be a turn-on. The water shut off, and I breathed a sigh of relief. Before he came out, I scooted to the edge of the bed so he knew I wasn't going to make him sleep on the floor. After everything, it would be inconsiderate and childish of me to do so.

The bathroom door opened. I feigned sleep as he moved about the room, shutting off the lights until only the streetlamps outside illuminated a shard of the bed through the gap at the top of the curtains. I sensed Walker hesitate before he moved closer. Then the bed dipped with his weight. He stayed on top of the covers, the comforter pulling at my shoulders, but the scent of his freshly washed body made me inhale deeply. His spicy scent was still there, just masked in soap.

We stayed that way for long minutes. I knew he wasn't asleep, and he probably could tell I wasn't either, so I asked the question I'd wanted to before he'd headed to the shower. "You were in the military, weren't you?"

He tensed, then made a short sound, one I took as affirmation.

"Why did you join?"

He didn't answer, so I turned my head a little. "I told you why I became a forest ranger."

It took a minute, but he finally answered. "Didn't have any other options." I thought he would leave it at that, but then he continued. "Didn't have money for university. My grades weren't good enough for scholarships. My family wasn't well-off enough for a loan. I wasn't fantastic at sports even though I like to watch them. And I didn't want to be stuck working at a grocery store or gas station for the rest of my life."

The room was quiet, the only sound the occasional car driving down the street outside our door.

"And," he said, almost startling me because I hadn't thought he would say anything else. "Deep down, I knew it might be the only thing I'm good at."

I rolled over then, onto my back so I could see the outline of his head in the dark. "Good at what?"

"Killing."

My heart clenched. I knew I should leave it, but had to say, "You're more than just a killer, Walker."

18

WALKER

A SLIGHT SHUDDER AND A SOFT WHIMPER WOKE ME. THE tantalizing scent of a feline's heat drifted through the bed covers and curled around my body. Every part of me froze with awareness.

The scent wouldn't quit. It only became stronger as the seconds ticked by. My cock hardened. My muscles tensed.

Growing up in a shifter town, I'd been around women in heat before. They all reacted differently to their reproductive cycles. The same could be said for those around them. High school had been the worst. But right now, I was more aware of Sabrina than any other woman I'd met in my entire life, even one in heat.

Another whimper, and I rolled to face her. The dim light coming through the window illuminated her face, which was contorted in pain. Shadows crisscrossed over her eyelids. I wasn't sure if she was still asleep or not.

"Sabrina?" My voice came out rough and raw, startling in the quiet.

She only whimpered again, and I moved until my face was above hers. "Sabrina?" I made sure to keep my voice soft.

Her eyes flew open, reflecting the low light in the room back at me. At first, I was frozen in her stare, then I leaned back, giving her space. Her hand shot out of the blankets in the next moment and gripped the back of my neck.

She yanked me toward her in one swift move, surprisingly strong. My mouth banged against hers, her tongue taking over in the next instant. She filled my senses as she took charge, claiming in a frantic, all-consuming way.

My heart thudded fast in my chest, my cock hardening even more. My body rejoiced that she was finally giving in to the bond between us, accepting it. Whatever irritated feelings she'd held toward me since the beginning didn't matter anymore.

The thought made me tense. Even though I knew Sabrina was my mate, she'd never given me one indication she wanted anything more than protection from me. No lusty looks, no soft touches. This was out of character. Even as my body inched closer to hers, even as my instincts told me to dive into this without looking back, deep down, I knew something was off.

Her hands were everywhere, up my back, over my head, down my chest. And her mouth just wouldn't quit, like she was trying to suck my soul out through my tongue. I burned everywhere—for her. My need kept escalating the more she touched me. I wanted to bury myself inside her for days, to forget everything and everyone.

That thought brought me back to reality. With effort, I wrenched my lips away from hers. "Sabrina. Stop." The words caused me pain. The urge to help my mate broiled me from the inside out, but I needed her to understand what she was doing.

Instead of listening to me, she pushed me back, stronger than anything I'd seen from her before now. I didn't know going into heat would give her more strength. There wasn't time to marvel, because she climbed over my body, straddling my hips, fumbling with the button of my jeans. I realized then she wore a shirt and nothing else.

My hips thrust upward of their own volition, wanting her to

continue, wanting to obey her demands. But my hands went to her wrists, stilling her movements. She growled, baring her teeth.

If that wasn't enough of a clue she wasn't in her right mind, I didn't know what was. Undeterred at being restrained, she rocked her hips against my pelvis. I groaned, closing my eyes, wanting to give in. But it wasn't right.

"Sabrina!" I shouted her name, a tone I would've used in the military. Her ragged breathing stuttered in her chest. "There's nothing more I want right now than to fuck you breathless, but you have to tell me that's what you need."

It was like I'd slapped her. Her whole body went ramrod straight. "No," she gasped. Then she tore out of my hold, off the bed, jumping to her feet, where she kept walking backward until she bumped into the wall. Her hair was a mess of curls around her head and her chest rose and fell quickly under her T-shirt.

I swung my legs over the side of the bed but stayed where I was. Our breaths echoed raggedly in the silence of the room. My cock strained painfully against the fly of my jeans. The bedside clock said three fifteen.

"Okay," I said, running a hand of over my face and head. "Now that you're awake, we can talk about what you need."

She stiffened, but otherwise didn't speak.

I swallowed, hoping beyond hope she would take me up on my offer. "I can run to the convenience store and grab some condoms."

If possible, she stiffened even more. "That won't be necessary," she said between clenched teeth.

My breath left me in a controlled exhale. *Of course not.* Because now that she'd come to her senses, she realized she'd been about to screw a washed-out ex-soldier with no life. I wasn't good enough. I'd never be good enough. *Story of my life.*

"Then what do you need right now?" I couldn't stop my nostrils from flaring at how her scent filled the room.

Her jaw clenched. "An hour alone."

"Fine," I said, standing to grab my shirt off the top of the dresser. I found my jacket next, then pulled on my boots, disgusted to see my hands shake. "I'm going for fresh air." I glanced at her over my shoulder. She hadn't moved.

I wouldn't go far, but if I stayed in the room for much longer, I was bound to beg her to use me, fuck my pride.

19

SABRINA

As soon as Walker closed the door behind him, my legs gave out and I sank to the floor, lustful hunger making my core clench.

God, that had been close. My heat reduced me to my primal urges. I could still feel and taste Walker on my tongue. I'd wanted to sample all of him. I squeezed my legs together, trying to stop a new surge of wetness. I was already drenched from those few minutes I'd touched him.

Why the hell did I have to go into heat right now? I swallowed. At least it hadn't happened while I'd been held captive. I banged my head against the wall behind me, once, twice. My limbs shook, and my skin felt itchy and tight. Even worse, my tongue felt swollen.

This sort of high need only happened once before in my freshman year, and the memory made my blood run ice cold. I'd vowed then to never let myself be that vulnerable, that exposed to a man, a *shifter*, ever again. It was either a strange coincidence or fate laughing at me that it was happening again with a cougar.

Besides that one heat, I'd always found them manageable. Brooke was the one who screwed anyone with a nice smile and a good set of arms. I was the one who was happy to just isolate myself for a few days, have fun with my fingers and vibrator, then I was good to go.

But this? Gnawing hunger rolled through my body like a sentient beast.

Walker could have taken advantage of the situation but hadn't. He could have given me what I wanted, and I knew I'd been seconds away from ripping his pants off. Instead of succumbing to our primal urges, he'd stopped me, left to give me space.

There was no way that other cougar from college would have done the same.

My breaths settled into a more natural rhythm.

I don't know how long I sat there before I rolled to my feet. My legs shaky, I climbed back under the covers, acutely aware of Walker's scent in the room. It made me purr.

I needed to get this under control before he returned. If I didn't, I was liable to jump him the second he walked through the door. With Walker and I sharing this room, I had no clue if giving myself a couple of orgasms would keep my heat manageable.

Unable to do anything else, my hand slid below the covers and between my legs. With my face pressed into his pillow, inhaling his rich and spicy scent, I imagined us together and made myself come.

20

WALKER

REMAINING IN THE SHADOWS OF THE BUILDINGS AROUND THE motel, I stayed away from Sabrina until the sun rose. Nothing stirred on the quiet street. My instincts told me we would be able to have some time here. I didn't have much intel to support the belief, maybe it was just hope. And that was dangerous.

When the sun broke over the horizon, I didn't go back inside our room. Sabrina needed space, and my body still hummed with the desire to satisfy her. I patrolled the perimeter of the motel for any signs of Mahn's men. There were none.

As soon as the stores opened, I made my way back to our stolen car and went to the mall across town to see about a burner phone.

Buying it took almost all of the rest of our money, but hopefully, it wouldn't matter for long. Phone in hand, I jogged back to the car. As soon as I slid inside, I dialed a number I'd committed to memory years ago. It only rang once before it was answered, a soft click on the other end, then someone spoke. "Yeah?"

"It's Hayles."

A beat of silence echoed hollowly over the line before Dalton Lavigne let out a breath. "Surprised to hear from you."

I didn't say I was surprised to be calling, that was understood, by both of us.

After what had happened, what Jordan and I had gone through and how the others had disobeyed orders to save us, we'd all been discharged. Lavigne, Guffey, Verdugo and Chi had all gone on with their lives, working for a black ops company that masqueraded as private security. Astrid Clyborne had offered me a job too, but...I couldn't do it. Not after what had happened. I couldn't take orders from someone else. I didn't *care* enough to follow orders.

Instead, I'd taken odd jobs from Landon, borrowed his cabin on the island when the city became too much, played pool with the street kids in downtown Van, drank with the regulars, mastered the newest video games with random people online— tried to fill my time with things that didn't matter.

But this... What had happened to Sabrina and I? This was something I cared about enough to reach out to my former special ops team.

"I'm in a tight spot," I said when the silence stretched between us.

"You know I always said I could help you out."

And he had. But money wasn't something I needed help with. Not anymore. I might've entered the military with barely a penny to my name, but I left it wealthy thanks to Landon. Investing my earnings into his company had been one of the smartest things I'd ever done. And being the genius with money that he was, Landon had made every dollar grow.

Rubbing my hand over my face, I said, "That's not the kind of tight spot I'm talking about."

As concisely as possible, I told him where I was and gave him the rundown of what had happened, and I didn't leave anything out. Because just like me, Lavigne, my whole ops team, even his boss at Clyborne Inc., were shifters. I told him about Sabrina, how we escaped, everything.

"Emerson Mahn is the one behind it," I explained, finishing up. "He's CEO of Mahn BioIndustries, but I have no clue what his objective is."

Lavigne didn't speak for long seconds, and I'd almost thought the whole call had been dropped when he said, "That's...a lot."

"You're telling me." I ran a hand over my head.

"So what do you need from us?" Lavigne asked after a moment.

"I'm almost out of funds. I need some supplies and manpower."

"And the plan?"

"I need to make sure there are no other shifters in that compound, burn the motherfucking thing to the ground, capture Mahn, and beat the shit out of him until he dies."

After a few seconds of silence, he said, "You know we're not in the Middle East anymore, right? Hell, you're even in the States. A former Canadian soldier blowing shit up on American soil isn't going to look good on your résumé."

My grip on the phone tightened. "Are you going to help me or not?"

"Funny enough, Mahn is on our current watch list."

"What for?"

"Can't tell you that. You don't work for the company."

My eyes narrowed at the dig.

"But I might be able to get this sanctioned. Give me twenty. Can I call you back on this number?"

"Yeah. Burner phone."

"'Kay. Sit tight."

The call disconnected and I let out a breath. If they could have the company sanction the op, it would make things so much easier. I knew Lavigne would help me as much as he could, even if his boss wasn't on board.

With twenty minutes to kill, I supposed I should call Landon. The fucker. If it wasn't for him, I wouldn't have gotten into this mess. The thought didn't anger me as much as it had the first time. If I hadn't been there the night at the warehouse, Sabrina would've suffered through this ordeal, trying to escape, on her own. I wouldn't have met one of the most badass and resilient women to cross my path. I wouldn't have met my mate.

Still wasn't going to thank Landon for it, though.

I dialed his cell number. It rang and rang with no answer, which was odd. I knew he'd been waiting to hear from me and was probably wondering where the hell I'd been for over two weeks.

Next, I tried his office. His secretary answered after the first ring. "Urick Enterprises, how may I help you?"

"It's Walker Hayles. I need to talk to Landon."

"Hello, Mr. Hayles. I'm sorry, but Mr. Urick is away. May I take a message?"

"Away? For how long?"

She hesitated, which made me straighten. "I'm not exactly sure," she said after a moment.

"What's going on?"

A heavy sigh fluttered over the line. "I'll only tell you this because you're, well, you, but Mr. Urick cleared his calendar for the week, fueled up his jet, and I haven't heard from him since."

"How long ago was that?"

"Two days."

My mind scrambled. Was he looking for me? It was possible if he thought something bad had happened to me—which it had.

"Did he go to Detroit?"

"Yes, how did you know?"

I rubbed at the ache forming between my brows. "Lucky guess. Look, I'm going to give you a number. If he checks in, tell him to call me, okay?"

"Certainly."

I hung up, glowering at the phone. What the fuck? If Landon had just stayed put, I could've gotten him to send his plane here.

Sabrina would've been safe in Vancouver within hours. Now I needed to figure out a different way of getting her out of the state. Clyborne might help with that. Maybe.

It wasn't long before Lavigne called me back exactly when he said he would.

His voice came over the line all efficient and business-like. "Here's how things stand: I'm setting you up an account at Denali State Bank. Give me about thirty minutes to finish that. You'll be able to access cash as well as a credit card. I have a vehicle lined up for you at Enterprise. I've sent them a copy of your new driver's license. You're William Hake for the foreseeable future, and you can pick up the car anytime. We have a contact at Fort Wainwright who is very interested in this operation."

"Shifter?"

"No, but MBI doesn't have a presence in Alaska. At least, not on paper."

Interesting. While I processed that, Lavigne said, "You'll be able to access a cache in an hour. There's a storage unit on the outside of town that works on combination locks." He gave me all the info for that as well. "Where are you staying?"

I gave him the name and address of the motel.

"All right," Lavigne said in conclusion. "The guys and I will be able to get there by tomorrow night."

"All of you?"

"Yeah, it'll be a regular family reunion."

I didn't know why I tensed. Maybe because I'd barely spoken to any of them over the past three years because I was the reason they'd been discharged. And now they were going to help me without hesitation.

Fuck, I was a piece of shit friend.

That brought me back to a time before the military, when my two best friends, the only people I gave a shit about, were Landon and Kane. We'd been inseparable until everything went to hell my senior year. Kane killed the mayor's psychotic son in a fit of rage. The asshole had deserved to die, but that was beside the point. After, Kane left to hide away from the world. He thought he was a danger to everyone around him. I knew better. He was a good guy. He needed to have faith in himself. And in *us*, that we would've had his back no matter what. We tried to reason with him, but he pushed everyone away.

I realized now I'd done the same with my old team.

"Hey," Lavigne's voice broke into my thoughts, "just so you know, Clyborne isn't doing this for free."

I stiffened. "I can pay her back."

"Money isn't what she wants."

My jaw clenched. Astrid Clyborne was a hard woman to read. When she'd offered me a job, I wasn't even sure she wanted me on the team. In the end, it hadn't mattered anyway. I wasn't going to be taking orders ever again.

Lavigne's voice cut through the chatter in my head. "She said you two can talk later."

"Fine." I should've expected it. But if she was going to try and strong arm me into working for her, she could shove it.

We wrapped up the call, and I started the car, heading toward the rental place in the center of town. I parked a few blocks away, wiping the Civic down for prints and tossing out the empty Oreo package before I abandoned the car. The rental's paperwork was already waiting for me when I walked through the door. Ten minutes later, I was sitting in a black SUV, heading toward Denali State Bank.

That visit lasted longer. They'd been told I'd lost my ID, so it took a bit to prove I was William Hake. Lavigne sent them proof of my identity, but it was time-consuming. By the time I left the bank with a new bank card, credit card, and a thousand in cash, a creepy-crawly antsy feeling had clawed its way through my body.

I tried to stave it off as I went to my last stop—the weapons. They were where Lavigne had said they'd be—a duffel bag of guns and ammo. I didn't need the whole thing right now, but I took two handguns and a bunch of ammo, then sped back to the main road into town.

Holy hell, I'd left Sabrina alone too long. Visions of Mahn finding her made my knees weak. I raced back to the motel, blasting through three yellow lights on my way, then screeched to a stop in front of room nineteen.

I grabbed the handguns off the passenger seat and made sure they were loaded before tucking them into my jacket pockets. Using my key, I unlocked the door with my hand on my weapon, unsure of what I'd find inside.

The first thing I noticed was her scent. The whole room smelled like her: her fragrance, her heat, her need, her orgasms. It was like I walked through a wall of lust, and it nearly brought me to my knees. A low, possessive growl erupted from my throat. The second thing I noticed was the neat and tidy covers on the bed and her shoes set primly beside the door. The whole room was a lot cleaner than when I'd left it. But no Sabrina.

My heart picking up to a panicked tempo, I stepped inside and locked the door behind me. The bathroom door was closed. It was the only place Sabrina could be, but I didn't take my hand off my gun.

"Sabrina?" I called out, waiting.

When she didn't answer, I skulked my way to the door, tried the knob, and when I found it unlocked, pushed it open.

"Ahhhhh!" Sabrina came at me with a hefty tree branch above her head. I jumped back, out of the way of her swing.

"Oh, shit." She dropped the branch. It clattered loudly on the floor, dirt spraying from the bark. "Sorry."

I swallowed, blinking. Her scent was even stronger in the bathroom, and it was hard to keep my cool. "Where did you get the branch?" My voice came out scratchy.

Brushing her hair away from her face, she said, "Behind the motel."

My entire body went rigid. "You went for a walk?" She

could've been discovered. Those fuckers could've taken her while I was gone.

"You've been gone for *hours*. I needed some fresh air. Sitting still is making me crazy. And I didn't have anything to defend myself with."

Something was going on in my head, something unreasonable I couldn't explain, but I felt the need to punch the wall. Maybe I was enraged at myself for leaving her alone so long. I didn't know. But violence streamed through my blood.

"That was..." I tried to choose my words carefully. "A risk."

She shrugged. "I was as careful as possible."

It was like she didn't care about her safety. And that shrug made me want to take her over my knee and spank her.

The image made me blink. I gave myself a shake and backed away from the bathroom before I could do something stupid. Keeping my gaze trained on the table in front of me, I took one of the guns and a magazine out of my pocket and placed it on the fake wood. "You can get rid of the branch because this is for you."

She moved closer. "Where did you get that?"

"A friend." I didn't want to elaborate. "And I've got a phone now. You can call your sister," I said over my shoulder, not looking at her. Because the more I looked at her, the more I wanted to touch her.

The moment I'd first laid eyes on her, I'd known she was beautiful. It was kind of hard not to notice. She was one of those women who walked around like a beauty queen without even trying. She wore no makeup, her hair wasn't done, her clothes ill-fitting, and she was still an eleven out of ten. *Way out of my league.*

But in heat, it was like she glowed.

"Really?" She came up behind me, her voice breathless. "I can call her again?"

"Yep." I pulled the burner phone out of my back pocket. "If you can find out where she is, that might be useful. I can get some people to help her out." This time, I did look at her.

"Okay." Her hand shook when she took the phone. "I'll need to call my voicemail again for the number. I didn't memorize it."

While she listened, she straightened. "She left a different number for me to call with a Detroit area code."

She wrote the number on the pad of paper beside the room phone, sat in the chair, then dialed.

"Can you put it on speaker phone? So I can hear if she's really safe or in trouble?"

Sabrina hesitated, then nodded, punching in the last of the numbers. It rang. Someone answered on the third ring. A woman.

"Hello?" asked the tentative voice.

Sabrina's shoulders shuddered. "Brooke. It's me."

"Sabrina. Thank God. I was so worried after that last call. You hung up so fast. Are you okay?"

"I'm okay for now. Are you okay?"

"Yes. I'm safe. *Very* safe. Where are you?"

She glanced up at me and I shook my head. It was better if we didn't talk about our location on the phone when we didn't know who else could be listening.

"What about mom?" Sabrina asked, sidestepping the question altogether like a pro. "Do you know where she is?"

Brooke let out a heavy sigh. "She's been in Mexico this whole time and won't be back for a couple more days. When she is, I have some...friends who will be able to keep her safe. You don't need to worry about her. But where are you?"

"What friends? Where are *you*?"

What sounded like a growl came over the line. Sabrina's eyes shot to mine, surprised. It didn't sound like her sister had made the noise. It raised my hackles.

"I'm back in Detroit, now why won't you tell me where *you* are?"

That confirmed the new area code, and it wasn't unusual since that was where I'd found Sabrina in the first place. But Landon had also gone to Detroit.

"We can help you." It sounded like Brooke was talking through gritted teeth.

Sabrina swallowed. "Who's 'we'?"

There was a pregnant pause on the other end of the line. The unease I'd been feeling throughout this conversation doubled.

Brooke let out another one of those heavy sighs. "I'm mated."

"What?" Sabrina shot to her feet. "What are you talking about? Who is he? What the hell, Brooke? I saw you two weeks ago, and you were dancing with some random guy at the club."

"I know. I know. Don't freak out." Her words came out in a rush, like she was afraid Sabrina would cut in. "It happened really fast, and it's a lot to explain, but just know he won't let anything happen to me, or Mom, or you if I knew where the hell you were!" The last sentence almost ended on a shout.

Sabrina blinked at me, then the phone, then the wall. "This is obviously something we're going to need to talk about later. Just know I'm safe for now—"

"Stop saying 'for now' and tell me where you are!" Brooke cut in.

But Sabrina kept going. "I'll call you as soon as I get back to Detroit." She looked at me then, like she wanted to confirm she would eventually get home. I nodded. "Love you. Bye."

"Don't you dare—"

Sabrina hung up. Her eyes wide, she stared up at me. "Was that a mistake?"

I had no clue. But I had to say something. "The good news is she's safe."

One nod was the only acknowledgment she gave me. I added, "Bad news is she's mated."

She blinked. "Is that bad news?" A frown pulled at her eyebrows.

"Honestly, I have no clue." I shrugged. "I don't know your sister or her mate."

A small shake of her head, then she sighed. "You don't understand. I would have bet my whole life savings that Brooke would stay single for the rest of her life just like my mom. She doesn't commit. At least, not with guys. To be mated..." She shook her head again, her expression stunned. "How does a person become mated in such a short time?"

A knot in my chest twisted. The question showed how oblivious she was to what was happening between us. The first time I touched and scented her at the same time, I knew she was meant for me, that we were meant for each other. But right now, she stared up at me in confusion.

I'd guessed our connection was one-sided, but being confronted with the truth made my gut clench. Each passing day, I became more aware, more consumed by her, and she felt...nothing.

But she still waited for an answer. I ran a frustrated hand over my head. "From what I saw when I was growing up, it can happen fast like that."

Interest lit her eyes. "You grew up around a lot of shifters?"

I nodded. "Yep. Half the town was shifters."

A wistful expression crossed her face. "That must have been nice."

I couldn't stop my snort. "Hell, nah. It was chaos."

21

SABRINA

"Chaos?"

He shrugged, then leaned against the doorframe to the bathroom. "There were a lot of different kinds of shifters. Not everyone got along. And on top of that, half of the population was human, so we were always keeping our true selves a secret."

"That must have been difficult."

"It was. I know of a few times where there'd been really close calls due to fights when we were kids. My one friend—" He shook his head.

"What?"

"My one friend, Kane, had a terrible temper, but his heart was in the right place. Defender of the weak, that was him. He just had a hard time controlling himself when he was angry. He ended up being driven out of town because of it." His expression shuttered.

"That's horrible."

He stared at a spot on the wall, then shook himself out of it. "I haven't seen him since my first leave in the military."

"I'm sorry." He shrugged like it was no big deal, but I could tell it hurt him, so I suggested, "Maybe you should track him down."

"I have absolutely no clue where he hid himself. He wanted it that way, to live as a recluse, like the world would be safer without him in it." Bitterness tinged the words.

I didn't know what else to say when he murmured, "Landon would probably know where he is."

"The person who hired you to find Jolyn?"

He nodded. "My other friend from Goldenlach Ridge. He's a big shot in Vancouver and could've helped your sister if she was still there." A frown clouded his features as he stared at an unspecified spot on the floor. "If I could track him down."

From the start, Walker had been helping me. And if my sister had been here, he would have helped her too, no questions asked. Pleasure spread through my body. He would have helped me with my problem last night if I'd said yes.

A purr began in my throat. I tried to smother it, but his head snapped to me, his eyes alert.

He pushed away from the doorjamb. "What are you thinking about, peaches?"

The intensity in his eyes made my stomach tremble, warmth spooling between my thighs. I'd thought I'd gotten control of my heat since last night, but now that Walker stood in front of me, prowled toward me step by step, it returned in full force.

But he wanted an answer, and I had to think of something fast. "The circus," I blurted.

He snorted as he stepped close. "Clowns do it for you?"

My cheeks flamed. "The trapeze artists." The words came out breathless. "Flexible."

He hummed agreement with a smirk, almost touching me but not quite. I didn't realize I'd taken a step back until my ass hit the door. With an unsteady hand, I reached for the doorknob. *Air.* I just needed some air.

Before I could get the door open, his hand came up, keeping the door closed. My breath left me in a whoosh.

The position we were in, him trapping me like this, brought back the memory from college. My heart pounded in my chest. Panic welled up in my throat. For a second, I forgot to inhale.

Walker backed off, straightening, a frown wrinkling his forehead. "Are you scared of me?"

The question caught me off guard, and I exhaled a shaky breath. He searched my face like he was looking for answers. He wasn't that other shifter. He wasn't the guy who used me then walked away. Walker wasn't doing anything to me, and it took me a minute to realize he hadn't really trapped me. Only his one arm was up. I could have easily slipped to the side, but my feet remained glued where they were.

He waited for my answer, and I shook my head. I wasn't scared. Since we'd escaped the compound, I'd felt safe with him. But it didn't stop the old memory from surfacing.

But like the time years ago, my body told me I should get closer. It was the heat talking, I knew it was. The intelligent thing to do would be to ignore it—what I hadn't had the smarts to do in my freshman year.

Walker continued to search my face. "Last night," he began, his arm still up on the door, but his body not touching mine. "It wasn't because I didn't want to pleasure you that I stopped you."

My whole body tightened like a bow, expectant.

"It was because I needed to be sure you knew what you were doing."

My insides softened, my palms flush to the door behind me. I didn't know what to say. How many other guys would have done that? How many would have taken advantage of the situation and my horny state?

He leaned closer. "But I'll tell you right now." His words came out in a sexy growl. "I really, *really* wanted to fuck you."

A soft gasp escaped me. Heat rushed through my stomach to settle between my thighs. His words made my legs turn into jelly.

"I can scent you everywhere in this room." Flecks of green blazed in his eyes. "I know you touched yourself while I was gone."

My core clenched painfully. An unwelcome puff of air left my lips. My will battled itself with dual purposes. One side of me wanted to lean into him, to bring his mouth against mine. To kiss him until we both couldn't breathe.

The other part of me wanted to run scared, remembering the time when I'd given myself over to a shifter. When I'd trusted him, and he'd walked away like I was nothing. It had taken me a long time to get over it, and I didn't want to go through that experience again.

"I know you have a need." Walker leaned a little bit closer and inhaled deeply. "I want to make you feel good, to satisfy you."

I wanted to do that too. God, did I ever. My whole body was thrumming with desire. Every word he spoke stroked a place hidden inside me.

He leaned in so close I could feel his body heat, but he still didn't touch me. "Will you allow me to help you?"

When I lifted my hands and braced my palms against his chest, I thought it was to push him away. Instead, the contact with him did something else to me. I gasped. He growled. The fire between my legs, the ache, intensified to painful heights. I could feel his heart beating wildly beneath my palms. My own echoed it.

Our gazes connected. He looked at me like I was the most important person in the world.

"Yes." The word tore out of me, a breathy hiss.

Satisfaction and need crossed his features. I curled my fingers into his shirt, then swallowed. "But this doesn't mean anything."

A bruised expression passed over his face, but he smiled. "Wouldn't want it any other way."

My stomach dropped at his agreement. I ignored it. "And no biting." That had been the only rule the other shifter gave me. At the time, I hadn't really understood, but now it seemed important.

Before Walker could reply, I wrapped my hand around the back of his neck and pulled his head toward mine. My mouth met his, hungry. He tasted of mint, his spice filling my head. His tongue stroked mine, giving and demanding at the same time. My blood pumped hard through my body, pounding a relentless rhythm.

A growl emerged between us, and for a second, I didn't understand it had come from me. He chuckled against my lips, his hands on my ass, lifting me up against the door until his thigh separated mine. I straddled his leg, my core hot against the warmth of his thick muscles. My hips moved on their own, back and forth, trying to gain friction between us. One hand clutched his head, the other the back of his neck.

Walker broke the kiss on a groan. "What you do to me…" He stared down at our bodies, my hips rocking, unable to stop. "Fuck."

We were still fully clothed, but from the way he stared at me, I felt exposed to my soul. My feet weren't even touching the floor. The only way I gained any leverage was to press my head and shoulders against the door. Each time I did, I made sure to rub against the hard muscles of his thigh. Over and over. The pressure kept building inside me.

He kissed me again, taking ownership. My fingers dug into the short hairs of his scalp, keeping him in place, like I was afraid he'd move away. When he stopped kissing me, it was to rub his jaw against my cheek, his lips hovering next to my ear. "Do you like it fast and hard, or soft and gentle?"

I inhaled sharply, my movements slowing, but my grip on his head tightened.

"Do you want me inside you?" He nipped at my ear, my chin.

"In one deep thrust? Or should I torture you with my cock little by little?"

I gasped, getting wetter at his words.

"Should I take you against the wall? Or spread you on the bed and feast for hours, plunge my tongue inside you? Worship every hole until you can't speak?"

Dear God, no one had ever talked to me that way before. The flame inside of me grew with each dirty word. "Keep talking."

He pulled away to see my face. "You like that, peaches?"

I could only nod, my body tight with need.

"You like the filthy talk?" His eyes burned into me. "Does it make your pussy lips slick and ready for me?"

"Oh, God." Each growly word he spoke ratcheted the inferno inside me. I was burning up and couldn't stop it. I didn't want it to stop.

"I take that as a yes." He hands went under my shirt, stroking, searching, up and over my ribs and shoulders. "I'm going to touch and lick. Should I make you beg and moan before I fill you up?"

The haze in my brain burned bright and hot. I needed his mouth on me again and directed his lips to mine. I wanted to drown in him and never resurface. My death would be so very erotic.

When his lips left mine, I yanked him back with a squeeze of my thighs on his legs. I ached so badly inside.

He chuckled against my mouth. "I can't talk dirty and kiss you at the same time."

"Both. I want both." I didn't even know if I was making sense as I pulled him down for another kiss. Was it possible to climb into another person? That was what I wanted.

My hands roved down his neck and shoulders, over his stomach and lower until I cupped him through his ill-fitting jeans. He was hard and bulging against my palm. Satisfaction hummed through me. This was what I did to him.

He groaned and rocked into my hand. "Fuuuuuuck." His head

dropped to my shoulder. "If you keep doing that, I'm not going to be able to fulfill all the shit I just said. I'll come in my pants like a teenager, spilling right here, right now."

Even when he said something like that, it made me hotter than hell.

But I didn't want to stop gripping him. He felt too good.

"Shit." The word tore from his lips at the same time his hand covered mine, stilling my movements. I squeezed. "Holy God," he groaned. "Sabrina, don't do that, or I'm not going to be able to make sure you're satisfied before me."

A wicked sensation whipped through me, powerful. I squeezed again. "Maybe I want to see you come in your pants like a teenager."

On a groan, he lifted his head, meeting my gaze. I gasped at the heat and lust I saw there. A heartbeat later, he released my hand. I rubbed his thick length again, up and down, and he rocked into me.

My hips were moving too, back and forth, sinking farther against his thigh until it felt like there was nothing between us.

"The things you make me feel..." His voice trailed off, then he was kissing me again, his taste filling my head as much as his cock filled my hand. "I'll give you anything."

We rocked in a stilted, frantic rhythm. My tempo increased. So did his. I was this triangle of need, my lips, hand, and between my thighs, three points of desire joining together in my lower belly.

The more I rubbed myself against his thigh, the more I ached inside, the harder I stroked him. We kept kissing until my need was making me bite at his lips, his jaw, his chin. His scent filled my head, intoxicating. I dove back into the kiss. I didn't know who was in control anymore and I didn't care. Pressure built behind my eyeballs. He groaned deep in his chest, then jerked against me. A spurt of heat warmed my hand. He swore.

Satisfaction thrummed through me. I'd done that. I'd made him lose control.

I wanted to do it again.

All thoughts left me when I felt his hand slide inside the front of my yoga pants. "I'm going to make you come. I'm going to make you come so hard." I stared up into his eyes as his fingers slid between my slick lips. "You're so fucking wet. Bloody hell."

I pressed against him, rocking my pelvis until his fingers slipped farther between my legs. Then I felt him inside me, the heel of his hand pressing against my clit.

"Yes, ride my hand. Shit, this is so hot. You're so beautiful." Then he was kissing me again, and I was consumed by everything about him. His palm rotated, rubbing me.

The pressure built behind my eyes, in my head, then spiked. A wave crashed over me, making me shake from head to toe, one of the most potent orgasms I'd ever experienced. I gasped, reaching out to steady myself, so certain I was going to fall. But he kept me tight against him as the stars in my head began to fade.

His fingers were still inside me, and when he slowly pulled out, my body jerked with aftershocks. Then his hands were on my hips. He lowered my feet to the floor but kept hold of me. My legs trembled. I was grateful for the extra support.

I lifted my gaze to his, a blush creeping through my cheeks. Dear God, we were still fully clothed. I'd had one of the most powerful orgasms of my life, and I wasn't even naked. Awkwardness began to curl through me. He'd just finger fucked me against a door. How would I even be able to look him in the eye again?

Before the awkward sensation could take over completely, his body pressed against mine, his hands beside my head. He'd caged me, but this time I loved it, loved the look on his face—the need, the ownership. My body arched toward him.

He took my face in his hands, head ducking to meet my eyes. The scent of my arousal swirled around us. "What do you need from me now? More? My face between your thighs? Cuddles? A bath?"

My stomach clenched in anticipation at the suggestion of more, but uncertainty began to weave its way through my chest. I swallowed, not wanting to send him away, but unsure if we should take this any further.

"Maybe cuddles?" I kept it a question, tensing when I thought he might insist on more.

Walker stared at me a moment, then nodded, sweeping me up into his arms and bundling me inside the bed covers. I'd barely accepted our new location when his body settled behind mine in a spoon, his arms holding me tight and his face pressed against my neck.

It only took a second to relax, the sense of protection he gave me making me feel safe and cared for. He kept the comforter between us, and I was both glad and disappointed at the barrier.

"Thank you," I murmured, my eyelids heavy.

Then my stomach flipped with delight when he kissed the back of my head.

22

WALKER

Dear God, making Sabrina come had changed me.

As I held her in my arms, my hand roving up and down her spine, over her head in soothing strokes, I didn't want to let her go—ever. *My mate. Mine.*

She'd told me having sex didn't mean anything, and I'd agreed. But in that moment, when she'd said those words, nothing had ever felt so *wrong*. It was a lie. It did mean something. From the moment her scent first hit me back in Detroit, I'd known she would mean something to me.

A soft purr radiated in her throat, and my hand stilled on her shoulder. I didn't understand how such a small sound could undo me, but it did.

"Sorry," she murmured. "I can't seem to help it when you're doing that."

I stroked her again. "Don't apologize. I love it." It was both cute and sexy as hell, and it made me want to feast between her thighs. In fact, I didn't want to ever leave this bed.

My brain began to fantasize ways to do it. I had money now, and a credit card. I'd book the room for a week, put the "Do Not

Disturb" sign on the doorknob, and we would fuck each other to oblivion. Not much of me protested at the idea.

Sabrina's stomach growled and my hand stilled again.

"Sorry." She adjusted her position slightly. "I had some left-over pizza for breakfast, but that's it."

"Quit apologizing." It was my fault she was hungry. I should have brought food back with me, but instead, I'd raced across town like a lunatic because I'd been gone all morning.

Not only did she need food, but I needed to give her space. It was her choice.

"I need to grab a few things at the store, some food. Would you like to come with me or stay for a nap?"

She stiffened against me, then relaxed when I gave her another stroke.

"Nap," she said finally, her voice already sleepy. "How long do we need to stay here?"

"Just another day." I couldn't resist giving her another kiss on the side of her head before rolling to my feet.

I looked down at myself. A wet spot glared back at me from near my fly. Her hand rubbing me had both been torture and heaven at the same time.

Shivering at the memory, I went inside the bathroom, took off my jeans, and tried to clean the come out as best I could. I only needed them for one more outing, then I could chuck them.

While they dried, I took a quick shower, but they were still damp when I yanked them on. No help for it. When I stepped out of the bathroom, Sabrina was asleep.

The sight shouldn't have been able to turn me on so much, but it absolutely did. With her hair tousled and her cheeks pink, I wanted to crawl under the covers and find the source of the intox-icating scent of her arousal.

I was rock hard in under five seconds.

Swallowing, I turned away to grab my jacket. In its pocket, I still had the gun and the money I'd withdrawn from the bank. When I left the room, I made sure the door locked behind me.

I'd parked the SUV on an angle, over the lines, like a douche who didn't want his doors dented. Not the way to remain unnoticed. I should've parked on the other side of the building instead of basically painting an arrow directly at our room. What was wrong with me? I was acting like a rookie with pimples.

Anger at myself making my movements jerky, I backed out of the parking lot, then circled around, surveying the motel for any signs we were being watched. Nothing.

I drove to the strip mall I'd seen closer to the center of town. It was a risk to do any kind of shopping because Mahn's men might be monitoring high traffic areas, but it was a chance I needed to take. It had everything I needed: clothing, food, a drugstore.

Parking near the lot exit, I kept aware of my surroundings and stopped at the women's clothing store first. Guessing Sabrina was about a size eight, I bought a few different things, including a smaller pair of runners. Next it was the men's store, where I bought some items for myself, including a duffel bag, then the drugstore a couple doors down for different personal hygiene products I hadn't been able to pick up at the gas station the night before.

My last stop was the grocery store a block away. I bought two bags of food we could eat without a kitchen. I wasn't sure if it was luck or something else, but I hadn't felt watched the entire time inside the stores. The back seat loaded with bags, I returned the long way to the motel, circling around on my path to make sure I wasn't followed before parking behind the building.

When I tried the door, the bolt was up. "It's Walker," I said, knocking.

The door opened a few seconds later. The sight of Sabrina wrapped in nothing but the comforter, the scent of her heat and arousal pouring out of the room... For long seconds, I could only stare, cock hardening like a Ferrari going from zero to sixty. I froze in place.

Delicious. Tempting. Need. Want. Every thought in my head plummeted to my crotch. I didn't snap out of the trance until she backed up from the door, allowing me inside.

Adjusting my jeans to relieve some of the pressure, I glanced at the open bathroom door and noticed her clothes hanging on the curtain rod. Of course she wouldn't have anything else to wear. My hands tightened on the shopping bags, regretful I held the means for her to get dressed again.

"I have some food here." My voice came out a croak, and I tried to cover it by shoving the old pizza box aside to make room for the new bags. Out of the corner of my eye, I noted she held the gun in her one hand as she closed and locked the door. *Good.*

"Thanks," she murmured, moving closer to take a look inside.

"And some clothes." When she grabbed an apple, I leaned close to inhale her scent.

She turned her head toward me, and I straightened, sheepish she'd caught me smelling her.

"Thanks," she said again.

I stepped away before I could give into temptation and licked her bare shoulder.

When she investigated the third bag, her spine stiffened.

"What?" I asked, curious as to what would make her react like that.

She reached inside and lifted out the box of condoms, then turned to me with a glower.

"You're still in heat," I said in explanation.

The box dropped into the bag. "You don't need to use it against me."

Her words, the way she said them, made all my instincts scream. "I didn't think I was," I said carefully, gauging her reaction. "But I want to be able to help you if you need it and don't want to risk pregnancy. It's entirely up to you."

She still had a need, and if she wanted me to fulfill it, I wouldn't turn her away. Her comfort, her safety, was already my top priority—even if it became a detriment to everything else.

But my words didn't seem to ease her discontent. They made her stiffen even more.

Something was going on here, more than just the two of us in this room at this moment. There had to be something in her past that gave her the almost glazed look in her eyes. I thought back to everything we'd shared earlier, the promises she demanded of me before she allowed any of it to happen, the wariness in her eyes when I'd stopped her from leaving.

"Did someone hurt you?" The question came out before I could think better of it, my tone angrier than I intended.

A soft gasp passed her lips as her head whipped toward mine. My question had found its mark.

"I'll kill him." The words tumbled out on their own, the need to protect making me move closer. "Tell me who he is, and I'll kill him for you."

Some wary emotion passed in front of her eyes. I realized how I sounded—savage, intense.

Before I could move back, she placed a hand on my arm. I twitched. Her touch scalded me through the material of my jacket.

"No, I..." She shook her head, looked away, then straightened when she met my eyes again. "Thank you very much, but that won't be necessary."

She'd refused my offer like I'd just asked if she needed her lawn cut. I blinked. Maybe there was more to this story than someone hurting her. "What happened?"

I knew there was a big chance she wouldn't tell me, and that was okay. Her past was her own and she didn't owe me anything. But I wanted to understand, needed this piece of her so I would know how she was hurt, why the sight of a box of condoms would piss her off.

Running a hand through her tangled hair, she turned away. The comforter slipped around her body. "It's nothing really," she began, but I understood she was trying to make light of whatever had happened. "I made a stupid call when I was freshman in college." A forced half-smile upturned her lips when she looked at me again.

"What stupid call?" I had a burning need to find out the truth, so burning I had to force my hands to loosen because my fists ached.

She took a breath. "I was at this frat party with some friends. I was in heat, but it had never bothered me before. But I'd also never been near a male shifter while in heat."

I forced myself not to react.

"When I scented him, I tried to leave because my mom had always told us male shifters could get aggressive. But he found me before I could escape, stopped me from leaving the house with his hand on the door."

My heart lurched in my chest. I'd stopped her with a hand on the door.

"He wasn't aggressive," she went on, "not really, just...persistent. And alluring. And my body told me it wanted him. So when he suggested going to a hotel room, I agreed."

A boiling rage bubbled in my stomach. Someone had used her. I could tell by the look on her face. But I didn't make her stop her story, knowing she needed to get it out as much as I needed to hear it.

"We made a pit stop on the way. At a drug store, he bought this super-sized box of condoms, a flat of bottled water, protein bars, lube... It should have put me on my guard, and I guess it did, but not enough for me to change my mind."

She swallowed, and every fiber of my being told me to gather her in my arms and give her comfort.

"We stayed in the hotel room for five days, and he only had one rule..." She stopped talking for a moment, and I thought I knew that rule. *No biting.* Because the guy hadn't been interested in a mate, not even a slight emotional commitment. "When I woke up the last morning, he was gone. Like *gone*, gone. I didn't know his last name. He'd left me with the whole bill. And yeah, the heat had been satisfied, but..." She shook her head again.

I could see the look on her face. She hadn't been just used, she'd been devastated. There was no way she wouldn't have gotten attached to a shifter who'd satisfied her hour after hour until he ripped out her heart by leaving without a word.

Fuck. Someone had taken horrible advantage of her. I ran a hand over my face. And that wasn't the worst of it. We were in a motel room. I'd bought a box of condoms. I'd stopped her from leaving. The parallels were frighteningly similar. I was surprised she could even stand to look at me.

"Shit, Sabrina," I breathed, keeping my place a few feet away from her but wanting to hold her so badly it hurt. "I'm sorry that happened to you. And if I knew the guy, I'd find him and rip off his arms for hurting you like that."

Every instinct I owned told me to go after him, to end him so he wouldn't use a shifter's heat against them like that ever again, because from what she'd described, he'd clearly done it before.

"But I'm not him," I went on, keeping her gaze. "Whatever you want to know about me, I'll tell you, peaches." I wanted her to know everything, the bad and the good. "If you want to call me for every heat you have after this, I'll come running." As her mate, if I found out she was going elsewhere, I'd go insane, but I knew she wouldn't want to hear that right now. Maybe she never would. "If you tell me to fuck off, I'll go. But I would never ditch you." I took a deep breath, needing her to believe me. "I have a condo in Vancouver, 2770 Burrard Street. When we get out of here, you can come to my place any time. When I get a new phone, a real one, I'll give you the number and you can call me. Day or night."

Unshed tears hovered in her eyes, and it broke me up inside. I gave into the urge to move closer and took her face in my hands. "Do you understand what I'm saying?" My throat was tight. "I want to give you want you need. But I also won't pressure you."

Her one hand came up to cup the back of mine. She swallowed, holding my gaze, her expression so vulnerable my chest ached. We stayed that way, staring at each other, for long minutes, her gaze searching my face.

"I—" she started then stopped, shaking her head. "I'm going to shower and get dressed." She picked up the bag of women's clothing and the stuff from the drugstore.

I stood stock-still until the bathroom door closed behind her.

23

SABRINA

CONFESSING MY PAST TO WALKER MADE HAD ME FEEL WRUNG OUT and tender, but after a shower and wearing my new clothes—underwear, yoga pants, and a T-shirt all in my size—I felt more like myself. Except, my heat wasn't going away.

By the time I stepped back into the room, Walker had cleaned up a bit. A few different foods lay out on the table where the pizza box had been—a veggie tray, ready-made sandwiches, a container of strawberries, and some bottled water.

He'd also fixed the sheets on the bed, except for the comforter, which I held in my hands. He jumped to his feet, intent on taking it from me.

"I can do that," I said, keeping it away from him. "You go ahead and have a shower or change or whatever."

He hesitated but nodded, then took one of the shopping bags into the bathroom with him.

I fixed the bed, ate some food, and by the time he came out of the bathroom, was already going stir-crazy again. I needed some fresh air. I needed to get home and back to Brooke and Mom. Shutting off the TV, I stood from the end of the bed and wiped my palms on my pants. "Now that we have money and a car, when can I go home?"

Setting the bag with his old clothes by the door, he hesitated. "I have some friends coming to help. They have connections that'll make it easier to leave Alaska."

"Okay." It made sense to wait if help was on the way. We didn't have passports. We wouldn't be able to step on an airplane, and Detroit was really far away. It would take days to get there, and we'd need to go through Canada to do it.

I ran a hand over my still-drying hair. "I hate staying in one place like a sitting duck. Can we get out of here? Get some fresh air? Go for a hike or something?"

Again, he hesitated. "Sure. That's a good idea. Maybe somewhere a bit out of the city."

Some of the tension in my neck lessened. As we got ready, I noticed that Walker tucked his gun in the back of his jeans, making me take mine too. I wedged it beside the granola bars in my right jacket pocket and put a bottle of water in the other.

We agreed on a trail west of the city and set off into the wooded area an hour later, christening our new footwear.

I set a brisk pace and Walker kept beside me, always alert. There weren't any other hikers on the trail. Usually, I wouldn't care if there were, but I was thankful for it now. If we encountered anyone, I'd be wondering if they worked for Mahn and if we were about to be shot at. It took a while, but I eventually relaxed into a rhythm.

"Tell me about your family," I said as we neared the top of a small hill in the trail. The landscape was absolutely stunning—a rich and vibrant forest, thin clouds scuttling above us but never blocking the sun for too long, a picturesque mountain range in the distance topped with snow. The desire to go skiing curled through me. This was the first time in weeks I'd felt like I could breathe properly.

Walker shook his head. It wasn't the action of him telling me "no", but more of a denial of something internal.

After a brief silence, where birds sang their songs and the wind rustled through the trees, he said, "It was just me and my mom after my dad died when I was three. We lived off social assistance for a long time. Then she met my stepdad, a useless piece of shit who liked to emphasize things with his fists. Not my mom, thankfully, just me and his own kid, Penner, who was six years older than me."

My stomach lurched. I couldn't help it, I had to reach out to him and wind my arm through his. I gave his biceps a comforting squeeze and waited to see if he had more to say.

"Penner buggered off as soon as he could afford to." He shrugged like it didn't matter, his muscles shifting under my hands. "That was the last time I saw him. My stepdad left when I started to fight back. My mom blamed me for his abandonment and told me to get out of the house the day I turned eighteen. So I joined the military."

I leaned the side of my face against his arm. "I'm sorry."

He shrugged again. "Wasn't your fault."

"It's still shitty."

"Landon and Kane made it bearable." He snorted, then shook his head.

"What?" I asked, wondering at his expression.

"They're both grizzly shifters. I made an unintentional pun."

I grinned.

"I would stay at their places when things got bad, and we were always up to something." A shadow crossed his features. I didn't ask him to elaborate.

Our pace had gotten slow during the conversation. We crested the hill then made our way down, unhurried. "Do you still see your mom?" I asked after a while.

"No." He shook his head. "She doesn't want to see me." A beat of silence passed. "She spends the money I send her, though."

I gave his biceps another squeeze, knowing her rejection must hurt. My chest ached for the things he went through.

"Tell me more about the Mahns. You said you grew up with them."

He let out a slow breath. "Yeah, but we didn't hang out." He shook his head. "Emerson was in my grade but wouldn't have anything to do with me. Wrong side of the tracks and all that, except in Goldenlach Ridge it was more like wrong side of the lake." He paused, then stared up at the sky. "I think I remember Jolyn having a crush on my friend Kane. She used to follow us sometimes, this scrawny little kid. I don't think Emerson treated her well."

A pensive expression crossed his face, like he hadn't realized the truth until now. After a while he added, "I haven't had any contact or thought about either of them since I left for the army."

When we'd walked a little further, I worked up the courage to ask, "Why did you leave? The military, I mean." He'd shown skill when we'd escaped. Like he'd said, he was good at what he did.

The question made his body go tense. We walked so far without him speaking that I thought he wasn't going to answer me. Then he said, "An op went bad. One of my team and I ended up captured by terrorists. He didn't make it." My hand brushed up and down his arm, trying to give what comfort I could. "Jordan was like a brother to me, and I failed him. Wasn't fit for duty after that. My whole team was discharged."

I leaned my head against his arm. "I'm sorry."

His hand covered my own and squeezed me back in gratitude. Our pace had slowed to a meander, but he didn't seem to want to return to our earlier hiking speed. I was fine with that. Being with him, hearing about his life, felt right. When I started to tell him more about myself, my sister and mom, and my job at Sleeping Bear Dunes, the tension in his body trickled out until he was leaning on me as much as I was leaning on him.

Back at the motel, an odd sort of tension grew between us. As rejuvenated as I felt after the hike, I thought we were both feeling raw about the things we'd talked about.

It was strange, the stuff we'd gone through together, the intimacy we'd shared. We knew each other, but we also didn't *know* each other. Because how can you really get to know someone in such a short span of time?

That was the thing, though. I *did* feel like I knew him. Deep down in my chest. A new warmth I'd never felt before settled beneath my sternum.

For supper, we ate more of the food he'd bought. I couldn't wait to cook a proper meal. Living on the lam was way overrated.

After eating, Walker stretched out on the bed, turned the TV on, and stacked his hands behind his head. I wanted to be closer to him, but indecision spiked through me, keeping me in the chair beside the little table. The more I tried to ignore the symptoms of my heat, the more they made themselves known: the itchy skin, the swelling of my tongue, the ache between my thighs.

And with him lying there, his biceps bulging under his T-shirt, his muscled thighs stretched out with his ankles crossed... A purr erupted in my throat.

His gaze snapped away from the TV and zeroed in on me. I swallowed and squeezed my thighs together. What I really wanted him to do was to come over and sweep me out of this chair, throw me on the bed, and do all the things he'd said he wanted to do earlier. Including more dirty talk. *Especially* the dirty talk.

One deep thrust? Or should I torture you with my cock little by little?

I flushed just thinking about it.

After what I'd confessed to him about the other shifter, I knew he wouldn't make the first move, wouldn't pressure me. If I wanted to have sex, I would have to tell him that was what I needed. He'd offered himself up to me in the hottest way possible. My body told me to take him up on it. A tingling tug in my chest encouraged me to move closer. I didn't want to deny the sensation any longer.

With his eyes on me, I stood and slunk toward the bed. When I stretched out beside him, the mattress shifted and bounced beneath me.

But I didn't just stop with lying beside him. I scooted closer until my body was pressed up against his and my head lay on the swell of his shoulder. One arm came down around me.

The TV still droned, some sort of show about refurbishing cars, and I closed my eyes and exhaled, relishing how good it felt for him to hold me, the way his scent made my stomach twitch. His hand trailed a path over my hip, up my ribs, and over my hair. I sighed.

This felt comfortable, nice, but it also wasn't exactly what I was looking for.

With my eyes still closed, I said, "I liked the way you touched me this morning." The statement came out a whisper.

His whole body went tense for a second, but then he relaxed again. "Yeah?" His breath made the hair at my temples move.

I peered up at him. "Yeah." His eyelids lowered, his gaze darting down to my mouth then back to my eyes. That look made me swallow. "I'd like for you to touch me again."

The green flecks in his eyes glinted in the light of the lamp. But when he didn't respond, only stared at me in that intense way of his, I pulled back. "Only if you want to. I—"

His arm tightened around me. "I don't think it's an exaggeration to say any time you want to, I'll want to, peaches."

The sincerity of his words made me soften and relax into the mattress. His mouth upturned at the corner in the sexiest smile I'd ever seen. My heart thumped wildly in my chest.

"You're in control here." His soft, seductive voice rippled over my skin, making me shiver.

I was falling—fast. I could feel it in the depths my soul. Walker was dangerous to me in a way most people weren't. I cared for him. The number of times he'd put himself in front of me to protect me... I'd lost count. Every selfless act solidified my affection even more. And what he'd told me of his family and friends...

If I wasn't careful, I'd lose myself completely. *But maybe I want that.*

Embracing the feeling, I rolled, straddling him. He groaned when my inner thighs settled over the bulge in his pants.

My hands braced against his chest. I knew I should tell him this didn't mean anything, but I couldn't get the words past my lips. Instead, I leaned forward and kissed him.

His mouth was like velvet against mine. I loved the taste of him, the seductive warmth mixed with spice. The rich scent of him filled my head.

Strong arms came around me, holding me close, his hands roving up and down. His finger dipped beneath the hem of my top. Each stroke up my back left a scorching trail across my skin. I rocked against him, reveling in the press of his hardness against my clit. It made me gasp, a purr building inside my throat.

He smelled so good. I broke the kiss to run my nose along his jaw, up to his ear, and back down across his throat. My teeth scraped his skin. He shivered beneath me, and I pulled away to look at his face.

With a shaky hand, he tucked a strand of hair behind my ear. "You're fucking hot. You know that, right?"

I shook my head.

"You're the sexiest woman I've ever met."

"That's because you haven't met my sister." The words came out before I could stop them.

The sexy, little thrusts he'd been doing beneath me slowed to a stop. "There is no way your sister is sexier than you. No possible way. I don't even need to meet her to know that. I'm burning up right now in a way no other woman has ever made me burn up."

In a one movement, he flipped me onto my back, his body looming over mine. I spread my legs wide. The way he'd taken control should have scared me, or at least startled me, but it only made my body hum. His cock strained, pressing between my legs, a satisfying bulge against my clit through the material of my yoga pants.

"I don't want your sister in bed with us," he murmured against my cheek, then my throat, inhaling deep into his chest. "I only want you, your tight, little ass, and this hot pussy of yours." To emphasize his point, he rolled his hips into me.

A whimper and a moan escaped me at the same time. His eyes focused on mine, the predatory light in them making my heart pound.

"You really like the dirty talk, don't you?"

Lips parting, I nodded once, too embarrassed to admit it aloud.

He leaned forward, his mouth against my ear. "Are you wet for me?" His voice was a low, seductive murmur.

I nodded.

"Say it."

A scorching flush washed over my body at his demand. When he pulled back, I licked my lips. His eyes tracked the movement. Clearing my throat, I said, "You make my pussy wet."

He groaned and rotated his hips into mine. "Dirty talk coming from your mouth should be illegal."

The same could be said for him because every time he spoke, moisture rushed between my thighs.

And the power I held over him from saying a few words...that power became an intoxicating sensation, making me lightheaded.

His stubble scratched my cheeks and neck as he inhaled my skin.

"I want you to ride my face."

A soft gasp escaped me. My body stilled in heated awareness.

"I want your legs spread above me," he went on, his hips doing those insanely hot circles into mine. "I want to feast on you while you squirm and moan and shout my name. I want your luscious juices dripping off my chin. I want your scent to cling to me for days."

A strange sort of whimper left my mouth, something like a moan. Every word he spoke made me hotter.

I'd never done that before. The way he described it, the look in his eyes, the heat there...my body trembled from the need it created. Goose flesh traveled up my arms and over my scalp.

His tongue swept into my mouth, owning me. When he broke the kiss, his eyes took in my features. "Is that something you'd like?"

I gave him a hesitant nod, my heart racing. He opened his mouth, and I knew in that instant he was going to demand I say it aloud. "I want to ride your face," I said in a rush.

"Fucking hell, why is everything you say so hot?"

The desperation in his voice made a half-giggle escape my lips.

His body tensed over mine. "You think that's funny?" The words should have been serious and put me on edge, but the twinkle, the heat in his eyes, told me this was more of his brand of foreplay.

I nodded once.

He groaned and rotated his hips. "You think it's funny I need you this bad? That I'm so hard I can't see straight? That being this close to you is going to make me spill in my brand new pants?"

Unable to help it, I laughed again.

One movement and his head was above me again, like a python tracking its prey. "Oh, you're a heartless one, all right. One of those bratty girls who needs to learn their lesson." I stilled beneath him, and he smiled. "Another time. I think we were talking about you smothering me with your pussy, and that's really all I can think about."

My heart thundered and my breaths came out fast. "Yeah, that's what we were talking about." I didn't recognize my voice it was so husky.

His eyes darkened. "Fuck, yeah." His lips brushed mine, his tongue stroking a second later. "Can't wait to taste you."

Heat unfurled in my brain. Then he was moving, leaning away enough to grab hold of the elastic of my waistband. He paused, waited for my nod and for me to lift my hips before he worked the material down my thighs along with my underwear.

He returned, running his hands up the insides of my thighs, creating shivers in their wake. I was bare before him and he inhaled once, spreading my thighs.

"Holy hell." His voice was ragged, like he was losing his mind. "Fuck, Sabrina, you're so beautiful. Your pussy... You're gorgeous. I can't even... I just want to stare at you all day. I want to play with you all day. *Fuck.*"

My stomach clenched with every word he spoke. The muscles inside me spasmed around emptiness, needing to be filled.

That stare of his made be burn up inside. All the kidding was gone from his voice and face, his eyes serious, his touch shaky. How was it he could look at me like a man starved? That I was the only one in the world who mattered? That the sun rose and set on me and no one else?

His gaze shifted to my face, still filled with reverence, and he helped me take off my shirt. He tossed it aside. His hands skimmed up my bare skin, my ribs and shoulders, down over my breasts where his gentle fingers caressed my nipples in light strokes.

"I swear you're the most beautiful person I've ever seen. No lie."

My insides melted. I was falling with no way to stop it. My heart clenched uncomfortably.

I spread my legs a little more. "I thought we were talking about some smothering."

His face split into a wide, slow grin. "Fuck, yeah."

His next movements were a blur. He whipped off his shirt, scooped me up, and had me straddling his chest in under five seconds. The swift change in positions made me blink.

"Ah geez, just look at you." His hands were everywhere, up my thighs, over my belly, up my ribs, over my shoulders, then settled on my waist. "You're so gorgeous."

The way he stared at me, the way my knees pressed against his ribs, the way my thighs opened against his smooth chest, made me even wetter.

Like he was aware of it, his body tensed for a second. He groaned. "Fucking hell."

Hands on my thighs, he slid further beneath me. "I need to taste you. I need you on my tongue so bad."

My breaths came out so fast now, I was almost hyperventilating. I didn't know what to think anymore. I didn't know *how* to think.

"Hold on," he said against my thigh, moving my hands to the headboard while sliding further down until all I could see was his forehead and hair.

One lick and I nearly shot off the bed. A guy going down on me like this was a totally new experience. The muscles of my thighs twitched with strain. He may have said he wanted to be smothered, but I didn't want him to suffocate.

Hands curving around my thighs, he leaned away from me a little. "You need to relax. You need to let go." Still my thighs strained, keeping my full weight off him. "I'll do all the work. I just need you to collapse this perfect pussy on my face."

My legs gave out, my knees sinking into the mattress on either side of his head.

He groaned against me, the vibration careening through my body. More shivers broke over my skin. His tongue did magical things to me. He licked, plunged inside me, sucked, and played with my clit. I didn't understand how he could breathe down there, but with all the satisfied noises rumbling through his chest, I knew he enjoyed it.

Every sweep of his tongue pulled a gasp and a moan from me. My hips moved back and forth, and he growled his approval, lifting me up enough to say, "Yes, fuck. Ride my tongue."

The enthusiasm in his tone did things to my insides, made me feverish and desperate all at once. He settled me back on him. His hands on my ass spread me open, his fingers toying with my crack and making me pant even more.

Sweaty chills broke over my skin. Every flick of his tongue brought me closer to the edge. This buildup inside me was new and frightening in its intensity. It felt like I was about to explode.

"Walker, oh my God, Walker... I can't... Oh my God... Please..."

He growled against me, his tongue making swooping circles around my entrance. When he sucked my clit into his mouth the next time, a wave rolled over my body, shattering my mind. Quivering thighs clenched the sides of his face. My fingers dug into the headboard. My back arched.

Shudder after shudder wracked through me. He kept laving me, milking every moan and tremor. I slowly came back into myself, realizing Walker gently stroked my thighs and arms. He lazily licked me, like he was cleaning me. My stomach clenched at the tender gestures. Leaning back, I tried to give him more breathing room, but his hands tightened on my things.

"Just give me a sec," he said, his voice a desperate murmur. I didn't know if he meant he wanted to finish what he was doing or if he needed a minute to collect himself.

When he finally allowed me to scoot back on his chest, I swallowed. He'd wanted my juices to cover his face, and they definitely were. I thought I should be embarrassed, but instead, a purr began in my throat. The satisfied look on his face only made it intensify.

A new heat curled in my stomach. After everything he'd given me, I wanted to return the favor. I wanted to taste him like he'd tasted me. But I also wanted him inside me. Even after that amazing orgasm, my insides clenched around emptiness, needing to be filled.

Knowing he liked me to verbalize my needs, I said, "I want to taste you in my mouth and fuck you at the same time."

The hands stroking my thighs stilled. His eyes widened. "Hell, peaches. I know I said I liked your dirty talk, but beyond that being anatomically impossible, if you say something like that again, I'm going to come in my pants before you even have a chance to touch me."

Power thrummed through me. I loved, absolutely *loved*, that he was so close to losing it. I wanted more of that feeling. I wanted him on the edge. I wanted him *over* the edge. I wanted to make him feel as good as he made me feel.

"Do you want to come in my mouth, Walker?"

Another dirty swear left his mouth. "I want to come in every part of you."

An explosive flush blasted through my body from top to bottom. There I went, trying to talk dirty for him, and he'd stepped it up to the next level.

Then he was moving, standing long enough to remove his pants. When he returned to me, he changed our positions. I was still on top, but on all fours, my hands straddling his hips, with a perfect view of his hard cock bobbing against his stomach, thick and angled slightly to the right. My legs straddled his face again, but in the other direction.

His fingers played with me, stroking, stretching, filling me. I moaned, thrusting against him. "Yes." The word tore from my lips. I needed to be filled.

"That's it, fuck my fingers. Shit, this is insane. You look amazing wrapped around my knuckles." The rest of his swears came out unintelligible.

I panted and moaned, barely able to see straight. I didn't know how many fingers he had inside me, but the pressure felt so good, my eyes rolled into the back of my head.

My ass was up and my head lowered, making it easy to give him a long, thorough lick from tip to root. He jerked, his hips thrusting off the bed. Another string of curses erupted from below me. I half-laughed, half-moaned. The things he was doing to me made me heady, but the power I felt over him, over his reactions, made me giddy.

Balancing my weight to one side, I took him in hand. He groaned. His movements inside me stilled for a moment. I rocked back, encouraging him to continue, but as soon as I took him fully in my mouth, he paused again. I licked his head, sliding my tongue up and down his cock, tasting every inch of him. I loved it. His flavor was a perfect blend of him, sweat and skin and spice and musk. My hand worked him as my tongue laved around his head.

"I can't...fucking think. Shit. Son of a—"

His curses didn't stop as I took him deeper and deeper down my throat. We developed this rhythm between us, forward and back, me taking his cock, his fingers plunging inside me. I stopped being aware of anything except the pleasure. It kept building, a scorching, unstoppable blaze. His tongue flicked against my clit again and again while his fingers pumped inside me.

I clenched, then moaned. My orgasm came from some bottomless place inside I'd never felt before. It was a flood, a wave, a crash of electricity overloading my senses. My hand clamped around his cock, and I released my lips around him because I had the sudden urge to bite down and knew that wouldn't be where I should do it. A rush of liquid between my thighs followed.

The orgasm consumed me entirely, and I wasn't exactly sure, but it sounded like Walker said, "Holy motherfucking fuck."

Then I was moving, being rotated onto my back, his lips on mine in the next heartbeat. My heart rate slowed, coming down from my orgasmic high, but even more anticipation swirled in my stomach. This was it, the moment when I'd finally feel him inside me. My legs spread, more than ready to take him.

"I need to grab a condom," he groaned against my mouth.

"I have an IUD." And shifters weren't prone to human STDs. All we needed to worry about was pregnancy.

He stilled a second before hooking my one knee over his shoulder, his next kiss desperate. He adjusted our positions, guiding my hand to his cock where it teased my entrance.

"Put me where you want me."

How could such simple words make me so hot? Why did everything he say stroke a secret place inside me I didn't know existed? I lifted my hips to take a bit of him inside me, one thick inch at a time. With his hands free, he toyed with my nipples, then squeezed my breasts. I loved it, realizing I purred but couldn't stop it.

He started to grin, but it morphed into a primal expression when I guided him inside me another inch.

Then my hand got it the way. I let him go, thrusting my hips toward him again, encouraging him on.

But he kept holding back, frustrating me. He gritted his teeth, almost like he was in pain, but he watched me, expectant. I didn't understand what he was waiting for. I thrust my hips again, then stilled when I realized he wanted me to say it out loud.

An inferno built inside me. "Fuck me hard," I moaned. "And don't stop."

Whatever control he'd kept so far snapped. He plunged inside me so deep my groan almost came out a scream. Nothing had ever felt that good.

He didn't wait for me to adjust to his size, but pulled out and back in. I could barely catch my breath before he was inside me again. My free leg wrapped around his hip, keeping him close. My hands were all over him, stroking smooth skin over muscle.

He plunged into me over and over again. Each press of his body felt better than the last. The more we fell into each other, the more I burned up.

"From the first second I saw you," he groaned, "I knew it would be like this."

He kissed and fucked me, and I closed my eyes against the emotions consuming my mind. My other leg got swept up over his shoulder. His speed picked up, this new angle so perfect I saw stars. Just like I'd asked, he didn't hesitate, didn't stop.

His hand went between us and found my swollen clit. His fingers pushed me over the edge. I climaxed with him inside me, squeezing every muscle in my body. With one last thrust, he came, a hot spurt inside me making me clench all over again. His fingers gripped my thighs, biting into my skin as my knees fell off his shoulders, but I loved the feeling, loved that he'd been pushed past his limits of control. I'd done that to him.

He leaned forward. I felt it then, his teeth on my shoulder. I stiffened. Not because I was afraid he would bite me, but because I *wanted* him to. Tension rolled through me, but he didn't bite, just scraped his teeth in an entirely seductive way.

The tension eased from his body. Slowly, our breathing leveled out. Foreheads pressed together, he didn't look away from me, and I didn't look away from him. His hands skimmed down my legs. I was spread out before him and didn't care. The satisfaction tripping through me felt too good.

After long moments, he backed away. His length slid out of me, and I gasped at the loss. With care, his fingers gently brushed my hair away from my face. His expression was both tender and awed. I was a little in awe myself. Never before had I experienced so many erotic moments in such a short span of time.

I pressed my hand to Walker's cheek, and he leaned into the touch. "You were supposed to come in my mouth," I whispered.

His whole body froze, taut. "How are you so damn perfect?"

He gave me a possessive kiss and collapsed beside me, his arm and leg trapping me. I loved the weight of him. After a minute, he got up, went to the bathroom, and returned with a warm wash-cloth. My cheeks burned a little at his tender assistance, but before I got a chance to be too embarrassed about it, he finished up and slid under the covers with me, arms wrapped around my middle with a kiss to my shoulder.

We were silent for a while, both of us staring up at the popcorn ceiling, our breaths in sync, when he said, "Fuck." It was a harsh tone, very different from the ones he'd been saying during out lovemaking.

"What?" I lifted up a bit to see his face better.

"I bought that whole box of condoms, and we don't even need it."

I flopped back, a chuckle bubbling out of me. I couldn't help it. It was absolutely absurd. After everything we'd just done, he was worried about a box of condoms.

And the way he'd said it, like he'd forgotten to pick up the dry cleaning on the way home from work... I laughed again. I'd rode his face. I'd fucked his fingers. We'd sixty-nined like porn stars, and he was mildly inconvenienced because he'd blown ten bucks.

No matter how much I tried, I couldn't stop giggling. I laughed so hard my stomach hurt.

Finally, he rolled onto his elbow to look at me, tucking a stray hair behind my ear. "You have a beautiful laugh." He didn't join in, but his lips twitched. "What's so funny?"

"You," I said on a sigh, the mirth finally subsiding. I pushed him back until I was mostly on top of him. "If you're so concerned about wasting money, we have all night to use up your stupid box." The extra layer of protection against pregnancy wouldn't hurt, and it would help with clean up. I snorted again.

He grabbed my ass and settled me where he wanted me. "Damn straight."

By morning, we'd made a pretty big dent in it.

24

WALKER

I woke up with Sabrina in my arms. I couldn't remember a time I'd held someone while sleeping. Honestly, I didn't think I'd ever had. Before I left for the military, I'd been a scrawny kid from the wrong side of town with no prospects. Girls never looked at me twice. At eighteen, my biggest growing spurt happened after I'd graduated.

Then there was basic training, then deployment. I had leave, sure. I'd screwed some women, sure. But I'd never spent the night with any of them.

This was new. All of it. And...I liked it.

I liked the way she felt, her length snuggled next to mine, her ass in my groin, my arm over her ribs. Enough light leaked through the curtains for me to see her clearly. Her soft, smooth skin came alive under my hand. Listening to her even breaths, all I wanted to do was nuzzle my face into her neck, then lick her awake. Her hair went everywhere, but I liked that too. The long strands curled into themselves, spilling over my arms and shoulder and chest. I loved the way it tickled me, like I wore her.

She smelled...amazing. The scent of sex was everywhere, but that wasn't what I meant. It was *her* scent—peaches and cream and something musky I couldn't get enough of. I wanted to bottle it, pour it over my body, then wear a vial of it around my neck.

A contented heaviness settled in my chest. That was new too, allowing myself to be still and silent and enjoy the moment. It would be no hardship to stay in this position, this moment, for hours and hours.

Her heat wasn't over yet, I could still scent it. But we'd definitely slaked it some. I hadn't been around a shifter in heat since living in Goldenlach Ridge, but it seemed to affect each person differently. In high school, sometimes girls would miss days of classes because of it. Others seemed to go around like it wasn't a big deal even though it put all the shifters around them on alert.

I thought Sabrina fit in the latter category. She could've walked away from me, from my offer, and I was honestly surprised she'd stayed. My whole life, people had been leaving, not staying. She would've been another in a long list.

But instead, despite her past, she'd stayed and let me help her.

During the night, whenever she reached for me, I couldn't deny her. Each time, I made sure she was in her right mind. I'd turn on the lamp beside us to make sure her eyes were clear. I didn't want anything to come between us. No regrets, no miscommunication.

At the beginning of all of this, she'd told me no biting. It had taken me aback at first. I'd never had the urge to bite a woman in my life. But last night...

Every time I came, right before, I'd had the urge to bite her—hard—right on her neck, the specific spot where her throat met her shoulder. She was my mate even though she didn't seem to share my feelings. Instinct told me to do it. Over and over again, I'd wanted to claim her, especially when I was behind her, curled over her spine, and that special spot was ever so close to my mouth.

Claim. The word felt strange on my tongue but oh so right.

From the second I'd scented her while she skulked through the dark around the warehouse on the outskirts of Detroit, I'd felt that primal urge. And now that I'd been inside her, made her scream and moan, tasted her...

But she'd asked me not to bite her, and I wouldn't go against her request.

She stirred in my arms, and I gave in to the impulse of pressing my face into the wicked section of neck below her ear. Inhaling deeply, I took her scent inside me, then exhaled slowly, trying to gain control of the urge to throw her back, spread her legs, and sink inside her before she'd even really woken up so I could wake her up with pleasure.

Her arm moved on top of mine, her fingers weaving through my own where they cupped her breast. She squeezed once, hard, then her hips moved against mine, searching. I accommodated her, adjusting our positions until my hardening cock grazed between her ass cheeks.

A fast breath left her. I skimmed my lips over the shell her ear, nipping. "Are you awake?"

She nodded, rocking gently against me in steady rhythm, each movement taking me further between her legs.

"What do you want me to do for you?" My lips traced a line from her ear, along her perfect neck, to the curve of her shoulder and back again.

Her knee lifted and I slipped further between her legs, right against her pussy. Her wetness coated my cock with each shallow thrust. "Tell me," I groaned against her hair when she only moaned.

"I want you inside me, just like this." Her voice was scratchy and raw from sleep. To emphasize her point, she tipped her hips back until the head of my cock slid inside her. My whole body shivered and rejoiced at the connection.

I kept my thrusts shallow. "Like this?"

Her grip over my hand tightened, her nipple hard beneath my

palm. "Yes." Her head lolled back on my shoulder. "That feels so good."

It felt amazing, and I didn't ever want to stop. Every little bit more I slid inside her made my arms around her tighten. While I thrust, I changed our hand positions until mine lay on top of hers and she squeezed her own breast. I guided that hand, down her chest, past her bellybutton, over the curls between her legs until her fingers slipped between her pussy lips.

She didn't need any more encouragement to touch herself. My hand stayed on top of hers, occasionally dipping down between her fingers for a stroke of my own. Our fingers slicked together with her wetness. It was erotic as hell, and my cock was so hard it ached. Little gasps escaped her lips one after the other.

Trailing kisses along her neck, I spoke against her skin. "I want to watch you touch yourself while I'm inside you."

Her fingers paused for a second at my words, then she was nodding and tilting her hips at me in encouragement. I adjusted our positions until her one knee was on the other side of my hip but she remained mostly on her side.

"Fuck, you're beautiful," I moaned while sinking into her warm depths. Her face was flushed, her lips parted, her hair spilled everywhere, the globes of her breasts jiggling with our movements. My body shook from how good she felt, how much I wanted to lose control and fuck her as hard as possible.

My hands on her knees, I spread her legs further, toward her armpits, and watched my cock slide in and out of her while she circled two fingers over her clit.

Fuck, it was hot. I couldn't even tell her how hot because my throat closed up with emotion. Her other hand squeezed her breast, and she watched me watch us. Her eyes felt heavy on me, significant, and a flush climbed from my balls to the back of my neck. I was burning up. She set me on fire without even trying.

Her fingers on her clit twirled faster; her breaths sped up. In response, I picked up my pace too. I pumped into her, filled her.

The walls of her pussy clenched me over and over again, pushing me to the edge of reason.

"Come around my cock. Squeeze me tight." My voice came out rough and raw.

Every time I eased out of her, her body pulled me back in, like she didn't want to let me go. Her hand shifted from her breast to cover mine on her knee.

"Walker..." I don't know what she was going to say because my next thrust ripped a groan out of her. Her fingers moved so fast over her clit, they were a blur.

Having her spread open like this was heaven. "I wish I could taste you and have my cock inside of you at the same time."

Her whimper turned into a moan, and she jerked, her back arching off the bed. I couldn't hold back anymore, not with her spasming around me. I let go and fucked into her as hard as possible. When my balls tightened and my cock jerked, I seized her fingers, the ones she'd been touching herself with, and sucked them into my mouth.

I didn't think it was possible to come harder than I'd already had with her. But with her flavor on my tongue and my cock buried inside her, I saw stars.

It was a slow descent back to earth. My brain wanted to stay where we'd traveled, the high place above the clouds where only our pleasure existed.

How the hell did this keep getting better? It didn't seem possible.

As I came back into myself, I became aware of the world around us—of the traffic out on the road, of people moving around and talking in the room next to ours, of the way Sabrina watched me, her fingers brushing over mine in a circular pattern.

I still held her knee up and away from her. I still had my cock inside her, balls deep. With reluctance, I slid out of her, then curled her warm, supple body against me, back to front.

She sighed and my arms tightened around her.

"Did I hurt you?"

She shook her head.

I leaned up on one elbow to see her face better, tucking a swath of hair behind her ear. "Are you sure?"

One nod, then she said, "You make me feel amazing. Every time."

Warmed by her words, I gathered her close, and she snuggled back until I cradled her from head to toe. I don't know how long we stayed that way, but it was a door closing from further down the motel, then a car starting, that made me ask, "You want to shower before we look for some breakfast?"

She nodded once, then slipped from the bed. My eyes followed her, tracking her perfect ass as it jiggled on the way to the bathroom. Watching her walk around naked would never get old.

She showered quickly, and I did the same. I thought she might act shy after what we'd done together last night and this morning, but I was happy to see she wasn't. A blush stole over her cheeks from time to time, but she didn't avoid my gaze, and when I reached out a hand to her, she took it in both of hers, pulling me to her.

We jumped into the rental, and I drove to a drive-through. I didn't want to sit somewhere and eat. It would be naive to think Mahn didn't have people crawling all over this city. Getting fast food was our best bet.

I should've just gone on my own and left Sabrina safe in the motel room, but I couldn't bear to part with her. I wanted her close, within sight, within reach. And from the way she took my hand every time I offered it, she felt the same way. That tug in my center mass, the one affirming she was my mate, roared with pleasure. And it was even more than that now too. It wasn't only about being mates. She was an amazing person. I wanted to spend time together. Our personalities fit like puzzle pieces.

After eating our egg sandwiches while I drove, we staked out a few places around town, seeing if we could sight any of Mahn's men.

Our efforts didn't see any results. Neither of us caught sight of Mahn, Sharpe, or the other assholes we'd seen at the compound. And no one who looked outright suspicious either.

We went to another drive-through for lunch and took the food back to the motel. As soon as we walked back in our room that smelled like sex and heat, I had to have Sabrina again. It must've been the same with her, because the second I locked the door behind us, she jumped me. Literally. Her legs wrapped around my hips, her hands gripped my scalp, and her mouth devoured mine.

My body responded to her aggression like I'd been starved for sex for years instead of hours. No person had ever gotten me revved up as fast as she could. We barely made it to the bed before I was inside her. Our movements were carnal and raw, and she came around me so fast I wasn't even sure if I'd locked the door.

When I regained my senses, I realized my jeans were around my ankles, my shirt still on. She wasn't any more put together, her underwear and pants hanging off one leg, her shirt lifted above her breasts.

I kissed each of her breasts before sliding out of her, but I didn't stop there. We might've fucked fast this round, but it wasn't going to be like that for the next one. I took my time undressing her, then myself. Then I worshiped her with my mouth until I was hard again.

Our burgers and fries were cold by the time we ate them naked on the bed.

Licking salt from her fingers, Sabrina stood. "I'm going to shower again."

I think I may've nodded, but I wasn't sure. I couldn't look away from her mouth as she cleaned each digit. When she threw a smirk at me before rolling off the bed, I growled, "Tease."

Her laugh echoed through the room right before she closed the bathroom door.

My heart lightened. I loved that laugh. I wanted to hear it every day of my life if she'd let me.

I rubbed my breastbone. I didn't want to send her away, but that was what she needed to do—get out of Alaska to be safe. It was what I'd been planning for her the second I dialed Lavigne's number.

A car pulled up outside close to our door. Checking the time, I rolled to my feet and grabbed my jeans from where I'd let them fall on the floor. A door opened and closed, then another. I grabbed my gun and gripped it tight while standing close to the wall.

I waited.

A knock on the door, then, "It's Lavigne."

A bit of tension eased out of me at the sound of his familiar voice. "You're early," I replied, and with the gun still in my hand, I unbolted the door and opened it.

As soon as it swung wide, I realized my mistake. Four familiar faces stared at me, people I hadn't seen for close to three years, their expressions morphing into ones of shock, their bodies frozen. I tensed in response.

Her scent. I'd gotten used to it, but the fragrance of sex and Sabrina's heat dominated our room like a living thing. Hell, we'd fucked so many times, the scents probably seeped under the door. And now I had four male, *unmated*, shifters in front of me taking it in.

A primal, protective instinct swirled in my body, making me ready to assert my dominance with them, ready to defend. Every muscle of mine coiled.

Lavigne was the first to move. "Dear fuck," he whispered, stepping back until his legs hit the SUV behind him.

Verdugo bent over like he'd been hit, one arm braced against the wall beside the door frame.

Chi turned, walked away until I couldn't see him anymore, then came back a second later, his eyes glowing. He remained ten feet away from the door, nostrils flared.

Guffey was the only one who stayed put, his jaw flexing as he chewed his favorite spearmint gum. When his face morphed into a wicked grin, my muscles twitched in warning.

None of us said anything, just stared while they processed her scents. The logical side of my brain knew these guys were my friends, knew they wouldn't do anything to threaten me or my mate. As patiently as I could with primal emotions threatening to take over, I waited for them to get a hold of themselves.

But the mood shifted as soon as Sabrina stepped out of the bathroom.

The tension in their bodies changed, now alert and aware. I didn't turn to Sabrina, didn't want to look away from them, especially Guffey, who appeared ready to fuck some shit up like he always did. We were never sure how he passed the psych tests every year.

"Hello?" Sabrina said from behind me, obviously unaware of what was happening between me and my old team.

I might've been able to keep control of my emotions if it wasn't for fucking Guffey. His grin widened, then he said, "Hello there, smidgen."

When Guffey's eyes trailed up and down her body, I reacted before I could think. My leg snapped out, making contact right in the middle of his chest. He stumbled back two steps, and I followed, ready to rip him to shreds for looking at my mate like that. My hands shifted into claws.

But two pairs of arms held me back, pressing me against the doorjamb and making it impossible to rip his throat out like I wanted. I bared my teeth and strained against their hold, hating them for stopping me.

And Guffey just laughed. He was fucking with me. I *knew* he was fucking with me. And still, I wanted to rip out his throat.

"Dude, cool it. No one's going to touch her." Lavigne spoke, his voice low and full of warning. He said those last words with his gaze directed at Guffey. The bastard kept smiling.

A growl emerged from my throat, a low savage warning like I've never given any of them before. Their eyes widened.

Protect! Defend! The emotions wouldn't stop. I didn't have control. These four friends, in one instant, had become threats.

"Hayles," Lavigne shouted in my ear, the kind of tone a drill sergeant would use. It brought me back enough that I could rationalize. I stopped struggling.

"And you," Lavigne growled, but I knew he wasn't talking to me this time, "back off."

"Not likely," Guffey drawled.

The claws on my fingers extended, ready to tear him apart. But I recognized the others weren't threatening my mate.

Hell, no one was threatening my mate. They'd come to help. Guffey was just a dickwad who relished in it. I knew him. I knew them all.

What the hell was I doing? I closed my eyes and slowly inhaled, needing to gain control of whatever was happening to me. The scent of Sabrina fresh out of the shower filled my head. She was safe. They'd come to help. I needed to accept that and get my shit together.

"I'm good. I'm good," I said, relaxing my body, my claws retracting. Finally, they loosened their grip. I shook off my aggression, my breathing ragged like I'd run a marathon. But I couldn't take my eyes off Guffey. He grinned at me again, but I was able to stop myself from attacking him.

His grin widened while still chewing his gum. He might've flicked his eyes toward Sabrina, but he didn't scan up and down. If he had... I don't know what I would've done.

Finally, I looked at Sabrina behind me. Her face was flushed, her eyes wide as she stared at me with parted lips.

I ran a hand over my head, uncertain. I'd acted like a possessive jerk, and she'd seen it all. It might've scared her. And that was the only reason I stayed put and didn't put my arms around her like I wanted.

I tore my gaze away from her and peered past Guffey. Miraculously, it didn't seem like we'd drawn any attention from the motel parking lot or the road beyond. The day went on like nothing had happened.

Even though he wore wrap-around sunglasses that hid his eyes, I could tell Lavigne stared at me like he was trying to see if I'd lose it again. I swallowed and gave him a nod that I was fine.

He stepped back. "We're going to need some different headquarters," Lavigne said before digging out his phone. "There's no way any of us can go in there." He gave me one last look before walking away to make the call.

25

SABRINA

THIS HAD TO BE ONE OF THE MOST EMBARRASSING MOMENTS OF MY life. It was worse than the time in high school when I accidentally dropped my whole lunch tray in front of the star quarterback and his friends and some ketchup had splashed up under his chin.

Four shifters stood on the other side of the door. Four very male, extremely virile shifters, their attention zoned in on me like I held ten flares in my hands while dancing the flamenco. I honestly didn't know what to do, so I held still and waited. For what, I had no clue.

Their scents came at me, masculine and sensual. I recognized wolf, but with them all standing together, I wasn't sure who it came from. There was another feline scent too, different than mine or Walker's.

They all looked about the same age as Walker. The pale one with the wide—kind of unbalanced—grin took most of my notice. His short, wavy brown hair went in every direction like he constantly ran his hands through it. The lankiest of the bunch, there was something...unsettling about his gaze. Not creepy, per se, but more like he could see right through me. And that smile. The more Walker growled, the more it widened.

Then there was the one who stood the furthest away. He wore a black knit cap over his dark hair and had a compact but strong physique. His eyes narrowed as he watched us with his shoulders hunched and his hands in the pockets of his black cargo pants.

The third guy was the biggest of them and had a hard look about him the others didn't. It made him appear older than the rest. Scruff of a beard dusted the olive-toned skin of his jaw. His biceps bulged under his close-fitting flight jacket. The one time he met my eyes, his nostrils flared.

My cheeks flamed, but I squared my shoulders and met his stare head-on.

The last guy talked on his phone. His eyes were hidden beneath wrap-around sunglasses. His head turned toward us, then away as he spoke, one hand casually tucked into his front pocket even though there was nothing casual about the way his muscles bunched, like he waited for something big to happen. He seemed to be the most in command...of both his baser instincts and these men in particular.

When I realized he spoke to someone about getting new accommodations, my fingers curled into fists. I had a serious bone to pick with Walker. He'd told me friends of his were coming to help, that we could trust them.

He didn't tell me they were all shifters.

He didn't tell me that as soon as we opened the door, they'd be able to smell the last forty-eight hours in the room.

If I had a gun, I might've shot Walker for keeping me in the dark about this.

Oh, wait. I did have a gun. The one he'd given me was still in the pocket of my jacket hanging on the back of the chair.

Walker must have realized my intent as I strode over to my jacket, because he stepped in my path, raising his hands surrender style. "Why don't you come meet the guys?"

I didn't know what I thought he was going to say, but that wasn't it. Tension in his body continued to make him stiff, but there was an apology in his eyes too. He cut off my path to my gun and slid a hand down my back to rest above the curve of my ass. It felt so good, I leaned into him.

My gaze shifted to the four guys. None of them missed the action between us. My cheeks grew hotter. The man with the sunglasses hung up his phone and tucked it in the back pocket of his jeans.

"Sabrina," Walker said, lifting his chin at him, "this is Lavigne. He likes to keep us in line."

"*Have* to, not *likes* to," Lavigne returned with a grin, his teeth flashing white against medium brown skin. He may have smiled, but the tension in his body didn't ease.

"That's Verdugo." Walker jerked his head to the man who still had his hand braced against the wall. "He's our problem solver."

The man with the scruffy beard gave me a nod.

I nodded in return.

"The one way out there is Chi." The man in the knit cap raised a hand but remained where he was. "He likes to make things go boom."

I lifted my eyebrows at that.

"And this..." Walker hesitated, then ran the back of his hand against his jaw. "This is Guffey." He didn't add anything else to the description like he did with the others.

They all stayed on the other side of the door. Except Guffey. He pushed past Walker and made of a show of appraising the room, his arms spread wide as he spun to take it all in.

"What have you two been up to?" He breathed in deeply then slapped his chest.

The heat from my cheeks ran downwards until it felt like my whole body burned with annoyance.

"You're such an asshole," Walker said, partially blocking me.

"I sure am." And Guffey didn't look upset about it at all. His eyes went to me, and that low growl came out of Walker's chest again.

Whatever he was trying to do with the posturing, it wasn't working on Guffey. The other man seemed to delight in Walker's rising aggression, like getting Walker to attack him would absolutely make his day.

"So you all work together?" I asked to defuse the tension. My question must have hit a sore spot because Walker tensed. So did Lavigne.

"We used to," Walker said quietly.

Before I could ask anything more, Lavigne jerked his head away from the motel. "We've got a place. I've texted you all the address. Meet up as soon as you can." With one last significant pause, Lavigne walked to the driver's side of their vehicle. Verdugo pushed off the wall to joined him. Chi strode to the second vehicle beside it.

Guffey was the last to leave, his eyes lingering on Walker's arm around me, his grin wide. "Should I ride with you two?"

"Fuck off." There wasn't as much heat in Walker's words as I would have suspected. Obviously, all these guys knew each other —and how to press each other's buttons—well.

Guffey laughed, then brushed past Walker, bumping his shoulder on the way out. Walker didn't react, and he didn't move until the vehicles were backing out of the parking lot. He closed the door.

"So, uh..." he started.

"I'll pack up." I turned away from him, stepping out of his embrace. The duffel bag tight in my hand, I strode into the bathroom to throw the toiletries inside. The more stuff I packed, the jerkier my movements became.

I was pissed—pissed he hadn't warned me. When I came out of the bathroom, I realized he hadn't packed anything yet. He stared at me with a pained and apologetic expression.

I stopped and crossed my arms over my chest, the duffel hanging on my shoulder.

Running a hand over his head, Walker let out a long breath.

"I'm sorry I was growling like that. It wasn't my place." He grimaced. "It'll probably happen again."

"I'm not pissed off about that." I pressed my lips together.

He paused. "You're not?"

I shook my head. If I was being honest with myself, that part kind of thrilled me. I'd never had a guy go territorial on me. Sure, it should have probably felt more domineering than it did, but I couldn't help the pleasure I felt from his seemingly involuntary reaction. And I really didn't want to examine those feelings deeper at the moment.

"You didn't tell me your friends were shifters," I said, my face flaming again. "You didn't tell me that as soon as we saw them, they'd know I was in heat and what we'd done together. You should have warned me."

His expression softened, and he took a step toward me. "You're right. I should have said something. And we should have met somewhere neutral. I wasn't thinking. I'm sorry."

When he took my hands in his, I didn't resist. I was a bit surprised by his quick apology. But I shouldn't have been, really. Besides him being short-tempered with me in the beginning during our escape, he'd been nothing but considerate, and I realized he wasn't going to change anytime soon. It was just who he was.

Something loosened in my chest. And when he cupped my jaw with his one hand, I tilted my head into the touch. He leaned forward to kiss me, and I met him halfway. The kiss was tender, an apology, and I drank it in.

When he lifted his head, he placed another kiss on my forehead. "Let's get packed before I start taking off your clothes all over again."

My core clenched at his words, more than willing to have another round with him. He must have seen the need in my eyes, because he let out a curse before backing away.

Inhaling slowly to regain my composure, I packed up the rest of our belongings, which didn't take long. Then we settled up our incidentals with the motel before getting in our rental SUV and heading to the house Lavigne had procured

It only took about fifteen minutes to drive to a big house on the opposite side of town. Situated well away from its neighbors, it was a sprawling, two-story, ranch-style home nestled amongst pine and birch trees. I didn't know how Lavigne was able to acquire the space in such a short amount of time, but it seemed perfect. After staying in the motel for days, I was looking forward to an actual home—one we didn't need to break into. I just hoped it had a lot of bedrooms.

Walker parked our rental beside the two other SUVs already there. Lights shone from the windows in the cloudy dim of early evening. After slinging our duffel bag over his shoulder, he ushered me up the wide steps, his hand on the base of my spine.

I liked the feel of it there *a lot*.

When we stepped inside, it looked like these guys had been setting up for hours, not minutes. Laptops were placed on the long dining room table enclosed in bay windows. Four black duffel bags were lined up beside the massive kitchen island that separated the cooking space from the living room with its wide-screen TV and brown leather sectional. Guffey had more equipment spread out along its surface.

Lavigne tossed a medium-sized duffel to Chi. "You're on perimeter," he said. Not hesitating, Chi slung the bag over his shoulder and went outside through the back door.

With a squeeze on my hip, Walker set our bag near the couch and melded into the movements with the others. I stepped further into living room area—awkwardly, my hands tucked into my pockets.

"We're ordering pizza," Verdugo called from the kitchen, his phone to his ear. "You got any preferences, Sabrina?"

More pizza. I shook my head. But this place had a kitchen. I could get honest-to-God groceries and cook a real meal for once.

Except, I had no idea how long we'd be here. Now Walker's friends were here to help, I was hoping we'd be able to go to Detroit as soon as possible. I needed to see that my sister was okay with my own eyes.

But these guys...they were settling in, *not* getting ready to leave.

As they set up their equipment, the kitchen island became more and more cluttered with electronic gear. A sinking sensation began in my chest and moved to the pit of my stomach.

Lavigne walked toward me. I tensed, and he stopped a few feet away. "Bedrooms are upstairs," he said, jerking his chin to the landing that overlooked everything. Four doors lined the narrow walkway. "You get first pick."

"Thanks." Picking up our duffel bag, I slung it over my shoulder and headed for the stairs, happy to get away from all the testosterone for a minute. At the top of the stairs, I opened each door in turn. The first was a blue room that shared a Jack-and-Jill bathroom with the next room, which had pink bunk beds. The third was a narrow room with a double bed all done up in whites. The last was the biggest bedroom with its own en suite bathroom and walk-in closet.

It might have been selfish of me, but after everything, I needed that space. Plus, I planned on sharing with Walker. It was only fair to have the biggest bed for two people. I wondered who'd get the short straw and the pink bunks.

Tossing the duffel bag on the end of the bed to claim it, I explored the room a bit, stopping at the window to admire the view of the woods behind the house. The sun brushed the top of the birches, turning the sky fuchsia. Movement made me squint at the tree line. Chi stalked around the house with a bag on his shoulder. I didn't know what he was doing, but his concentration was on the woods surrounding us, not the house.

A quick look in the bathroom, and I gasped at an amazing

rainfall shower head. Even though I'd just showered, I couldn't resist indulging and stayed under the hot spray way too long.

Redressed and rubbing a towel on my wet hair, I walked back out onto the walkway. From up here, I could see everything. Everyone was busy with something. Walker and Lavigne pored over a map on the coffee table in front of the sectional. Verdugo sat at the laptops in the dining room. And Guffey...

He was setting out guns beside the electronic equipment on the island. Lots and lots of guns, the kind in movies like *Die Hard* and *John Wick*.

Gripping the railing in front of me tight, my stomach plummeted.

"Walker?" He lifted his head when his name left my lips on a croak. I cleared my throat. "Can I talk to you for a minute?"

He didn't even hesitate, just dropped the conversation and made his way up to me. "What is it?" he asked when he was a few feet away, his eyes concerned. He reached for my hand, and I took it in my cold one.

With a jerk of my head to our bedroom, I led him inside then closed the door. As nerves continued to roll in my stomach, I licked my lips. His eyes tracked the movement and darkened. I shook my head at him. That wasn't what this was about.

"I thought we were leaving the state," I said when I found my voice. "I thought we were going to Detroit, to find my sister." Instead, it looked like these guys were gearing up for battle.

Understanding in his eyes, he tugged me closer. "You are. Lavigne brought you a passport. I wish their boss would have left her plane here for you to take, but apparently, Clyborne needed it for something else. But there's a direct flight heading out in the morning. You'll be with your sister by tomorrow night."

I should have felt relief, but instead, I searched his face, the dread not leaving the bottom of my stomach. "What about you? I thought you were coming with me."

His expression softened, his hand coming up to cup my cheek. "I can't leave without taking care of a few things."

Fear ripped through me. Fear for him. "What are you going to do?"

"Burn that whole fucking place to the ground."

It wasn't the words that chilled me, it was the lethal promise in his eyes, the starkness in his tone. It made me believe that even if he didn't have his friends to help him, he'd do it himself. I'd heard his screams, and I'd been debased over and over again. I didn't disagree, but we'd both seen the kind of firepower contained in that place.

I swallowed around the lump solidifying in my throat. "Come with me," I pleaded. I didn't want him to get hurt or recaptured. I didn't want Mahn or Croskey to get their hands on him again. And above all, I didn't want him to die.

He stared at me long and hard, but in the end, he shook his head.

My heart seized in my chest. I took a step back, needing space between us. We were free and could stay free, and instead, he was rushing back into the arms of someone intent on hurting our kind.

He'd wanted to wait for his friends before we left Alaska. Now I knew why. He had his own personal swat team. But what could they do against a compound equipped with a small army?

The look on my face must have said it all, because Walker's jaw clenched. He opened his mouth to say something but didn't because someone yelled "Pizza!" from downstairs.

My appetite was gone, but at least it was a distraction from the tension between me and Walker. Heart in my throat, I turned away before he could say anything more and was halfway down the stairs before I heard him follow.

26

WALKER

THE GUYS WERE ALL DIGGING INTO THE PIZZA, PILING SLICES ON paper towel, eating on the couch with their man spreads, and drinking beer and Coke by the time we joined them. I had more to say to Sabrina but wasn't sure she wanted to hear it.

That fear in her eyes—it was what I'd seen while we were on the run, but this time, it was directed at me. She was afraid *for* me. I knew I must be messed up to feel sentimental about it, especially when it caused her distress, but her concern warmed me. It meant she cared. Maybe the mating bond was starting to kick in for her too.

"What'll you have, Sabrina?" Guffey asked, making room on the couch beside him. "Hawaiian, pepperoni, or deluxe?"

She hesitated, looking at the spot he'd cleared for her, then at the challenge in his eyes. With a shrug, she picked up a paper towel and a piece of Hawaiian.

Then she sat next to Guffey.

I tensed. I couldn't help it. The guy made busting balls an art form, and now that he had leverage against me, he wasn't going to quit. Once she'd settled, crossing her legs under her, Guffey gave me the biggest fucking grin on the planet. Bloody hell, I really wanted to punch him in the face.

Sabrina wouldn't meet my eyes. I knew she was distressed, and I didn't like it. Didn't like it one bit.

"Want a beer, Sabrina?" Chi asked, tilting one toward her. "Or a Coke?"

"A Coke. Thanks."

He kept the beer for himself and handed her a can of cola.

There wasn't any room on the couch, so I grabbed a slice of pepperoni and a beer, then sat on the other side of the coffee table from her.

Along with those first few bites of pizza came the resulting mouth-full silence. Sabrina's eyes darted to everyone but me. After a swig of her drink, she asked, "So do any of you have first names, or is that for sissies?"

Verdugo snorted, then saluted her. "Gabriel."

"Alex," Chi responded a second later.

When her eyes jumped to Lavigne, he said, "Dalton," with a nod.

Then she looked at Guffey. "Jackson." He leaned closer. "But smidgen, you can call me anything you like. Most girls fall back on, 'Oh God. Oh God. Please don't stop.'" He said the last bit in a falsetto voice.

A growl came out of my throat I couldn't help. No one even acknowledged me.

Sabrina's eyes were trained on Guffey, and she gave him a tight smile. "Must be because you're really good at doing laundry."

Chi and Verdugo guffawed at the same time. Even Lavigne cracked a smile.

But the joke didn't erase the haunted and pleading look Sabrina had worn since our chat in the bedroom.

Her fears were misplaced. This was what these guys did for a living. They executed precision ops in small groups. They lived for this shit. So did I, if I was being honest with myself. But after Jordan's death... It wrecked me. The others might've been motivated to do good, to find something similar to devote their time to after our special ops team was discharged, but not me.

Maybe that had changed over the past three years. I didn't know. But right now, the burning need to destroy the people who'd captured me and Sabrina outweighed everything else.

And somehow, having her on board with it was important to me. I couldn't say why. It was happening either way. I just didn't want her to look at me with those desperate eyes.

I cleared my throat. "Verdugo." His eyes whipped to me, a slice of pizza halfway to his mouth. "You should tell Sabrina about the time you took out the town of mercs in Lebanon."

Eyebrows raising into his hairline, Verdugo tipped his head, giving me a perplexed, 'What the fuck?' kind of look.

It was Guffey who leaned forward, relishing the idea with a slap of his knees. "You should have seen it, Sabrina." He turned to her a little. "A true sight to behold. We'd known they were holding women for slave trading, and we'd been trying to take down these motherfuckers for a while. There was a least a dozen of them—"

"Two dozen," Verdugo interjected.

"—and we'd drawn straws," Guffey went on like he hadn't been interrupted, "to see who went in first to thin the herd and take out the guys around the perimeter. The problem was, Verdugo didn't just thin the herd. He neutralized them all, one after the other. By the time we waltzed into camp, there was no one left but the captives."

Sabrina twitched at the word "neutralized" but otherwise, all through the story, she'd stared at Guffey, her face expressionless. I couldn't tell what she was thinking.

With a glance at me, Chi leaned forward. "Then there was this time in Turkey," he began like he knew what I wanted. "These pirates took over a yacht, a diplomat's, held him and his family for ransom. While the others sneaked aboard the pirates' vessel, Hayles and I breached the yacht. It took under five minutes for the team to secure both boats, and we got the family free."

That story led to one Verdugo participated in, then Guffey went on with another. The only ones not to contribute were Lavigne and me.

But as the stories went on, Sabrina's expression turned hard, more distant. With a sinking sensation, I realized my plan to ease her fears was backfiring. Now that the guys had started, they kept going with all their favorite "we saved people" stories. Of course, they were always bloody and disturbing. And the way the guys were trying to one-up each other meant they kept getting worse.

Before I could put a stop to it, Sabrina shot to her feet. "I know what you're trying to do, and it's not going to work."

Everyone stilled, including me. A tortured look went across Sabrina's face as she met my gaze. "You're not going to convince me what you're planning to do is nothing but a walk in the park compared to what you've already gone through together. I know you've lost someone you were close to. And that means none of you are indestructible."

My stomach sank at the mention of Jordan. She must've seen it in my face because she dropped her gaze to the table. "Guns, bombs, and killing villages of terrorists aren't something to make light of." She took a deep breath. "I was at that compound. I know what these men are capable of and that they hate shifters."

Tension turned the guys into living statues as she spoke, but none of them interrupted her.

"They want to hurt us," she went on. "They planned to take me to some arena to die."

My breath froze in my hollow chest at the reminder.

"They tortured Walker for days on end." She waved a frantic hand toward me. "I had to listen to him scream. He was almost *dead* when I freed him. And you guys are laughing about some old stories like it's some sort of joke." She swallowed audibly. "I can't laugh with you. This shouldn't be happening." She looked at each of us like she searched for an ally.

But it wasn't in any of us to back away from something like this. Not now. Not ever.

"It's for all those reasons we need to take that place down," Lavigne said quietly. "It's what we do."

It was the first time he'd spoken since we'd started in on these stories, and maybe Sabrina realized the significance of that because her face fell.

Without another word, she pushed past Guffey's knees and headed for the stairs. The guys were all staring at me, but that wasn't what made me jump to my feet and follow. I couldn't take her tortured expression. I couldn't leave her in this state.

When I caught up to her, she'd stopped at the foot of the bed, her arms wrapped around her middle, her back hunched like she tried to ward off freezing temperatures. When she heard me, she turned her head.

I stopped just inside the door, closing it behind me. "If you want to scream or throw something at me, go for it."

She didn't even crack a smile. Instead, she walked right up to me and wrapped her arms around my torso. The unexpected action made me suck in a breath.

"I'm scared for you," she said into my shirt.

Warmth spread through my chest and abdomen. My hand stroked her head, her hair, then down her back. She relaxed a little into the touch, but her body was still riddled with tension.

We were quiet for long moments, nothing but the occasional murmur from the level below to interrupt the silence. Finally, I said, "I can't let Mahn do to others what he did to us." I kissed the top of her head. "I can't leave it."

She remained still for a long time, her fingers splayed across my back. Maybe she was thinking about those two bobcats she'd been tracking. Maybe it was something else. But after a long minute, she nodded once, yielding.

More warmth spread through my body at her concession. She didn't want me to go. She didn't want me to get hurt. But she was accepting this as part of me and not fighting it anymore. I didn't know what a potent sensation that would be. My arms tightened around her. I wanted, no *needed*, to be closer to her.

She seemed to be of the same mind, because she was yanking at my shirt, trying to get it over my head, her movements jerky. Then her lips were there, on my chest, my neck, my jaw, her hand pulling my head to hers. She kissed me like her life depended on it, and I was right there with her.

We moved together toward the bed. When the back of her knees hit the edge, I followed her down, only breaking our kiss long enough to pull her T-shirt over her head and shove the duffel bag to the floor. Her eyes a mix of lust and desperation, she yanked me back to her. My heart thumped wildly in my chest. I wanted to touch and taste her everywhere.

Her fingers fumbled with the button of my pants, then they were tugging, yanking frantically.

I pulled back only enough to skim off her pants and under-wear. Before she could demand otherwise, I spread her thighs, my face between them, burying myself in her scent while I tasted her. Fingernails dug into my scalp, creating shivers down my spine. There was nothing better than tasting Sabrina, hearing her moans, her hands encouraging me on.

I couldn't get enough of her. I lapped at her core, tongued her clit, rubbed my face in her juices over and over again. My cock was rock hard, and I thrust into the bed with each stroke of my tongue. I wanted to fuck her, taste her, and talk dirty to her all at the same time.

Her thighs clenched. Her hips lifted. She gasped my name while her fingernails curled into my scalp so tight I felt pinpricks of pain. It took me a second to realize she'd lost control enough to partially shift her claws. It made me growl in pleasure against her. Her hold tightened even more as I drank every tremor.

When her thighs released me, spreading wide in an offering, she tugged at my hair. "Walker," she gasped. "I need you inside me."

Her words did things to me, made me hot and needy and desperate. With one last, long lick, I crawled up her body, kissing her as soon as I was close enough. I shared her scent with her and hooked one leg over my shoulder. She clutched at me like she didn't want to go slow. I didn't either.

With one deep plunge, I was inside her to the hilt. She cried out and I swallowed the sound, loving it, burying it with my own groan. *Heaven.* This is what heaven felt like.

She wrapped her other leg around my hips, holding me close. Then I was thrusting, long movements that pulled a moan out of her with every stroke. Her fingers found mine, and I took her hand and captured it above her head. Her other clutched my scalp.

In and out I plunged, over and over again, our gazes locked. With every rock of my hips, her heel dug into my ass, encouraging me to go faster, harder.

This was where I'd usually talk dirty, but the words wouldn't come out. Nothing formed in my mouth except the awe I felt at the expressions moving over her face, the feel of her clenching around me.

The only things I wanted to say were love words, but I kept them inside, not knowing if she felt the same. Instead, I tried to give her *everything* without words.

The heat inside me built, and when she cried out, her pussy tightening, the urge to bite her, to claim, overcame everything else. My lips moved to her shoulder. My canines extended. Instead of stiffening, instead of pushing me away, she clutched me closer as shudders wracked her body.

With one last thrust, I emptied inside her. My teeth clamped around her shoulder. A primal voice inside me told me to bite. *Bite, bite, bite.*

It took all my will power to hold her there and not do it. I don't know how I resisted when I'd recognized from the beginning she was mine and I was hers. But her will, her choice, meant more to me than instinct. I held her to me as tight as possible until the urge passed. But it never went away fully. I still wanted to claim her as I loosened my grip and canines receded back into the mouth.

Lifting up onto my elbows, I rested my forehead against hers. She peered up at me with wide eyes, bright splotches of color on her cheeks. Did she understand how close I'd come to biting her? From the look on her face, it was highly likely. But she wasn't running from me. She wasn't screaming at me or telling me to get off her.

I kissed her then, putting every emotion still bottled up inside me into the action. I wanted her to feel what I'd held back. I wanted her to take it in some fashion.

And she did, all of it. She gave back more. The kiss went on and on, this all-consuming thing that swept us both away from reality.

I didn't pull out of her, and with each second of that kiss, I hardened inside her more. She tilted her hips against me, and I responded. This second time, I made love to her with tender movements and long touches, leaving the desperation behind. I wanted to worship her and her body. I wanted to savor everything.

So I did, over and over again, making love to her with my hands and body instead of my words. When we were both wrung out, we settled together front to front. She stared at me with those beautiful golden eyes of hers, softened with satisfaction and fatigue.

I couldn't stop looking at her or touching her. My fingers ran through her hair, massaging her scalp and neck, then smoothing down her spine until her eyes closed. In the back of my mind, I realized the guys had put loud music on downstairs.

As she fell asleep in my arms, one tear escaped her. My heart clenched at the sight. Then I realized the way she'd made love to me over the past couple of hours, it was like she'd been saying goodbye.

But I knew this wasn't goodbye. This wouldn't be our last night together. After the guys and I took down the compound, I'd find her in Detroit. I wasn't letting her go, not until she told me she didn't want me.

That thought sent a spear of pain through my chest.

The more she slept, the more her body sank into me, her hand on my hip, her cheek resting on my biceps, her knee tucked between mine. I could only stare at her as I threaded my fingers in her hair.

I knew I should leave her and find Lavigne to keep planning the op, but I couldn't let her go. She was Sabrina, the most amazing woman I'd ever met, my mate, and I never wanted to leave her again. The thought of sending her on a plane tomorrow tore me up. I didn't want her out of my sight. I wanted to stay with her and take care of her, and never put that desperate, tortured look of concern on her face ever again. I wanted to see her smile and make her laugh.

But I couldn't do any of that with the compound in existence. I wouldn't be able to rest thinking Mahn and those fuckers would come after her.

So the guys and I would make our plans and hit the compound tomorrow night. By that time, Sabrina would be safe with her sister in Detroit. Only by doing those two things could I even begin to build a future with her.

27

SABRINA

Everything was supposed to look better in the morning, but it didn't.

I woke up alone as dawn broke through the tall windows lining the wall. Walker's distinctive spicy scent and the fragrance of our lovemaking wrapped around me as closely as the bed's comforter. I snuggled down deeper, never wanting to leave this cocoon of warmth. Except there was one thing missing: Walker.

A strangely tight sensation in the middle of my chest told me to go find him, that I wouldn't feel right until I touched him and held him close to reaffirm he was well, that he was safe.

Our lovemaking the night before had been different. His touch made me feel things I hadn't wanted to but fully embraced anyway. I was scared for him, of what would happen, and it was because of that fear I hadn't been able to hold back. Every sensation resonated deep in my bones, and it had felt...*right*. I couldn't explain it, really. When I'd thought he was going to bite me, in that instant, I'd wanted him to.

And when he didn't, I'd had to mask my disappointment. Which in and of itself was bonkers. Biting meant something I wasn't ready to give, not yet. Maybe not ever. But with Walker, it was a possibility that maybe someday I'd be willing to consider.

But only with him, no one else.

My stomach somersaulting at where my thoughts had gone, I rolled from beneath the covers and padded to the bathroom. If I believed a shower would fix where my mind had wandered or the permanent feelings I was beginning to have, then I was completely wrong. None of it washed away—not my connection to Walker, not my thoughts of wanting this thing between us to continue, not my fear for what he was about to do with his friends. The only positive thing the morning held was that the itch in my skin had vanished, the fever that had plagued my skin now nonexistent.

After getting dressed in clean yoga pants and a T-shirt, I opened the door, the murmur of voices down below telling me everyone else was awake too.

I hadn't thought I'd made any noise, but Walker straightened and turned toward me as soon as I stepped out on the landing. Our eyes caught and held. Whatever he'd been doing with Lavigne, he abandoned and headed straight toward me, taking the stairs two at a time. When he was close enough, he took one of my hands, guiding me toward him until he pressed a kissed to my forehead, then tucked my hair behind my ear.

I sighed. I couldn't help it. Now that he was near, the tight sensation in my chest eased. It was like I could breathe easier and that made no sense whatsoever.

"How are you?" Walker asked, running his hand down my arm to my elbow.

I nodded. "Good." I noted that the murmuring of voices had stopped below us, but I didn't look, my eyes trained on Walker's instead.

"You hungry?"

I nodded again, and his lips quirked as he led me to the stairs. "Your choices for breakfast are cold pizza, Frosted Flakes, or toast." He gave me a bigger smile then. "We shouldn't have sent Guffey to do the shopping."

"Toast is fine."

We walked down the steps, and I took in our altered surroundings. What had looked like the beginnings of an HQ now resembled a war room. More maps were spread everywhere, more computers, more monitors. There were live feeds coming from somewhere, and I realized the images were of the outside of the compound. The sight of that God-awful place made me shudder. I realized someone would have had to go there last night and get close enough to install cameras. My stomach rolled.

Something that looked like a large bug sat near the front door, a drone of some sort. That must be how they'd gotten the aerial images of the compound that were pinned to the dining room wall. It appeared way bigger than I had even guessed while escaping, half of it laid out like a zoo. An empty one. I couldn't see any animals in the images.

My stomach lurched again thinking about the habitat Croskey had made me use.

Each of Walker's friends either said "good morning" or gave me a head nod as we made our way to the kitchen, and I returned their greetings in kind. One spot on the counter was left for breakfast; a jug of milk, the box of cereal, one box of pizza, a jar of honey, and a bag of bread were squeezed into the space.

After hesitating a moment, I grabbed the bread and slid two pieces into the toaster. Walker hadn't left my side, his fingers tucking into one of my back pockets and eliciting all sorts of erotic shivers down the back of my thighs. He leaned against the counter, his legs outstretched before him. With one tug, he pulled me closer until my body fit between his legs.

The murmur of voices picked up behind me. I heard words like "tactical," "fallout," and "parameters," but paid little attention while Walker slid both hands into my back pockets, cupping my ass.

His eyes held me in a spell, the green and yellow of them as mesmerizing as their intensity. It looked like he wanted to say something, but with everything happening around us, he hesitated. His gaze lowered to my lips, then swept up to my eyes. He was going to kiss me. Right in front of everyone. Then I'd lose myself, just as I always did, and it wouldn't matter that all his buddies were only feet away. And heat or no heat, I'd want to climb up his body and ride him until every worry and concern faded away.

The toast popped, breaking his spell over me as effectively as a knife to a soap bubble. I moved away from him, grabbing a plate with shaky hands.

"There's no rush. It's still a couple hours until your flight."

His words made me stiffen, my hand dropping the toast onto my plate with a quiet smack. *Right. The flight.* The one he wouldn't be joining me on.

Furiously, I spread honey on my cooling toast. If I dwelt on what was about to happen, that I'd be traveling without him and he'd go racing toward the very people who'd tortured him for days, I'd lose my composure.

Leaving felt so very wrong. Everything told me to stay where I was. If Walker was here, then that's exactly where I should be. I knew it didn't make sense. My sister was only a flight away. Finding her, seeing she was okay with my own eyes, had been my goal since day one. But leaving Walker to do this...it hurt my chest even to think about.

I took a breath, trying to calm, to ease my fears and make this situation work. I wouldn't be able to convince him to scrap their plans, but what if there was some other alternative?

He remained beside me, his arms crossed over his chest, and I stepped between his legs once more. His hands automatically dropped to my hips so I could move in closer.

"What if..." I cleared my throat when his fingers tightened on me. "What if I stayed?"

It was his turn to stiffen. "What do you mean?"

I could sense the guys behind me had paused in what they were doing to stare at us, knew they listened. I tried not to care. "What if I waited here for you to get back?" I placed my hands on his chest and searched his face. "Then we could go to Detroit together tomorrow or the next day."

For a split second, he seemed to consider it, then he shook his head. "You'd be alone here, and that isn't safe. I need all the guys for the op."

"But—"

He cut me off, pressing his forehead against mine. "I'd also be worried about you. My concentration would be shot. The best, the *safest*, place for you to be is far, far away from here." He tucked a stray bit of hair behind my ear, then cupped my jaw. "I need you safe. Understand?"

It took all my will power to nod instead of argue. I didn't want to go without him. "When will I see you again?" I hated how fragile that made me sound.

"If everything goes to plan, and it will." He dipped his head down until I met his eyes. "Then I'll be in Detroit tomorrow night."

It wasn't so long to wait. If I kept telling myself that, then eventually, I might believe it. I nodded again.

"And then you won't be able to get rid of me."

He said it softly, for my ears only, but a shadow of worry passed over his features, his expression vulnerable.

My stomach dropped at his uncertainty. After everything, we still had our own insecurities to deal with. I leaned forward and planted a gentle kiss to his lips. "I'll hold you to that," I whispered.

His arms came around me and hugged me tight before letting go. This was as much as we'd ever talked about the future and this thing developing between us. Maybe we were both scared. And right now really wasn't the time. He had to focus on the mission, and I had to concentrate on not freaking out for leaving without him.

Pushing away, I grabbed my plate and ate my breakfast even though it had grown cold and I'd lost my appetite. I'd promised myself over the past couple of weeks that I'd never take food for granted again, and I was going to stick to the pledge.

With one last squeeze of my hip, Walker left me against the counter, and I tried not to let anxiety eat away at me. Though they weren't loud about it, everyone bustled in their operation prep. I heard and understood some snippets of the conversation. They weighed the odds of attacking the compound this way or that. They talked about timing, how the earliest they would raid it would be an hour after sunset. It all made my stomach roll.

I didn't want to listen. And I didn't know what to do with myself. Defeated, I headed upstairs, ignoring the stares pressing into my spine. I packed the clothes and things I might use again into a small over-the-shoulder bag Walker had left for me.

When I returned downstairs, I set my bag by the door. It felt so final, like I hadn't fought hard enough to stay. But from the determined look on Walker's face, I knew it would be useless to argue.

Even though Walker had mentioned it earlier, I was still surprised when Lavigne handed me a passport, complete with a picture of me. He'd somehow gotten it from my driver's license. I wanted to ask how it had been made so quickly.

Along with the passport was a wallet with a credit card and some cash and a new phone with all my flight information on it. I clutched them tight to my chest with a "Thank you."

"Ready?" Walker asked, coming up to me.

I nodded even though I wanted to kick him in the shin like a child and run upstairs and hide so he'd have to let me stay.

After parting goodbyes to the guys, we went outside and down the steps to the SUV, then headed to the airport. Both of us remained quiet, like we'd already said everything we meant to say even though I knew that wasn't true. At least, it wasn't for me. I wanted to tell him to be careful, to tell him about all these feelings I had churning in my belly since the first day of our escape, to thank him for staying with me this whole time, for protecting me, for being there for me during my heat but not asking for what I couldn't give. All of it.

None of that came out.

Walker held the steering wheel tight, knuckles white and jaw clenched. "I have a friend who's going to pick you up when you land, stay with you until you meet up with your sister and this mate of hers, okay?"

I grimaced. "That's not really necessary."

"It is. I want you safe. I've texted you his number and picture so you'll know who he is."

"Safe," I repeated. But who was going to keep him safe?

I tried not to let the thought drown me. He had a full team at his back. They'd keep him safe. I had to believe that. I'd spent the day with them. They knew what they were doing.

No matter how much I tried to convince myself, the nauseous ball in my stomach continued to churn. My chest ached like we had a cord connecting us together. I wanted to try again to convince him to let me stay, but from the set of his jaw and the look in his eyes, I knew he wouldn't back down. He wanted me as far away from here as possible so he and his buddies could destroy the compound.

The thought should have left me bitter, but after everything he'd been through, I couldn't resent him for it. Even so, it didn't stop the desolation in my stomach.

This shouldn't hurt so much. After an eight-hour flight, I'd see my sister.

The closer we drove to the airport, the more Walker tensed and kept looking into the review mirror every few seconds. His unease spread to me, and I glanced over my shoulder. "What is it?"

He signaled and took the next left, away from the airport, toward the Tanana River. "I think we're being followed." On a straightaway, he gunned it, pushing the speed limit and making me grip the sides of my seat. His phone was up to his ear in the next moment. "We've got a situation." He listened for a moment. "Yeah. Be quick." Hanging up, he tossed the phone on the dashboard, a scowl on his face. We sped by warehouses on the right, an RV superstore on the left.

Twisting around, I tried to catch what he saw. There were a couple cars behind us, but nothing that stuck out to me. The area was industrial, with little traffic except semi-trucks hauling goods. "What do you—"

Movement flashed out my window, making my head turn. The grill of an SUV was too close. *Bang.* The world spun sideways. My teeth clattered in my skull. Airbags deployed. The seatbelt snapped me against the headrest, cutting into my skin. My brain ached at the loud noises screaming around us. Glass shattered. Metal screeched. I didn't know which way was up or down. I screamed, but everything else drowned out my voice. The right side of my body pressed against metal that hadn't been so close a moment before, scraping into my skin.

Everything slowed, then stopped. Tires screeched on pavement. Something warm trickled into my eye. Grabbing at the tight seatbelt against my chest, I tried to get my bearings.

We'd landed right side up. The airbag pressed against me. My limbs felt heavy, my mind slow. I reached, trying to touch Walker beside me. The skin of his arm brushed my palm. I squeezed.

"Walker?" My voice cracked.

He didn't move, and I couldn't see him clearly because of the airbags. I smelled blood but didn't know if it was his or mine. I swallowed and tried to do an inventory of my injuries while the door pressed tight against my body.

With a snap and a hiss, the airbag in front of me deflated. A knife tore through the fabric, then my seatbelt. Rough hands grabbed me under the armpits and pulled me out of the broken window. I struggled. Shards of glass dug into my back and hips, then tinkled to the ground. I caught sight of our vehicle, the one side crushed near where I'd been sitting. If I'd been sitting in the backseat, I would have died.

Something cold snapped around my neck. I twisted around and caught sight of Sharpe and his trucker hat, along with two other guys in tactical gear.

I screamed in rage and thrashed, trying to break free from Sharpe's hold. I kicked one of the others in the jaw when he got close enough.

Two other guys turned their guns on our SUV, bullets clattering against the body of the vehicle and slicing into the windows that weren't already broken.

I broke from Sharpe's hold and dove at them. "Walker!" I screamed, hoping he'd hear me and wake up enough to fight.

The two guys paused their attack when I tackled the one, but another wrapped an arm around my waist before I could do much damage. I fought against them as they dragged me toward another vehicle.

When it looked like they were going to fire again, a semi-truck turned the corner, and they scrambled into the Hummer instead. I screamed Walker's name again, needing to know if he still lived.

I couldn't let them take me.

It was the last thought I had before the pain of the shock collar blackened my vision.

28

WALKER

SABRINA BELLOWED FOR ME FROM FAR AWAY. I BLINKED, TRYING TO clear the haze from my eyes. An airbag pressed against me, suffocating. I smelled blood and felt it trickle down my cheek. A pulsing pain pounded through my head.

None of that mattered. Only Sabrina mattered. I shoved everything else down: the pain, the nausea in my stomach from the crash, the fear of failing.

Shots came at me, sinking into the airbag, the upholstery, the windows, and tore into my skin. I ducked, protecting my head, then flinched, instinctively shifting to heal myself. A bullet squeezed out of my shoulder and the cut on my head sealed shut.

I need to get out of this fucking car. As fast as the shots started, they stopped.

We'd been blindsided, T-boned. They were abducting Sabrina. Rage consumed me. There was no way in hell I'd let them take her from me. Pushing the deflating airbag away from my face, I grabbed the door handle. No matter how hard I tried to push, it wouldn't open. Panicked, I shifted into my cougar form and used my claws to tear the airbag and seatbelt away from my body.

With unsteady legs, I staggered to the opposite window. Even though I'd shifted, my brain still felt rattled. I lunged up and through the window, landing on shaky paws. The sight of a Hummer speeding off down the road made my heart thump hard in my chest.

I tore off after it, past the discarded SUV that had slammed into us. I couldn't waste time looking for my phone. I wouldn't let Sabrina out of my sight. But no matter how fast I pushed myself, the Hummer went faster, until I lost sight of it as it turned onto the highway.

I didn't stop. I knew where they were taking her—to the compound. The bond between us tugged me in that direction. I didn't care if it didn't make physical sense to sprint the whole way. It didn't matter I was running along a road as a cougar and someone would probably call animal control. I wouldn't stop until I had Sabrina back in my arms.

The farther I ran, the more the twisted mass of rage and desperation grew in my stomach. I couldn't let them have her. I wouldn't fail.

An SUV sped up beside me. "Hayles!" Verdugo shouted out the window.

I slowed my run, gasping for breath, and the SUV stopped beside me. The back hatch opened.

"Get in," he ground out. I leaped into the back, shifting once inside to slam the door closed.

My emotions, my feelings for Sabrina, were making me sloppy. Even on these side roads, we couldn't risk humans seeing us shift. But the need to get to my mate outweighed everything else. It didn't matter what happened to me as long as I could get her free.

The SUV lurched forward, knocking me off balance. I braced my knees, staring forward at my four friends. Our mission had just changed. Everything was jeopardized. Mahn's men had found us. They might know the location of our temporary head-quarters.

Destroying the compound didn't matter anymore. Only Sabrina mattered. "They'll take her to the compound," I said through gritted teeth.

"We need to play this smart," Lavigne said from the driver's seat.

"We don't have time to play this smart." We needed to move now, not make one of Lavigne's foolproof plans. "They'll take her where we won't be able to track her, the arena or somewhere else."

"Clyborne is still looking into the location of the arena. But if you go in there half-cocked, they'll kill her."

I knew he was right, but we didn't have time to plan a different op. My gut told me Sabrina would be shipped some-where, probably where they were going to send her the night we'd escaped.

"Fuck!" I slammed my fist against the window.

I might lose her without ever telling her the truth between us, that I cared about her and that we were mates.

She wanted to stay. For the first time in my life, someone had wanted to stay with me and stand by my side.

Once I got her back, I'd tell her everything, all my feelings, that I want us to be together. There'd be no holding back.

29

SABRINA

THE LOUD DRONE OF A PLANE LANDING WOKE ME, SO DEAFENING I covered my ears with my hands. It felt like I was right under the plane itself.

Opening my eyes, I realized that was close to the truth. A cargo plane touched down on a runway in front of me, a gray beast of a thing with two huge propellers swirling at the front. I swore my ears were bleeding from the noise level.

Even worse than that, I realized I was back in a cage, the same kind I'd been in when I'd first awoken on the plane those weeks ago. Dropping my hands from my ears, I shook the bars, trying to get out.

Bang. Someone hit the top of the cage.

"Stop it," Sharpe snarled over the noise of the engine. My stomach dropped. His eyes hadn't lost their hate. I swallowed against the cold metal of the collar around my neck, the one he'd put there. Loathing washed through me.

I tore my gaze away and took in my surroundings. Men wearing all black held machine guns and patrolled the runway, most either wearing ear protection or helmets. They walked in pairs, their gazes trained to the wilderness beyond the fence of the landing strip. Behind me, the compound loomed, an ugly mark on the otherwise beautiful landscape. Not much time had passed since they'd grabbed me, the sun still high in the sky.

My hair stuck to my face, wet. I touched my forehead, and my fingers came away with blood. I must have hit my head during the car crash. Was Walker okay? Was he dead? I swallowed the bile threatening to crawl its way up my throat. He hadn't spoken, hadn't moved when I'd been snatched out of the SUV. *Oh, God.* I closed my eyes and pressed my forehead to the bars. I prayed he was all right.

The plane's engine quieted slightly as it pulled away from us, taxiing toward a white fuel truck. I took in a deep breath, trying to calm my racing heart and rolling stomach. I'd picked the lock on a cage like this once. I could do it again.

Finally, the plane cut its engine, and my ears rang in the sudden silence. The *clip clap* of dress shoes on pavement sounded hollow in my skull.

"Why is the pilot powering down?"

The calm voice made me turn my head. I'd only seen the man standing beside me a few times. Emerson Mahn. The person Walker had told me was behind this all and who he'd grown up with. He wore the same kind of expensive suit he'd worn before and didn't look at me as he addressed Sharpe. "Get him to start it up again. We need to leave."

While Sharpe jogged toward the plane, Mahn turned to me. "It won't be long now."

Nausea swam in my stomach. The first time I'd seen him, I'd thought his gaze cold. My opinion hadn't changed.

He took out his phone like he hadn't a care in the world, scrolling through his social media with a woman in a cage beside him. I didn't bother pleading for my life or demand that he free me. After everything he'd done to bring me here, everything he'd put us through, I knew it would be pointless.

I swallowed. "What happened to those bobcats I was tracking?"

Mahn was silent so long I didn't think he'd answer, then he shrugged. "Gone to the arena, same place you're going." While he spoke, he kept his eyes on his phone. "Probably mounted on the buyers' walls by now."

My heart squeezed tight, then sank into my toes. *They're dead.* Bile rose in my throat. It was what I'd suspected after Walker said he'd smelled shifter in his cell, but I'd hoped for something else. Those bobcats didn't deserve to be hunted. No one did.

I watched as Sharpe climbed the steps to the plane, then disappeared inside.

"I'm going to tell you a secret," Mahn said, and I jerked at his voice, surprised. "Your kind are unnatural. You don't belong on this earth, and you need to be eliminated. I'm not a religious man, I'm a scientific one. There is nothing we've tested or done to you that explains how your *species*," he spat the word, the first crack in his demeanor, "lives. You should not exist." He stared back at his phone.

My hands clenched on the bars. "We weren't hurting you."

"No?" He turned his head to me for a moment. "You've been associating with a highly financed group of animals."

I stiffened. How did he know about Walker's friends? Were they being watched?

"Do you think they just happened to be together?" he went on, and I tried to stifle my growing panic. "Who's bankrolling them? You might be a civilian, but the *people*," the words came out a sneer, "you've been associating with have been trained to kill humans."

My heart stuttered in my chest. They *were* highly financed. I'd received a new passport no questions asked. They had guns and equipment that must have cost thousands. Lavigne had rented a new house in under five minutes. None of that was normal.

"What do you know of their boss?" he asked, briefly looking at me, his eyes squinted against the sun.

I swallowed and shook my head. "Nothing." It was mostly true. I'd heard the name Clyborne once, but that was it. They hadn't shared information, and I hadn't asked.

He might be right. There might be more to them than guys playing hero, but it didn't change the fact that my sister and I had been abducted in Detroit by Mahn's men, that we'd been collared and caged. Mahn admitted to wanting to eliminate shifters. We weren't the bad guys here, no matter who Walker's friends worked for.

"The fact of the matter is," Mahn went on, "I've been watching your kind for a long time now. They are connected in places, high-up places, they shouldn't be. They organize themselves all over the world and kill without conscience. But don't worry, I have things set in motion. I'm doing humanity a favor by taking them out."

"Bullshit," I spat, my hands tight on the bars of the cage.

His mouth upturned in a smirk. "If it wasn't for Walker and his friends in Goldenlach Ridge, my life would have taken a completely different direction."

My mind raced. The only friends Walker had told me about from Goldenlach Ridge were Landon and Kane. What did they have to do with all of this?

"It took me a long time to figure out what was wrong with that town," he continued, his gaze going back to his phone. "How everyone was so oblivious to schisms below the surface. Then, one day, it all became incredibly clear thanks to the three of them."

I shook my head, not understanding. My attention snapped to Sharpe as he jogged back toward us. "He says he needs to refuel and go through a systems check before another take off."

Mahn pursed his lips, his expression displeased. "Monitor

him. Make sure he's moving as fast as possible. We don't have time for delays."

With a nod, Sharpe jogged back toward the plane.

I stared up at Mahn, still reeling from everything he'd told me. His calm demeanor pissed me off. I clenched my jaw against the need to scream at him. "Those bobcats did nothing to you."

He turned to me slightly, no remorse in his eyes. "Ah, yes. Well. We all need to make a living somehow, don't we?" A small smile curled his lips. "It's what I do to nosy rodents." His smile fell. "And animals like you should learn not to put your snouts where they don't belong."

I shuddered, the bile rising in my throat once more. Forcing myself to swallow, I said, "Why take me and leave Walker to die?" God, I hoped he was okay, that he'd survived the hail of bullets. If anyone could, it was him.

"I don't know what made him different than the other cougars in my employ, but Walker had his chance to bend, to become a part of my team, and he blew it. But you..." That smirk was back and I shuddered at it. "You're worth ten million, already bought and paid for."

My jaw popped I gritted my teeth so hard. "Not everyone who works for you seems to agree with your ideology." There was one person who'd helped us.

"You're talking about my sister."

My stomach dipped. If he knew, then Jolyn was in danger too.

He shook his head like he was saddened. "As soon as I get my hands on her, the traitor will be dealt with. And after all I've done for the little thief." He said the last part almost to himself.

Movement on my other side had me turning. A man crouched down in front of my cage. I scooted as far away from him as possible. Croskey. Instead of his lab coat, he wore a windbreaker and slacks. He waggled the remote for my collar in front of my face.

I snarled at him. He jerked back and the reaction pleased me.

He'd tortured Walker, kept me imprisoned like a lab rat, degraded me. My whole body shook with the need to attack. He stood and moved away from the cage.

The plane started up again. I whipped my head toward it. The noise escalated with each passing second. The fuel truck moved off as the propellers at the front of the plane whirred faster and faster.

I couldn't get on that plane. Arriving at the arena would only mean my death. But trapped in this cage with a collar meant I had no options. I watched as the airplane moved forward toward the end of the runway, then turned to face us. The closer it came, the louder the volume, until I covered my ears.

When it slowed to a stop in front of us, the cargo door was already lowering. Sharpe hopped off the back end. He shouted something I couldn't hear and waved at Mahn. The cage jerked, and I fell backward. I was on some sort of rolling cart, and Croskey pushed me toward the back of the plane. My heart leaped into my throat, beating erratically. Now that I was close, I could see the same caged animals from before were there, each with desperate eyes. I probably looked the same. Did they live on the plane?

The wheels bumped over the lip of the cargo door, throwing me forward on my hands and knees. Panic gripped me by the throat. I took hold of the bars and shook with all my might. I wouldn't go quietly. I'd rather die here, fighting, than be at the mercy of a hunter.

30

WALKER

I PACED BACK AND FORTH HIDDEN IN THE TREE LINE. THIS WAS A shit plan. Everything was shit. Sabrina was in danger, and all I wanted to do was run in there and free her. The only thing holding me back was the fear of failing if I tried to do it all on my own.

We could see the plane on the tarmac. It refueled and looked to be taking off shortly. My heart pounded. Dread and rage settled in my gut.

"We need to move now," I said between gritted teeth.

Lavigne stood beside me, calm, his wrap-around sunglasses giving away none of his expression. "We wait for the signal."

"There's no time."

"We wait for the signal," he repeated.

I clenched and unclenched my fists. When I saw them wheeling Sabrina in a cage, I lost it.

Fuck the plan. I needed to free my mate.

"Hayles!" Lavigne shouted, but I didn't stop, my body shifting in the next instant. He cursed, then I heard footsteps gaining fast behind me, but it was the soft pad of paws hitting the ground, not human feet. He must have shifted into his lion form. We didn't need to stay human. They knew what we were.

I launched myself up and over the chain link fence, the barbwire at the top scraping chunks of skin off my belly. I didn't care about the pain, shifted slightly to heal the worst of it, and kept running.

Every hundred feet or so, a pair of guards monitored the perimeter of the runway, and as soon as they saw me, they opened fire. *Thud, thud, thud.* Bullets hit the dirt in front of me, spraying tiny rocks in my face. I didn't stop, my focus entirely on Sabrina's cage and where they pushed her up the ramp at the back of the plane.

She could see me now. Her hands gripped the bars of her cage, her lips moving. Rage and courage etched her face. She shouted my name, but I couldn't hear her over the noise of the plane.

Shots fired further away, and I knew they were my guys, not the enemy. *Finally.* I may have upped the timetable, but we'd had no time left. I wasn't going to lose Sabrina. We needed to stop this plane from taking off.

Most of the guards were now occupied by Verdugo, Chi, and Guffey in their full tactical gear as they came from around the back of the compound in our other SUV.

I rounded the edge of the runway. Mahn disappeared inside the plane, but Sharpe was coming out, an M16 in his hands. When he walked by Sabrina's cage, she reached out a hand and grabbed him by the balls. He dropped to his knees like he'd just seen God.

That's my girl.

The plane lurched forward. Sabrina's cage was on wheels at the top of the ramp, unsecured, and it skidded downward, tipping over the edge to crash on the tarmac with enough force to bend the bars and knock the door open.

Just as Sharpe regained his feet, she launched herself at him, landing on his back with her arms wrapped around his throat in a chokehold.

A slice of pain shot through my side. I spun around, searching for the source of the shot. Croskey shot wildly, escaping toward the compound with a briefcase in one hand, a handgun in the other. Knowing Sabrina could handle Sharpe, I tore after him.

This was the man who'd gleefully plugged me into volts of electricity, who got others to beat the shit out of me, cane me, whip me, and starve me, who'd torn my skin off to watch it heal. This was the man who'd taken careful notes of all my reactions, who'd put a collar around my neck, pumping me full of drugs and God knew what else.

This was the man who'd kept Sabrina in a cage, who'd fed her kibble and only gave her a litter box to use, who'd kept her behind glass like a specimen, where the only option she'd had to escape was to use her body.

Fury boiled inside of me. My chest heaved with the need to hurt this son of a bitch. He'd once told me he liked to hear me scream. This twisted piece of shit had tried to break us.

He'd failed.

The easy thing to do would be to put a bullet in his head.

I didn't want to do the easy thing.

The smart thing to do would be to take him in for questioning to find out more about this whole operation.

I didn't want to do the smart thing.

In the back of mind, I realized the plane had taken off, that Emerson Mahn was getting away, but my focus was solely on the piece of shit opening the door at the side of the compound, running away like a coward.

I leaped. My front paws pushed against the door just as he walked through, slamming it into his body with such force, he screamed. *Good.* I wanted more of that screaming to make up for the pain and suffering he put Sabrina and me through.

My jaws clamped on his leg, and I dragged him away from

the door, back toward the tarmac. The fight behind me was dying down, and I trusted the guys to cover me while I took care of this.

Croskey whimpered, his hands covering his face and head. The pleas for his life fell on deaf ears. Instead of going for his throat to make a quick kill, I went for his stomach. I tore into his soft belly, whipping my head back and forth. Blood coated my tongue and face. I didn't stop until the screams did.

With a huff of breath, I fell back on haunches and stared at the gore in front of me. I'd thought killing him would ease the emptiness I'd felt since I'd been brought here. But nothing felt different in my chest. I was still the hollow shell I'd been weeks ago.

Except, I wasn't. There was one thing, one *person*, who'd filled that hole—Sabrina.

These past few days had been the first where I hadn't felt like the faint memory of who I once was since Jordan was murdered in front of me.

And it wasn't a temporary thing. Even now I could feel her presence, what she'd done for me. It went beyond physical.

I backed away from the mess I'd made and searched the area for my mate. My heart beat a disjointed rhythm in my chest when my eyes landed on her standing between Chi in his human form and Lavigne in his lion one. Sharpe lay dead at their feet, his throat ripped out. From the blood on Lavigne's jaws, he had to have been the one who'd finished the task.

Letting out a relieved huff that Sabrina was unharmed, I gently bit around the remote that had fallen out of Croskey's pocket and loped my way toward her. There were tears in her eyes. I shifted until I was standing naked in front of her. The second I could, I released her from her collar, then threw it well away from us.

My arms curled around her, holding her tight, our heartbeats echoing against each other in a fast rhythm. She trembled against me, and I realized I shook just as much. I'd been so close to losing her.

Too close. I wouldn't be able to let her go, ever.

I inhaled the scent of her. I knew I was naked and a mess of blood, but I didn't care, needed her next to me, against me. Nothing else mattered but her safe in my arms, and she didn't seem to mind either because she held me just as tight.

This close to her, the bond between us hummed, and nothing had ever felt so right.

31

SABRINA

I COULDN'T LET GO OF WALKER. I DIDN'T CARE HE WAS COVERED IN blood, my body craved him, needed contact like I needed air to breathe.

Everything had happened so fast. And now the plane was gone, and both Sharpe and Croskey were dead, along with all the guards around the property. Verdugo, Chi, and Guffey stood around us, alert, along with a lion.

A *fucking* lion. That had to be Lavigne. He was majestic and poised, his eyes scanning the area around us as Walker held me against him.

A strange silence shrouded our group, like we waited for something else.

"Are you okay?" Chi asked me, a tactical helmet covering his head.

I nodded. "I am now." My fingers flexed where I held onto Walker's naked body.

"Everyone has been neutralized," Guffey said with a pop of his gum. "We're good to go ahead with the remainder of the plan." He grinned.

I didn't understand how anyone could smile after what had

just happened, so I looked to Walker for a more in-depth explanation. "You guys take care of it," he murmured as he pressed his
forehead to mine. "I need to get Sabrina out of here."

A scent came off him, one I'd never smelled before. Steeped
in his signature spice, it held something heavier too. After tossing
his head toward Verdugo, the lion trotted to the SUV the guys
had arrived in. They opened the back hatch to reveal crates of
supplies.

Verdugo stepped up beside us, removing his weapons. "I'll get
you two back to the house while the others level this place. But
we have to go back to the other SUV, all right?"

I nodded, but Walker didn't move, his eyes trained on mine.
"Are you ready for a run?" he asked, his hand cupping my jaw
lightly.

"Yeah." I took a deep breath, more than ready to be rid of this
place forever.

"Then let's head out." He grabbed my hand, and we ran for
the fence on the other side of the tarmac.

I didn't understand why Verdugo left his weapons with Chi
until he took the lead and shifted in front of us, his clothes
tearing away from his body. A brown speckled wolf took his
place, bounding up a stack of crates he used to jump over the
chain link fence.

Still running, I yanked my T-shirt over my head, and shifted
in my next leap, my yoga pants getting lost somewhere behind
me. My newly heightened senses made the world around me
crystal clear. When I glanced to my left, Walker was already in his
cougar form. We jumped the fence together, landing in a huff of
air and a spray of dirt.

Sprinting between a wolf and a cougar shot exhilaration
through my body, my heart beating fast. It felt incredible after
being in that cage again. I put on a burst of speed, and Walker
matched me. We barely separated during the rest of the run. If a
step took me slightly away from him, he was right back there a

moment later. But it wasn't only him. I didn't want to go far, not even inches away.

We didn't stop running until an SUV came in sight. Walker shifted back to human, and when I did the same, he stepped in front of me, his hand on my jaw, our chests heaving as we took deep breaths from the exertion. That same new scent was even stronger now. I didn't know what it meant, but it was everywhere. Adrenaline pumped through my body, making me jittery.

"Hayles," Verdugo said, jerking his head to the SUV.

Walker didn't take his eyes off me, gave me a deep kiss, then led me to the back door. Inside, there were blankets and towels, and he made sure I was covered as soon as I was settled.

He wiped the blood from his body, then strong arms came around me in the next instant, pulling me into his lap. When Verdugo tossed some pants at him, he barely took the time to put them on, instead holding me close, his hands skimming my shoulder, hip, thigh, his face buried in my hair like he tried to inhale me. My heart pounded in my chest. I clutched him as tight as he held me.

"I thought I'd lost you," he murmured against my skin, voice ragged. My hands gripped him tighter.

I was only dimly aware of the SUV starting, the vehicle being put into gear, and Verdugo driving us away from that godforsaken compound.

Walker's new scent kept coming off him in waves, filling the small space in the vehicle. His severe focus should have scared me, but it didn't. His hands stroked my jaw, my shoulder, and he pressed my forehead into his. His eyes glittered.

I couldn't look away. His stare was too much and not enough. The scruff of his jaw scratched my palms. Something was happening inside me, a desperation I'd never felt before made me breathless.

Verdugo's low voice barely registered as he spoke on his

phone about us, about this new scent of Walker's and that it might become an issue.

A growl emerged from Walker's chest, and I snatched it away by pressing my lips to his. I didn't care what Verdugo said, I just wanted Walker's focus entirely on me. It became a necessity. He kissed me over and over. There wasn't an ounce of relaxation inside him. And I felt exactly the same.

It seemed like forever before we arrived back at the big house. The SUV hadn't yet fully stopped when Walker was out the door, tugging me after him. I'd barely gotten my feet under me, the blanket slipping, when we were halfway up the steps. Then he spun, turning toward Verdugo, and snarled.

I gasped at the violent intent behind it, but my heart sped up in anticipation.

"If anyone steps inside in the next twenty-four hours," Walker growled, his hand tight on my wrist, "I'll kill them."

Shocked, my gaze jumped to the man who'd helped us, who'd risked his life for his friend. He didn't seem surprised or even a little alarmed at Walker's declaration. If anything, his demeanor only shouted "resigned."

I didn't have any more time to think on it because Walker guided me up the steps, unlocked the door, then tugged me inside the moment it was open. Verdugo didn't follow.

As soon as the door closed, Walker kissed me, pressing me against the wall. His hands were everywhere. That new, intoxicating scent of his kept getting more and more intense. It filled my head and made me want to crawl inside him and never leave.

I broke the kiss, wanting him to slow down, and took his face in my hands. "Walker. It's okay. I'm okay."

He shook his head and kissed me again. I allowed myself to be swept away because every part of me needed to lose myself to these feelings. Every molecule wanted what Walker was doing to me, embraced it.

He rotated his hips against mine. "You're mine," he growled against my lips.

Then he paused like he needed me to say something, his entire body vibrating.

Liquid heat gathered between my thighs at the intensity of his stare. My heart fluttering fast in my chest, I watched as his jaw changed, partially shifting. His canines extended, his teeth sharpened.

Realization made my heart pound in my chest so hard it hurt. His new scent, his possessiveness, his teeth, this was all about mating—*really* mating. Not sex. Not blowing off steam. This was something big.

Nervous energy erupted through my body, warring with the adrenaline and the lust. There was something else there too, poignant emotions swirling in my belly. My body reacted to his declaration, the sight of his canines and glowing eyes, and shifted on its own. My canines curved over my bottom lip. His eyes flared, focusing on my mouth while his body pressed into mine. I couldn't stop what was happening to me. He'd initiated it, and my body wanted it.

I wanted it.

"You're mine," he growled against my ear, thrusting against me for emphasis. Shivers ran across my skin. The truth settled into my gut. From the beginning, through the horrors we'd both experienced, we'd been drawn toward each other. There seemed no stopping it, and now we were here.

His hips pressed into mine, his eyes boring into me. His lips parted and he waited. He wanted me to submit but was giving me the choice.

Tension oozed from my body, leaving me soft and pliant. "Yes," I whispered. "And you're *mine*."

Any restraint he held snapped with my agreement. He grabbed the blanket around my body and threw it away. I gasped as a thrill shot through me. He'd never been this aggressive before. The cool of the wood door pressed against my spine and bottom.

He stepped closer, his face in my throat, and the bulge in his pants pressed between my thighs. All my instincts told me to stay still, to submit. My fingernails dug into his biceps.

When his teeth scraped against my shoulder, I gasped. Heat settled in my stomach then snaked its way between my thighs. My heart pounded in anticipation of what he'd do next.

His inhale shook through his body as he breathed in the skin of my neck. Up and down, he grazed his teeth along my shoulder and throat. I closed my eyes, allowing the light touch to calm me. He took my hands and pressed them against the door by my shoulders, pinning me.

"Mate," I whispered.

With a groan, he sank his teeth into my skin. Undiluted plea-sure shot through my body along with the spike of pain from the punctures. I moaned, sparks shooting behind my eyelids. A mini orgasm made me jerk into him. Moisture slicked the inside of my thighs, the scent curling upward.

We were mates and I should have realized it sooner.

On a growl, he sank his teeth in deeper. It extended the sensa-tions inside me, and my hips rubbed against his bulge, seeking more, the aftershocks twitching through me.

I sagged against him, letting him take my weight. His hand stroked, seeking the moisture between my thighs. I was so wet his fingers slid easily inside me.

"Yes," I hissed, the sensation of his fingers below and his teeth in my shoulder almost too much.

Without letting go of my throat, he released my other hand and fumbled between us, freeing his cock from his pants.

In one thrust, he was inside me. I couldn't stop the growly sounds emerging from my throat. Eyes rolling in the back of my head, I groaned and purred at the same time. Nothing had ever felt so perfect. His teeth penetrating me the same time as his cock... The only thing that would make it better would be me biting him at the same time.

The second I had the thought, I wanted it with my whole being. I pushed off the wall. The movement made him release my neck. I gasped. With his pants around his thighs, he stumbled backward, falling on his ass, and I followed, somehow still keeping his cock inside me.

I settled down on him. His pupils were dilated, his expression both savage and tender. Sweat beaded his brow, and a bit of my blood settled in the corner of his mouth. We both groaned when I shifted my weight forward. I needed to bite—to claim. I couldn't stop myself, didn't want to stop.

My hips moving on their own, gyrating delicious circles, I draped myself over his body. "This means something," I whispered into his ear. My tongue laved the space between his shoulder and his neck, the place I was drawn to the most.

"Yes," he groaned, his fingers digging into my waist, his hips thrusting up into mine.

It felt amazing, this connection I'd never experienced before. It felt like we touched everywhere, our minds, our bodies, our spirits. I couldn't remember where we were, and I didn't care. This moment between us was the only thing that mattered.

Our rhythm picked up speed. I couldn't hold back any longer. Scenting the space where his neck met his shoulder, I latched onto him, my teeth digging in tight. The taste of him, his blood, rushed over my tongue. My eyes rolled back in bliss.

"Fuck!" Walker arched off the floor, orgasming underneath me. His body jerked inside mine. With him spilling and me taking his flavor in my mouth, another orgasm slammed through me, almost knocking me out. I lost all concept of time. It made my vision blacken and my breath halt in my chest. I held on to him and didn't let go.

That tug I'd been feeling in my chest for the past day now felt like a solid, unbreakable thing. We were mates. I knew it in my heart. I knew it wasn't something we could undo. And even though I hadn't understood it until these past couple of days, it was exactly what I wanted.

I took a deep breath. This was big. But it was right.

The more I breathed, the more I returned to myself. My canines retracted, releasing his neck. Without even thinking, I licked his wounds. He gasped in response, his hands tightening around me. I'd officially claimed what was mine. Walker was *mine*. And I was his.

Awareness crept in little by little. His pants were wrapped around his knees. His cock was inside me, and neither of us moved to change that.

I lifted off of him enough to see his face. His eyes were hooded, his face slack and satisfied, and a small smile graced his lips. It made my own quirk. God, I loved that look on his face. My heart rate pick up all over again.

I couldn't stop myself from leaning forward and kissing him. The blood I'd taken mixed with what he'd taken from me. His hands cupped my face, shivers of pleasure erupting over my skin. He held me like I was the most precious person in the world, and it made my heart constrict so much it hurt.

When he broke the kiss, the words I'd been holding inside me tumbled out. "I love you."

His eyes widened, then he groaned and kissed me again. It was full of desperation, like he was taking my soul into himself. He broke the kiss, pressing our foreheads together. "I love you so much, and I thought I lost you."

His ferocious words made me swallow and shake my head. It had been too close. "You're not going to lose me."

He gave me another harsh kiss. When he moved beneath me, I realized he was pushing his pants the rest of the way off with his feet. I adjusted myself to accommodate him. In a move I didn't know was possible, he rolled to his feet while his hands held me beneath my thighs.

"I want to lick every inch of you." He carried me towards the stairs, then up them. "I want to be inside you and bite you again, and hear you say you're mine."

I buried my face in his throat and held on tight. "And you're mine."

His arms flexed around me as he cleared the top stair.

I lifted my head a little. "You're not really going to make everyone stay out of here for twenty-four hours, are you?"

"I sure fucking am."

With that, he closed the door with his foot, deposited me on our bed, and fulfilled his promises.

32

WALKER

THE WHEELS OF THE PRIVATE JET TOUCHED DOWN, THE PLANE jerking slightly then settling as the roar of the engine grew louder. Sabrina's hand tightened on mine for a heartbeat, then relaxed. I slung my free arm around her shoulders, tucking her in as close to my side as possible within the confines of the seat.

We were the only two passengers on the plane. Everyone else had been dropped off at different locations in Canada, and we were the only ones traveling to Detroit—a courtesy Astrid Clyborne had decided to give us, even though she was pissed at me for killing Croskey without getting answers from him. I already had a debt to her, and I knew at some point, she'd be in contact to collect.

The thought of working in special ops again didn't terrify me as much as it used to. But I didn't want to think about it right now. I only cared that Sabrina was safe. Even the demolition of the compound became secondary.

Emerson Mahn was still out there somewhere, and from what he'd told Sabrina, I knew he wasn't done with shifters. He had some other plan, I just didn't know what. My old crew was working on it, trying to track down the location of the arena and anywhere else he may be holding shifters. That warehouse in Detroit was next on their hit list. If they were going to take it down, I'd already told them I'd be happy to participate.

After everything Clyborne had learned from me and Sabrina, and everything her own team had seen at the compound, Mahn had a target on his back the size of North America, topping both Canadian and American "person of interest" lists. With the resources available to him because of his company and finances, it made all of us nervous that he remained at large. Thankfully, his kind of scum were exactly the kind my old crew was good at finding and eliminating.

The tricky bit was keeping what he knew about shifters a secret. There were some people in both governments who knew of shifters or were shifters themselves, but not many. It was going to take a delicate hand to keep everything on the down low. Luckily, Astrid Clyborne was known for her delicate hands.

Beside me, Sabrina took a deep breath. I knew she was anxious. She'd called her sister before we left Alaska, letting her know when we'd land. Ever since we'd dropped off the last of the guys, she'd been a ball of nerves. The closer we traveled to her sister, the more tension crawled up her body. I understood why. The last time she'd seen Brooke, she'd basically pushed her out of an airplane. And even though they'd had a few short phone calls, she needed to see for herself that Brooke was okay, and that this new mate of hers was a good person.

She hadn't spoken a word to me about any of it, but I knew regardless. Ever since we'd gone through the mating ritual, the bond between us, the thick connection that felt like a rope, kept solidifying more and more. Each sexual encounter felt like a religious experience, like we were inside each other's minds while making love. Every touch, every connection, intensified. I'd never experienced anything like it.

This was it. The two of us. We wouldn't be making any further decisions without the other weighing in. There hadn't been a lot

of discussion yet as to where we'd live or what we'd do, but I
knew she loved her job at Sleeping Bear Dunes, and living so
close to a national park sounded perfect to me. If Clyborne
wanted me for the odd job, she'd have to work with me being in
the States. But it didn't matter where Sabrina and I lived as long
as we were together. Going forward, we were partners, two souls
in tandem.

At the house in Fairbanks, when I'd told the guys I'd kill
anyone who disturbed us, I'd meant it. Fortunately, they'd taken
my warning seriously and stayed away for a full twenty-four
hours. And when they did return, it was only to remove their
equipment and leave again as fast as possible. Sabrina and I
ended up having the house to ourselves and took full advantage
of it. We didn't leave until we needed to head to the airport.

Now, as the plane came to a full stop, we unbuckled and
found our bags where they'd been secured behind us. Slinging
my duffel over my shoulder, I pulled Sabrina to me, wrapping my
arm around her waist and pressing my lips to her forehead.

"Everything's going to be okay. You're home."

She nodded against me, then pulled away to give me a
wavering smile.

The stairs to the plane lowered. A whoosh of fresh air battled
with the recycled stuff inside the plane. The early June temperatures were so much different in Detroit than in Alaska. We could
feel the heat already, even though it was barely nine in the
evening and the sun was just setting.

Taking Sabrina's hand, I led her to the stairs, then down. We
squinted against the early evening glare and made our way to the
large block of buildings to the right. There were a few questions
from the customs agent, then we were heading through the doors
to the main terminal.

As soon as we cleared the sliding doors, a gasp escaped
Sabrina's lips. Her hand slipped out of mine. She ran toward a
couple before I could stop her. The woman, a slender blonde

with long, wavy hair spilling over her shoulders, let out a squeal and made a mad dash toward Sabrina. She had to be Brooke. They were about the same height and had similar facial features.

They collided in a twirl of limbs and laughter, or crying. I'm not sure which because it sort of sounded like sobbing and someone being strangled at the same time.

The man beside Brooke moved forward. When our eyes met, we froze at the same time. My heart pounded hard in my chest. The two women were talking, practically shouting at each other, but I couldn't tear my gaze away from the one living person I never thought I'd see again.

"Kane?" It came out a question because I couldn't believe it was him. I blinked, positive he'd disappear. But he didn't.

This was the man who I hadn't seen since my first leave in the military. The one who'd been determined to cut himself off from the world, to live on his own for the rest of his days as penance for his mistakes. He was the one I'd told not to throw his life away. My heart pounded. And here he was standing in a Detroit airport with Sabrina's sister.

He'd grown a beard and it suited him. The scar on his neck was still visible, but only partially. He'd bulked up too, maybe as much as I had in the military.

With an echoing disbelief in his expression and movements, he signed, *Walker?*

Then it was the pair of us who were moving, who grasped each other in a hug a decade overdue. Part of me wanted to punch him for cutting me out of his life, out of everyone's lives, but there was more of me just so damn happy to see him. The punching could wait.

Those better times in Goldenlach Ridge came back to me. My throat tight and my eyes burning, I squeezed him against me as hard as possible. I wasn't going to waste this second chance of having my friend back in my life.

When we pulled away from each other, we both realized our women stared at us with slack jaws.

"You two know each other?" Sabrina asked, her eyes darting from me to Kane while she held her sister to her side.

"Yeah," I said with a hearty slap to his shoulder.

Kane gave me a side grin when he signed to Brooke. She blinked at me. "You're Walker? The one Landon sent off to find Jolyn?"

"Yes," I said, uneasy. How did they know about the side job Landon had given me? How did Sabrina's sister know about Jolyn? I looked at Kane. "What's going on?"

He signed to me. It had been a while since I'd used ASL, but I was happy to realize a lot of the knowledge remained. Kane told me how Brooke had landed on his doorstep after falling from that plane, how cougar shifters had been after her, how the collar around her neck had appeared to be something he'd designed himself, which led them to Landon. Brooke spoke quietly to Sabrina, translating what she could.

I shook my head, trying to fit everything that had happened together like random pieces from two different puzzles, striving to make sense of it.

"And you're mated?" The question came from Sabrina, her eyes darting between Brooke and Kane.

"Yes," she said, stepping into the circle of Kane's arms, wrapping her own around his waist.

"I've never seen you look so happy." Sabrina almost whispered the sentence, her voice in awe, as she stepped into my side.

"I've never been this happy." She stared up at Kane and blinked. "And if I hadn't fallen out of that plane, I would never have met him." She shook her head, then returned her gaze to Sabrina. "What happened to you?" Brooke asked. "Where were you taken?"

"Alaska." She put her arm around me, and I pulled her close. "We both were."

Brooke's eyes widened. Her gaze snared on the open neck of Sabrina's shirt where her mating mark was visible. "You're mated too?"

Sabrina nodded and hugged me tighter.

A squeak left her sister. "You'll need to tell me everything."

Sabrina snorted. "Well, not *everything*."

Brooke grinned. "At least most of it."

Our focus switched to Kane when he signed, *What happened in Alaska?*

I pressed my lips together before saying, "I have information for Landon about all of that and would rather not say it twice." Landon was the one who'd hired me after all. I glanced around the terminal. "Where is he?" After hearing everything, if Kane was here, then Landon should be as well.

"That's the problem," Brooke said, her eyes turning grave. "Landon's missing."

All the tension returned to my body. "What do you mean he's missing? For how long?"

"We arrived with him and were all staying at the same hotel since we didn't think it was a good idea for me to go back to my apartment." She tucked a bit of hair behind her ears. "But he left to do an errand yesterday morning, and we haven't heard from him since. He's just..." She lifted her hand then let it drop. "Gone."

Gone. I'd swapped one disappearance for another. I met Sabrina's gaze knowing my job wasn't done yet. I'd need to contact Clyborne Inc. to let them know of this new development. It had to all be connected, but besides Jolyn Mahn, I didn't understand much of how it could be.

Sabrina took my hand and nodded once. As long as I had my mate by my side, we could conquer anything. I looked at Kane and knew he was thinking the same thing. We'd find Landon together. All of us.

EPILOGUE
JOLYN

Back to the Beginning

The only way this was going to work was if I could get out of there before anyone realized I was where I shouldn't be. I kept my footsteps slow and steady even though I wanted to run. My heart beat a rapid rhythm in my chest, and I took a slow breath to calm myself. Moments like these were what my military training were made for—even if I wasn't following anyone's orders but my own right now.

Since it was late, quiet settled over the compound as I made my way to Emerson's office. Most everyone had gone home for the day, to their families, with their rationalized excuses as to why they worked at the decommissioned wildlife rescue. *It paid the bills. They had kids to feed and clothe. What they didn't know couldn't hurt them.* Only a handful of guards remained on the property, and I'd made sure they didn't see me.

None of the little red lights on the security cameras at the end of each hallway were on. I'd put sleeping pills in the coffee of the guy in the control room. He'd fallen asleep on the job once before. No one would suspect me. I'd turn the cameras back on before I left. The guy might lose his job, but it was better for him to be unemployed instead of working at this place.

Wildlife rescue. *What a joke.* It was my brother's sadistic little pet project. The only real animals he kept were the ones that stayed on his cargo plane twenty-four-seven in case he was ever stopped crossing the border at customs.

This place wasn't what I'd signed up for. Since the beginning, our plan had been to equalize, not this messed up little game Emerson wanted to play with people's lives.

Not kidnapping, not torture, not murder.

After four years in the Canadian Armed Forces, he'd thought I'd be ready and raring to join him at the helm. Instead, my brother's latest plans made me sick to my stomach. I hadn't understood how far his obsession went, not until I saw a woman in a cage and heard the tormented screams of a fellow soldier. I'd had to stand there and smile, to look like I agreed with Emerson's demented tactics. If I didn't, I knew he'd have no problems killing me even though he looked at me like another of his investments. I'd held it together long enough to make it to the bathroom and retch. In the time I'd been away in the army, my brother had changed from obsessed into a monster, worse than those he'd hunted for the past decade.

Or maybe he'd always been a monster and I just hadn't seen it until my years away from him opened my eyes.

I turned the last corner down the long hallway, my hands loose at my sides. When he figured out what I was up to—and he would eventually—Emerson wouldn't hold back his rage because I was his sister. No, it would fuel it even more.

At the door to his office, I didn't hesitate to pull out my stolen key, unlock the door, and slip inside before anyone could see me. It was a neat and tidy space, sterile. Emerson didn't care about it. There wasn't any warmth or personal touches added.

I crossed the room, the urge to look over my shoulder tickling at the base of my spine. *Focus.* With the help of Marley and Alina,

I'd been planning this for weeks. And since Emerson was off the compound, and plans were to move the woman to the arena tomorrow, the timing had to be perfect.

Pulling two USB drives out of my pocket, I slid into my brother's ergonomic desk chair and turned on his computer. This was only step one of the plan. After I freed Emerson's two prisoners, I'd head to Detroit to finish it. I slid the first USB drive into the laptop and tapped my foot impatiently while it booted up. Seconds ticked by. My heart beat in my throat, making it hard to swallow.

I knew I shouldn't worry. I had all night to execute my plan since Emerson was in Anchorage, wining and dining his latest "buyer," but the feeling of dread snaking through my body wouldn't go away.

This was it. There was no turning back after tonight. No more pretending I was going along with my brother's plans. He'd mark me as a traitor and try to kill me. Of that, I had no doubt.

The laptop hummed softly as the welcome screen and password prompt appeared. I typed in the command Marley had given me, and a few long seconds later, I was in. Another command and the download started. I didn't like the extra time this was taking, but I needed to understand my brother's endgame as much as possible. When so many lives were on the line, failure was not an option.

The download finished. I swapped the drive for the second one, a red, sticky dot affixed to its casing. Marley was a genius when it came to viruses. The program embedded inside would infiltrate my brother's computer and spread to the local servers he kept in the basement. It was set on a delay so I'd be long gone when it happened.

Watching the seconds on my watch, I waited until five minutes elapsed before yanking it out of the port. I stood and popped both drives into my pocket. *So far so good.* I only had two things left to do: free the prisoners and get the hell out.

As soon as the office door closed behind me, the emergency lights turned on. Somewhere deeper inside the compound, an alarm sounded. My heart raced. How had he found out about my betrayal so soon?

No. There was no way the alarm could have been my fault. Something else was happening.

"Shit." If all the security guards were on alert, it would make it impossible to free the two prisoners. But I had to try. I couldn't leave them to their fate—a horrific death followed by a session with the taxidermist.

I took my gun out of the holster at my side and headed toward the lab. The lights continued to blink. The alarm blared.

The next corner I turned, I stopped dead. The two people I'd been intending to free ran toward me. The woman's long, brown hair streamed behind her, and she wore only a plaid shirt and underwear. *Oh, God. What had they done to her now?* The man, Walker Hayles, wore tactical pants. Each had bare feet and held a gun. He lifted it toward me.

A guard rounded the corner behind them. Without thinking, I fired then ducked back behind the wall. Two shots hit the concrete near my face. My bullet had found its mark in the guard's forehead, so the other shots had to have come from the prisoners.

"Stand down!" I shouted. Getting shot tonight wasn't part of the plan. Not even close.

I slid my fist around the edge of the wall. Neither of them took the shot. I chanced a peek. They stood with their backs to the wall, caught. Hayles had his eyes on me, his gun raised halfway to the ready position, his body blocking most of the woman's while her gaze was glued to the dead guard. I'd never learned her name. They'd only processed her in the lab under a number: eighty-seven.

Keeping my gun pointed at the floor, I took a step into the hallway. They'd gotten their collars off. That hadn't been in the plan. At least, not while I was around. They might not deserve their fate, but they were still part animal and couldn't be trusted. A spike of fear stabbed me in the belly. Would they transform and attack? Try to rip me to shreds? If they did, I'd have no choice but to protect myself.

The woman tore her gaze from the dead guard and whipped her head toward me. Eyes widening in recognition, she lifted her gun.

Hayles stopped her with a hand on her wrist. "She was the only one who gave me food."

I stiffened. How had he known that? I'd been careful to only bring the food when he was passed out and no one would notice. Emerson and Croskey had been intent on starving him before killing him. Probably another one of their tests, to see how long one of their kind could survive without food and water.

The last time I'd seen Hayles, he hadn't looked like he would survive the night. Now he appeared healed and strong.

Obviously his...animal characteristics helped with the healing process. "This way." I cocked my head the way I'd come.

"We can't trust her," the woman said, her hands tightening on the gun, her arms shaking.

"No," Hayles agreed, but he lowered his gun the rest of the way. "But we're going to follow her anyway. Are there any more like us here?" One hand went around the woman's back, he ushered her forward.

I shook my head, thankful I didn't have to free others. It would have made it impossible for me to leave. "You two are it right now." But from what I'd heard, that wasn't always the case.

Without looking to see if they followed, I led the way down the hallway toward the exit. I paused at the last corner. "Turn right. Go to the end of the hallway. The last door on the left leads to the garage. You can find a vehicle there." I pulled a set of keys out of my pocket, the one I'd stolen from the security guard I drugged. "These will work on something. Head southwest to Fairbanks."

Hayles took the keys and nodded his thanks. Then he said something that made the fine hairs all over my body stand on end. "Someone's looking for you, Jolyn."

He knew my name. It wasn't much of a stretch because we'd grown up in the same town, but I'd never thought he knew who I was.

Then he added. "I'd run if I were you."

Dear God, he was talking about Landon. Every curse word in my vocabulary surfaced in my mind. If Landon was looking for me, there was only reason. *Shit.*

I was already moving when I heard the woman ask, "What's going to happen to her?" right before the door closed.

"Nothing if I can help it," I muttered, heading to the other side of the building where I'd parked my Subaru.

Even though the alarms still blared, I encountered no one else as I made my way to the rear exit. I didn't have time to put the cameras back on, not now. But at least Hayles and the woman had gotten free. I hoped. They were on their own. I had bigger fish to fry, and I'd just added Landon *fucking* Urick to the pan.

The cool night air slapped at my face and pulled at the edges of my jacket. I zipped it up as far as it would go while jogging to my Subaru. The scent of pine erased some of the evil stench that seemed to live in my head since I'd come to this place.

My heart beating a hummingbird rhythm in my chest, I unlocked my SUV with my key fob and jumped inside. The push of a button started the engine. I took a few seconds to put on my toque and mittens. Alaska was always so damn cold at night. I shifted into reverse and tore out of my spot.

When Emerson had bought this place, he'd renovated it until there was only one way out of the compound. I drove around the building until the chain link gate came into sight. It was smashed all to hell. Two guards usually stood in front of it, but right now, one was on the ground with a wound, and the other knelt beside him. He hopped up when he saw me, waving at me to stop.

Making a split decision, I accelerated. If I stopped now, I might never get out, and I couldn't take the chance. He dove out of the way just in time. The undercarriage squealed and groaned as I drove over the remains of the chain link gate. Metal scraped concrete. A shot banged behind me. I ducked, but it didn't hit my rear window. One more speed bump, and I was free. Tires accelerated against pavement when I pressed the gas pedal all the way down.

This was it. There was no more pretending. Emerson would return tomorrow and hear what I'd done. He'd find the virus and he'd know it was me. There was no going back.

I needed air. I opened the window all the way. Wind whipped against my face. No matter how far I drove from the compound, the dread in my belly wouldn't leave. I'd do anything to stop my brother's plan, because the truth made me want to vomit.

None of this would have happened if it hadn't been for me.

Thank you for reading! Did you enjoy? Please add your review because nothing helps an author more and encourages readers to take a chance on a book than a review.

And don't miss book three of the *Goldenlach Ridge Shifters* series, CONQUERED BETRAYAL, available now. Turn the page for a sneak peek!

You can also sign up for the City Owl Press newsletter to receive notice of all book releases!

SNEAK PEEK OF CONQUERED BETRAYAL

I knew it was weird to follow them, but I couldn't help it.

Whenever I saw Kane, I had the urge to stay close, to see what he was up to, like he was some sort of superhero, and if I remained nearby, I'd finally get to see him change from his glasses to his cape.

Which was ridiculous because Kane didn't even wear glasses.

Ever since he defended me, stopping Tom Akins from beating the crap out of me when I was ten years old, I'd held him in high regard. And by "high regard" I meant "crush." I've had the *hugest* crush on Kane Baird for the past seven years.

Because he couldn't speak—some injury he'd suffered a few years ago no one ever spoke about—I'd learned ASL in secret. He'd been homeschooled for years now. On the rare occasions I saw him, a thrill went through me and I tried to prolong the sighting as much as possible. I'd take any excuse to stay away from home, to ease the tightness banded around my chest. Sometimes that meant following him.

Okay, so it sounded a little creepy. But seriously, what else was a girl supposed to do?

Skulking not far away, I followed him out of town. He was with his two friends Walker and Landon. They were always together, each a year apart in age. Walker, the youngest of them, would graduate in a month.

They made a handsome trio. Kane was the biggest, he'd only bulked up over the past couple of years. Landon, the most slender, always wore dress pants and a button-down shirt. Walker, shorter than the other two, was the most wiry in strength. His shoulders and chest seemed wider than they should for his height, like he wasn't done growing yet.

Deeper they hiked into the forest with me following. They passed the old trapper's shed, then the creek. Where were they off to? I could hear them talking, but not what they said, the wind carrying their voices away. I guess it kept my presence a secret too, because they didn't look back at where I trailed them, trying to keep just around the last bend so I could duck out of the way if they turned around. *Not a creeper at all.*

The trees grew closer together, the noise of town fading to nothing. My heart pounded while nervousness swirled in my stomach. I should probably head home and leave them to their day, but my feet kept following. What would I say if they discovered me? I'd daydreamed about being bold enough to ask Kane on a date. He didn't have a girlfriend from what I could see. But in that daydream, his friends hadn't been around.

They disappeared from sight. Picking up my pace, I puffed a breath of relief when I glimpsed them again.

A scream—a woman's voice—tore through the air. I froze, the fine hairs on my arms standing on end. A second scream followed, this one more masculine and primal. The three boys tore off in its direction, up a hill and away from the creek. I followed, running frantically through the bushes, branches scraping at my shoulders and arms. I cleared the hill, and the shallow valley spread before me. What I saw made my heart pound in my head. A huge grizzly bear dragged a limp woman by her foot through the layer of dead leaves on the forest floor. It let go when the three boys screamed at it, not twenty feet away. Were they crazy? That bear was massive and feral. Probably the one scaring campers at the local campground. But that was on the other side of town. These boys should be running in the opposite direction, not shouting at it.

In an instant, everything changed. The world blurred. Kane,

the boy I fancied myself in love with, morphed into something else. He leaped through the air, skin changing into fur. He *transformed*. A gasp caught in my throat like a boulder. His clothes ripped from his body. Before I could scream, he'd turned into a massive bear, one whose growl stopped my heart.

I couldn't breathe, couldn't think, couldn't process what the hell I was seeing. A haze fogged my vision.

The fact that Walker also changed, turned into a cougar, was secondary. It hardly registered. All I could see was one bear attack the other. A roar ripped through the air. *Fur. Claws. Blood.* I didn't realize I'd grabbed hold of the tree next to me until I squeezed the bark so tight it cut painfully into my palm.

I couldn't look away. Every instinct in my body told me to get the hell away from here, but I couldn't move. Landon stood apart from the battling bears, yelling at them, shouting Kane's name over and over again.

But that wasn't Kane anymore. It was a monster. My infatuation with him shed from my body, fear and horror taking its place. The edges of my vision darkened. My head felt disconnected from my neck. The invisible band around my chest squeezed tighter. I forced myself to breathe. It came out strangled.

Landon turned, and I stumbled back, falling down the slight incline in my attempt to get away. I couldn't let him see me. If he could be friends with monsters...I didn't want any of them to find me.

Crawling on my hands and knees, I gulped breaths, then stood on jelly legs. I ran as fast as I could. By the time I reached the edge of the town, my lungs burned. I ran through Goldenlach Ridge to our property on the lake, ignoring the heads that turned my way. For once, I was grateful to see my brother. Emerson noticed me from his spot at the picnic table and stood up from the game of chess he'd been playing by himself.

"What's wrong?" He strode over and grasped my shoulders, steadying me.

Terrified, I shook my head, my entire body trembling. What I'd seen shouldn't be possible. It didn't make any sense. People shouldn't be able to change like that. Kane and Walker looked like normal boys, but they weren't normal at all.

"They're animals," I gasped between broken breaths. "They changed. The boys. They're animals." My words came out garbled. Would he believe me? It sounded insane.

Instead of dismissing me, a strange light entered Emerson's eyes, one I usually hated to see. "Changed?"

I nodded, panting for air, swallowing against the fear lodged in my throat. "I can't explain it." It felt like my tongue was made of sandpaper. "They were human, then they...weren't."

The hands on my shoulders tightened. I braced myself for more pain, but he let up, putting his arm around my shoulders in an oddly comforting gesture, and ushered me toward the house.

"Let's make some tea. Then you'll tell me everything."

Don't stop now. Keep reading CONQUERED BETRAYAL.

Don't miss book three of the *Goldenlach Ridge Shifters* series, CONQUERED BETRAYAL, available now, and find more from J. E. McDonald at www.jemcdonald.net

Betrayal tore them apart. Now more than their hearts are at stake.

Under her brother's control for far too long, Jolyn Mahn is determined to sabotage his evil agenda regarding shifters and take down his twisted empire. But just when she thinks she's making progress, her past comes back to haunt her—the only man she's ever loved turns up at the worst possible moment. She has no time for the skeletons in her closet, especially ones over six feet tall and wrapped in an expensive suit.

He can only spell disaster.

Landon Urick has two things on his mind: find his missing friend and figure out how the lost love of his life is involved. Between flying bullets and high-speed chases, their lives become intertwined once more. He tells himself he only wants answers, but the bear inside him clamors to claim this feisty human, a woman who hurt him like no other. But Jolyn doesn't know he's a shifter, one of the very people her brother is bent on destroying— and a species she fears more than any other.

With an obsessed megalomaniac on their heels, and their survival hanging in the balance, can they find trust in one another, or will their past deceptions mean death for them both?

Please sign up for the City Owl Press newsletter for chances to win special subscriber-only contests and giveaways as well as receiving information on upcoming releases and special excerpts.

All reviews are **welcome** and **appreciated**. Please consider leaving one on your favorite social media and book buying sites.

Escape Your World. Get Lost in Ours! City Owl Press at www. cityowlpress.com.

ACKNOWLEDGMENTS

Writing is such a strange, solitary thing, but putting a book together takes solid people at your back. I'm so grateful for the people in my life who offer me constant support, advice, and encouragement.

My first big thank you goes to City Owl Press/Mystic Owl for putting my words out there. Thank you to my editor, Heather, for being my number one cheerleader when it comes to my new ideas. You're a thoughtful and kind person as well as a fantastic editor. Thank you to Tina and Yelena for being exemplary leaders in their field, to the amazing copy editors, and to MiblArt for knocking each cover out of the park.

Thank you to my amazing foundation of beta readers, Caryn, Bevin, and Melodie. I honestly don't know what I'd do without you.

To all the amazing authors at City Owl/Mystic Owl. You're so supportive, and I'm honored to be counted among you.

Thank you to all the bloggers and reviewers who give up their spare time to read and review books! A special big thanks to Marcia D, Miranda O, and Brook W.

Thank you to all the readers out there for falling in love with the Goldenlach Ridge Shifters like I have. I love the positive feedback I've been receiving, and every review you leave means SO MUCH!

Thank you to Mickey at Creative Edge. You're a force to be reckoned with.

And thank you to my writing groups both on and off line. A

big shout out to my Saskatoon Write Club peeps and your enduring loyalty to the group.

These past two years have been hard in many ways, for everyone, and I couldn't do what I do without the support of my family. Thank you to my parents and my husband for making this all possible. Love you.

ABOUT THE AUTHOR

Photography by Zehra Rizvi

J. E. MCDONALD was born and raised in Saskatchewan, Canada, The Land of the Living Skies. As a child, she was either searching the clouds for identifiable shapes, or star-gazing way past her bedtime. She's an anti-morning person who wakes up at 5am to write. Needless to say, coffee is a morning requirement. She cut her teeth watching Star Trek, James Bond movies, and reading the Harlequin novels her mother left in the bathroom—which resulted in an extremely skewed sense of sex education by age eleven. All of these factors contribute to her love of writing paranormal romance with humor, mystery, and lots of spice. J. E. resides in Saskatchewan with her husband and three daughters.

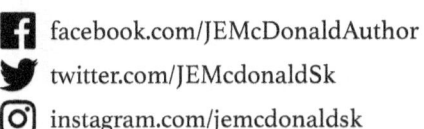

facebook.com/JEMcDonaldAuthor
twitter.com/JEMcdonaldSk
instagram.com/jemcdonaldsk

ABOUT THE PUBLISHER

City Owl Press is a cutting edge indie publishing company, bringing the world of romance and speculative fiction to discerning readers.

Escape Your World. Get Lost in Ours!

www.cityowlpress.com

facebook.com/YourCityOwlPress
twitter.com/cityowlpress
instagram.com/cityowlbooks
pinterest.com/cityowlpress

www.ingramcontent.com/pod-product-compliance
Lightning Source LLC
Chambersburg PA
CBHW020822260626

47169CB00003B/780